Sword of David

This know also, that in the last days perilous times shall come.

2 Timothy 3: 1

(*Vatican City, Rome*)

Last Monday, the Bishop of Rome addressed the Catholic followers regarding the dire importance of exhibiting religious tolerance. During his hour-long speech, the smiling Pope was quoted telling the Vatican's guests that the Koran, along with the spiritual teachings contained therein, are just as valid as the Holy Bible.

"Jehovah, Allah, Vishnu; these are all names employed to describe an entity that is distinctly the same across the world. Jesus, Mohammad, and Buddha are all messengers of the truth. Catholics can no longer believe that all Muslims, Hindus, Atheists, and so on, are all going to hell. We have this on the authority of the former Pope Benedict XVI. A couple years ago, he had given a long interview that has only just surfaced in English. Benedict's view must be definitive, not just because he was a pope but because he was a notably conservative one."

DAILY MAIL UK- Tomorrow's soldiers could possibly be able to run at Olympic speeds and be able to go for days without food or sleep if new research into gene manipulation is successful. According to the U.S. Army's plans, their soldiers will be able to carry huge weights, live off their fat stores for extended periods of time, and even regrow limbs blown apart by bombs. DARPA is working on triggering genes that will make soldiers' bodies able to convert fat into energy more efficiently enabling them to go days without eating while in the warzone.

US NEWS AND WORLD - Just within the past six months, DHS has stockpiled more than one billion rounds of ammo, including 450 million rounds of .40 caliber hollow point ammo, to fight "home-grown terrorism." It has also been reported that DHS also purchased 7,000 semi-automatic "assault weapons". This is the very style of weapon they are currently attempting to ban from public purchase.

WASHINGTON (CNN) A new intelligence assessment has been circulated by the Department of Homeland Security this month and reviewed by CNN. It focuses on the domestic terror threat from right-wing sovereign citizen extremists and comes as the administration holds a White House conference to focus efforts to fight violent extremism.

Some federal and local law enforcement groups view the domestic terror threat from sovereign citizen groups as equal to -- and in some cases greater than -- the threat from foreign Islamic terror groups such as ISIS, that garner more public attention.

WASHINGTON- NASA issued a warning of possible imminent solar flares of X-class power within the next few weeks, perhaps as critical as X15 or above. A direct hit on Earth from an X-class flare could cause major disruptions to the U.S. electrical grid, which already is very vulnerable. As well as to life-sustaining critical infrastructures dependent on the grid to function. NASA said the warning regarding the X class solar flares could last for several weeks. In 2012, NASA said the sun unleashed two massive clouds of plasma that barely missed a catastrophic encounter with Earth. "If it had hit, we would still be picking up the pieces." NASA physicists had announced two years after the event had occurred.

CHURCH LEADERS.COM- Less than 20 percent of Americans regularly attend church—half of what the pollsters report. While Gallup polls and other statisticians have turned in the same percentage—about 40 percent of the population—on average, have been weekend church attendees for the past 70 years. A different sort of research paints quite a disparate picture of how many Americans attend a local church on any given Sunday.

"We knew that over the past 30 to 40 years, denominations had increasingly reported a decline in their numbers," Marler says. "Even a still-growing denomination like the Southern Baptist Convention had reported slowed growth. Most of the mainline denominations were all reporting a net loss over the past 30 years. At the same time, the Gallup polls had remained stable. It didn't make sense."

WASHINGTON DC- The Pentagon Admits Preparing for Mass Civil Unrest. In a research program being ran by the Department of Defense, they have basically admitted that the Pentagon has long been concerned about widespread civil unrest. More shocking than that bombshell, is the fact that they are now funding universities to model the risks and tipping points that would come with a breakdown of American society at large. The program costs millions of dollars, and is designed to derive, "warfighter-relevant insights". According to the Pentagon, the purpose is for senior officials and decisions made in "the defense policy community" to come up with contingency plans should widespread social unrest occur.

TIME OF JACOB'S TROUBLE PART ONE

SWORD OF DAVID

James R Dale

Chapter One

Sooner or Later

"Before you were formed in your mother's womb, I knew you.

Before you were born, I set you apart."

Jeremiah 1:5

The rhythmic *'thump, thump, thump'* of the UH 60-B Blackhawk helicopter rotor blades had quickly lulled Master Sergeant Jack Braedan to sleep. It was not uncommon for "Blackjack" Braedan, as he was nicknamed by the members of Team 322, 1st Special Forces Operational Detachment-Delta, to nod off before an insertion. In fact, it was hoped for. Because, if "Blackjack" fell asleep during their flight, it meant their leader was calm and confident. If he remained awake, studying maps, and going over their mission brief, his men knew trouble was coming.

Today's mission had all the earmarks of trouble. The men of 322 were flying to a remote village in the Sana'a Governate of Yemen, where they hoped to capture one of the most prominent leaders of the Houthi rebels. Though the Houthi movement had started as a protest to economic underdevelopment and government corruption, their chosen flag proclaimed "Death to America. Death to Israel." That motto, and the Houthis proclivity for terrorism, made them America's enemies. It was the business of 322 to strike fear and dread into the heart of American's enemies, and to seek out justice where normal American soldiers dare not tread.

Tonight their business was with Sayeed Mohammad Ali. Ali was the Houthi warlord responsible for the death of six American security contractors during the 2011 attack on the US consulate in the Yemini capital. It is often said that Americans have notoriously short memories. That wasn't so among the special operations community. Two of those contractors had been former members of Delta. The mission to capture Ali had been put together quickly, based on spotty intelligence. But "Blackjack" Braedan had fallen asleep soon after the Blackhawk had lifted off the deck of the USS Ronald Reagan in the Arabian Sea. Since their leader was sleeping peacefully, the men of "Double Duce" were calm and confident as well. They knew Ali's days of avoiding justice were about to come to an end.

"Five minutes," a voice announced over 322's headphones.

"Roger," Master Sergeant Braedan acknowledged, instantly awake.

A blast of cold air assaulted the team as Staff Sergeant Jonathan "Jon Jon" Roberts, the team demolition specialist, slid open the right-side fuselage door of the Blackhawk. Still flying at over 200 kilometers per hour and 4,500 feet above sea level, the early spring air of the Yemeni mountains was a frigid wall as it rushed inside the chopper. About 100 meters to the right of the UH 60-B, flew an AH-64 Apache Longbow gun ship, Chalk 1's wingman for the night's operation. The Apache, armed with an M230 30mm chain gun and 8 AGM-114 HELLFIRE Missiles, would be the Close Air Support for the team, as they took down Ali. As Staff Sergeant Alan "Smurf" Taylor opened the Blackhawk's other fuselage door, Blackjack looked out to the left. He saw Chalk 2, Delta 321, in their own Blackhawk with their own Apache escort.

High above the flight of four choppers circled a General Atomics MQ-9 Reaper UAV, more commonly known as a Predator. The Predator drone's job was to provide real time video feed back to the 1st Special Forces "*Head Shed*" sitting safely in the Tactical Operations Center aboard the USS Ronald Reagan. In addition to providing the video feed, the Predator drone also had a Hellfire missile tucked neatly under each wing, ready to contribute to the unholy havoc that the Apaches could create, if needed. Though, Intel had said that wouldn't be necessary tonight. In fact, Intel said Ali had been living alone in these rugged mountains these past two weeks, protected only by a single guard and his oldest son. They had said that he would not link up with his band of one hundred Houthi fighters for *at least* another 72 hours.

Blackjack was glad that the Apaches and the Predator had come along just the same. Intel in this godforsaken corner of the world was famous for being notoriously optimistic.

"Que it up, Chief," Blackjack instructed the Blackhawk co-pilot.

"Roger," CW3 Richards replied. You could almost hear the grin in the chief's voice, as Johnny Cash instantly filled the headsets of the men of 322.

"Blackjack" Braedan's music of choice would have been Disturbed or Marylin Manson, but it was Terry "Mad Mac" McDonald's turn to pick the team's "walk up" music and he loved Johnny Cash. Jack had to admit, the song was a fitting tune for the judgment they were about to meet out on the murderous Ali. '*You could run but you couldn't hide*,' Johnny Cash promised. '*Sooner or later God would cut you down*'. Fitting indeed. 322 was coming, and judgement was coming with them.

"One minute. We have the target in sight."

"Roger," Blackjack replied.

In sixty seconds, the Delta Operators would roar into the target area, hovering above Ali's mountain hovel at exactly 0245 hours, fast roping the last thirty feet to the ground. Whether they would have tactical surprise was anyone's guess. *Everyone* in the Yemeni government, from President Bharzani on down, had a hand in approving tonight's mission. Blackjack, Jon Jon, Sergeants First Class Terry "Mad Mac" McDowell, the team Intelligence Sergeant, and Julian "Julie" Hesterman, the team medic, would breach and clear Ail's home, marked as T1 (Target 1). The rest of 322, which included Major Anthony "Big A" Brant, Sergeants First Class Jerry "Cowboy" Jones, Tomas "Swede" Johansson, and Staff Sergeants, Tommy "Yankee Dog" Ni Yung and Cody "Nasty" Harrell would provide outer cordon and clear T2, which was an outbuilding adjacent to T1. Delta 321 would provide outer cordon for T1 and T2 while supporting 22's breach team of T1, if needed.

"Okay, gentlemen, time to punch the time clock," Blackjack announced, pulling back the charging handle on his modified M4A2 Carbine, and feeding a 6.8mm round into its chamber. He released the handle and it sprang forward, seating the round. Blackjack tapped the forward assist and flipped the selector lever from Safe to Auto. The rest of 322 followed his lead and soon they were "hot" as well.

The Blackhawk helicopter began to slow, and Jack Braedan knew the green "Go" light was seconds away. The UH 60-B flared and assumed a hover. The status light, just inches from Black Jack's face, went from Red to Green just as expected. Jon Jon tossed out the coil of repelling rope, and the men of 322 leapt into the dark night and into combat.

Although the moon was waxing on the twenty-ninth day of March, providing less than 10 percent illumination, the four tubed and improved Night Vision Goggles worn by 322, provided the Delta Force operators all the amplified light they needed. In a surreal world of green and black, Jack grabbed the repel rope and followed Jon Jon to the ground. A few heart beats later, he was against the outside wall of Ali's mud hut, watching Jon Jon place a two-ounce doughnut charge of Composition 4 plastique explosive on the crude lock of the hut's wooden door. A light tap on his shoulder informed him that Mad Mac and Julie were "stacked up" behind him, ready to follow him into the unknown.

Blackjack slung his carbine and withdrew an M84 stun grenade from one of the many utility pouches on his kit. More commonly known as a "Flash bang," the M84 would produce a blinding "flash" of more than one million candela within five feet of initiation and emit an intensely loud "bang" of 170–180 decibels. It was sufficient to cause immediate, temporary flash blindness, deafness, tinnitus, and inner ear disturbance. Ali would now undoubtedly be aware of their arrival. But the door breaching charge and the "flash bang" would provide the 322 with the precious few seconds of disorientation they needed upon entry, to hopefully overwhelm whoever may be inside the mud walled hut, quickly and efficiently.

Blackjack pulled the safety pin on the "flash bang" and nodded to Jon Jon.

"Fire in the hole," Roberts mouthed silently. Blackjack closed his eyes and turned his head.

Roberts pressed the detonator, and the doughnut charge blew the lock off the wooden door. A half a second later, Jon Jon kicked the door open, as Blackjack released the spoon of the M84 stun grenade and tossed it inside Ali's home. "One thousand one, one thousand two, one thousand...." The "flash bang" exploded, filling the inside of the hut with a blinding light. Jon Jon entered, breaking left. Blackjack Braedan broke right and was followed immediately by Julie and Mad Mac.

The assault was over in less than 30 seconds.

"Two Tangos KIA," Blackjack reported to Big A, over his voice activated throat microphone. "*The Champ* is zipped, muzzled and ready for transport." *The Champ* was the code name selected for Sayeed Mohammed Ali by the Head Shed. "All Tangos are photo'd and swabbed. Julie and Mac are staring their sweep."

"Roger," Major Brant acknowledged. "All quiet at T2. Looks like the Spooks got one right for a change. Extraction will be at Pah Pah Zulu Delores in one five mikes. I say again, Pah Pah Zulu in fifteen minutes. Tell the Boys to make it quick. Acknowledge."

"See you at Delores, Boss," Blackjack replied, raising his arm, and making a circling motion with his index finger to the assault team. "Julie! Mac! You have ten minutes and then we roll."

"Lot of stuff to go through here, Blackjack," McDowell complained.

"You can stay longer if you like, Mac," Braeden shrugged. "I'm sure the *Champ's* entourage will be happy to help you sort through it when they show up."

"Well, since you put it that way..." the huge Texan grumbled.

"Clear the net," Big A announced. "Traffic from HQ. Wait one."

After a moment of silence, as the Team waited for perhaps a follow-on mission or some other such calamity, Major Brant came back on the net. "Blackjack, you're taking Yankee Dog's seat on the bird next to me. Cowboy, round up Double Duce."

"What's up?" Jack asked, curiously.

"Just meet me at the bird, Jack," Big A insisted, quietly.

* * *

Jack Braedan awoke to a glorious spring morning shining through the second story window of his parent's spacious country home. He hadn't been back to his childhood residence in Franklin, Tennessee in over two years. He had arrived well after midnight, driving nonstop from Fort Bragg, as soon as he'd suffered through the mandatory out briefs and med checks that come with returning from an overseas operation. After a brief, unemotional meeting with the Delta Chaplin, Jack signed out on emergency leave and was driving 80 miles per hour down Interstate 40 West in his tan, 2016 Jeep Rubicon. By 2AM, he was curled up in his old bedroom, fast asleep.

"John Michael," a female voice called loudly from downstairs. "Are you going to sleep all day? Breakfast will be ready in ten minutes!"

Jack stretched and looked at his watch. It was almost seven o'clock. Jack had gotten five strong hours of rest making him alert and on point. He could smell the bacon frying downstairs. His mom was cooking for her boy. Even though Jack was a Special Forces operator with nine deployments to the Middle East and the Horn of Africa over the last three years, he was perpetually twelve years old in the eyes of his mom, Maryellen Braedan.

Suddenly, a surge of emotion swept over him as Jack realized it wouldn't be his mom downstairs cooking. Mom and Dad were gone. Major Brant's insistence to meet him at the bird had been followed by "I'm so sorry, Jack," and the grim news that a drunk driver had collided with his parent's BMW, killing them instantly. The voice downstairs was his Aunt Kate. Her Audi RS3 had been in the driveway when he'd pulled in at 2AM. Jack swung his legs over the side of the bed and ran fingers through his thick brown hair. Ten minutes was enough time for a shower. Exactly nine minutes later he was dressed in grey sweats and running shoes, bounding down the stairs toward the Braedan's enormous kitchen.

"Hey, Aunt Kate," Jack said quietly. "Long time, no see."

"Oh Jack, come here." his aunt sighed, turning away from the bubbling pan of milk gravy on the stove and holding out her arms.

Katrina Braedan was a walking, breathing, southern belle. Five foot ten and slender; Kate had been the 1980 Vanderbilt University football homecoming queen. She still ran 15 miles a week, played tennis every Tuesday, and didn't look a day over forty-five, despite being closer to 60. Katrina Holder and Maryellen Messenger had been roommates at Vanderbilt and could have passed for twins. Jack used to tease his dad, saying that's what attracted him and Uncle Sean to the pair.

"How are you doing, Kate?" asked Jack, stepping into her embrace, and wrapping strong arms around his aunt, hugging her tightly.

"Well, as well as can be expected," his aunt replied. "How are you, hon?"

"Tired," he sighed, planting a kiss on her cheek before setting her back on her feet. "What are you cooking?"

"Your mom's Sunday morning special," his aunt replied, then tears welled in her eyes and she wrapped her arms around him again. "I know its Saturday, but I thought...Oh Jack, I'm so sorry."

"Kate," Jack said, reaching up to brush a tear away from his aunt's cheek. "It's going to be okay."

"You always were the strong one," she replied with a sad sigh. "I guess it comes with the territory." Kate took a deep breath and let it out slowly. "Sit down, honey, and let me get your breakfast. The service is at 11:00. It's going to be a long day."

"Where's Uncle Sean?" he asked, pouring himself a cup of black coffee, and taking a seat at the spacious Braedan kitchen table.

"He's at the funeral home making some final arrangements," his aunt replied.

"I'm sorry I couldn't get back sooner," Jack said, quietly. From the moment "Big A" broke the news to him, it had taken five days to travel from Yemen to the Braedan's driveway.

"Oh sweetheart, don't be!" she insisted, returning to the task at hand, by moving the pan of gravy aside to place a new pan on the stove. "Sean took care of everything, and we know the military got you back here as quickly as they could."

If there was someone who could "take care of everything," it was his Uncle Sean. Sean Braedan was the attorney for the city of Franklin, Tennessee. Along with his dad, he was one of the most influential men in Williamson County. The only thing Sean loved more than influence was the law and legal wrangling. And the only thing he loved more than legal wheeling and dealing was Franklin First Methodist Church and the Lord God, Jesus Christ. The Braedan family surely loved the Lord God.

Jack, however, was the proverbial black sheep. Religion just never "took" with him. That didn't mean he didn't respect his family. His dad and his Uncle Sean were the two biggest heroes in his life, outside the men on his Team. Jack might scoff at Jesus Freaks when drinking beer with his team, or if he happened to be scanning through the channels on the television and caught sight of one of the many *Tee Vee* evangelists, but he wouldn't *dream* of disrespecting the church in front of either of them. Even at sixty, his dad or uncle would still *thump* Jack on the head if they caught him talking bad about the church or church-goers.

"So, he's not coming here before...before the funeral?" Jack asked.

"No, honey," his aunt replied, removing a pan of golden-brown biscuits from the stove. "He's got a meeting with the mayor at 9:30. There's been some trouble with the re-zoning issue for the mosque they want to build out on Buckner Road."

"A mosque?" Jack exclaimed, almost choking on his coffee. "Here? In Franklin?"

"The one they built in Murfreesboro a couple of years ago just won't hold them all," Kate sighed. "All of those new Syrian immigrants flooding into Middle Tennessee need a place to pray," she finished.

He couldn't help but note the sound of consternation in her voice. Katrina Braedan was a southern belle to the core, who treated everyone with respect and dignity regardless of their station in life, but she just couldn't *stand* that false prophet, *Mohamed,* and his false religion. But she knew the state of the world. Things were changing in the U.S.A.

"I hope you're hungry," she said, carrying over a plate piled high with scrambled eggs, bacon, and biscuits, all smothered in gravy.

***

Jack stood in the receiving line, dressed all in black like he was some 21st Century Angel of Death: black suit, black shirt, black tie, and black Wayfarer sunglasses to hide his bloodshot eyes. He had bought the entire $900 ensemble at Joseph A. Banks in the Cool Springs Mall, barely two hours ago. It mirrored his black mood to a T.

"It was a lovely service," said an elderly matron, patting his cheek with a withered hand.

"Thanks," Jack replied mechanically. "Thanks for coming."

"Maryellen and Big Jim were real saints," the next person informed him.

"Thanks," Jack nodded, "Thanks for coming."

Even though he knew they meant well, every expression of condolence was like pouring salt on an open wound. "I have to get out of here, Sean," Jack whispered to his uncle. There were at least another hundred more people still waiting in line. Only a few short months ago this large gathering would have sent the doomsayers into a panic as a super spreader event.

"You go on, son," his uncle nodded, placing a sympathetic hand on his shoulder. "We'll see it through."

"Jack, I know you will hate it, but supper will be promptly at seven," Aunt Kate said, giving him perhaps the fiftieth hug of the day. "Don't be late. There will be company. Everyone loved your mom and dad."

"I won't be," Jack replied, though he inwardly cringed. Company meant at least 20 or 30 guests to Braedan women. And yet *another* opportunity for the family to talk about how much God loved them, even in the hard times. "I'll be back way before six. I love you."

Before he left First Methodist, Jack stopped by the church cemetery, avoiding the two newly dug graves, and paid his respects to the only friend he had left in Franklin. Staff Sergeant Timothy Horn, a Silver Star and Purple Heart recipient, was buried under a simple, white government headstone. Tim had died in a fiery IED blast in Ramallah, Iraq in 2011, while Jack was attending Delta Force selection course at Camp MacDill, Florida. Jack had been thirty days in and been given the painful option of going to the funeral and being recycled to zero day or completing selection. Tim wasn't his first friend to die in battle, and he would not be the last. Jack took his sorrow and bundled it up tight, tucking it away in a dark corner of his heart. He finished the course as the Honor Graduate among the 13 soldiers remaining out of the 52 who started.

Jack stood in front of Tim's marker, remembering that sorrowful day. The fact that it has been two months later, when he'd finally gotten leave to come home and pay his respects, filled Jack with a bitter, burning anger. Iraq, where so many good men and women had bled and died, was once again an enemy in all but name. Afghanistan, where he'd spilled blood and where so many other friends and comrades had given their last full measure, would likely fall back into chaos six months after the final American combat soldier pulled out. What was the point of so many wasted lives? What was the gain from so much destruction and death? The America that he and Tim, along with so many others had signed up to defend in the years following 9/11, was barely recognizable anymore. Eighteen years after every single member of congress, Democrat and Republican alike, stood on the capitol steps and sang "God Bless America," his beloved country was 21 trillion dollars in debt and tearing itself apart from the inside.

Life was a bag full of hot crap.

Jack found himself wishing he'd just stayed at home and drowned himself on a bottle Bourbon. He wiped a tear from his eye and headed for his Jeep. He was driving aimlessly when he spotted a refurbished red brick and glass building across the parking lot from the old Azzo Computers store. Noticing the red and white "Grand Re-Opening" banner, he immediately turned his Jeep into the crowded parking lot. "*Guns USA*" the store sign proclaimed. If there was anything that could chase away the black mood that had descended on him, it would be a new gun.

America may have been spiraling down the toilet and bleeding out like a stuck pig, but one passion remained. She loved her guns. Eight years under the thumb of a gun hating, socialist president had been relived a bit by a term under "The Donald", but the libs were back and charge and crying again about "*If it only saves one life*." How long the 2nd Amendment would survive was anyone's guess.

Guns USA was 20,000 square feet of gleaming tile floors, aisles of grey metal shelves stacked with ammo, and display racks of myriad shooting accessories. Glass counter-top cases filled with pistols lined two walls, and behind the counters stood smiling, polo shirt and khaki pants wearing salespeople. Behind the *Guns USA* salespeople, were walls of shotguns, hunting rifles and a large selection of evil and misnamed, "assault" weapons. The fourth wall was thick glass, and behind it was an indoor range. Save for a handful of staunch constitutionalists in congress, mega stores like *Guns USA* would be only a memory after last January's massacre at the Dallas Convention center.

"Can I help you find something?" asked a salesman behind the counter. He was fit, with steel grey hair, a tan leathery face, and was at least a decade older than any of the other *Guns USA* employees. There was a confident air about him that spoke of someone who might possess actual knowledge of firearms.

"Got anything that'll scare the crap out of a liberal?" Jack inquired.

"Got plenty of those," the man grinned. "Looking for something in particular?"

"Let me see that 36 Delta," Jack said, inclining his head towards a short barreled, compact carbine with a folding butt stock.

"Heckler and Koch," the man smiled, reaching behind him to lift the lightweight carbine off its pegs. "Gotta love the Germans. Seven and a half pounds," he said, handing the weapon to Braeden. "800-meter range; 1.5 power scope with a fixed 300-meter reticle. 30 round mag or 100 round C-Mag drum. Civilian model of course. No full auto."

"Fired it yet?" asked Jack, clearing the carbine out of habit, and pointing the barrel in a safe direction to look through the sight.

"Nothing goes on the wall without a test fire," the man informed him.

Jack flipped open the collapsible stock and went to low ready, then to firing position. It felt good. Laying the carbine on the counter, he began to quickly field strip the weapon. In a few short seconds, Jack Braedan had it broken down and was inspecting the bolt.

"You in the service?" the man asked, examining him more closely. "You look like some sort of secret agent man."

"Coast Guard Reserve," Jack replied deadpan, removing his sunglasses, and laying them on the counter.

"Coast Guard," the man laughed. "That's funny. My name's Dave," he said, extending his hand. "Proud owner of this fine establishment."

"I'm Jack," he nodded. Dave had a firm grip. Not challenging like a man trying to prove he was an Alpha, but assured and confident. Braedan liked him instantly.

"Okay, Coastie," Dave smiled as he released Jack's hand. "Let me know if you need help putting her back together."

"Where does this springy thing go?" Jack asked, beginning to reassemble the carbine even quicker than he broke it down.

"Can I help you find something, ma'am?" Dave asked, turning to his left.

"Actually," a female voice replied, hesitantly. "I'm looking for him."

Jack stopped his reassembly of the H & K and glanced over curiously. His heart skipped a beat when he saw who had spoken. The woman *may* have been the most beautiful creature he'd ever laid eyes on. She was tall, just an inch or so below six feet. Wavy, auburn hair flecked with fire trailed halfway down her back, free and unencumbered, except for a few thick braids. She was wearing a black, form fitting dress that clung deliciously to every curve and stopped at mid-thigh. Her pale, perfect skin didn't have an ounce of makeup. She was inspecting Jack with emerald eyes so green, Braedan involuntarily caught his breath.

"Two folks all dressed in black," Dave observed. "Are you a secret agent like 007 here?"

"Worse," she replied, "I'm a lawyer."

"I thought I recognized you, Counselor," Dave nodded, his mood darkening.

"Ummm, have we met?" Jack asked, hesitantly. "I'm Jack Braedan," he said, introducing himself. He walked over and offered her his hand. *"My God she was beautiful."* She was New York runway beautiful, in fact. Sports Illustrated model beautiful. Not a delicate flower though. There was an air of strength about her that only the unwary or unobservant would miss. She took his hand in a confident grip, not timid at all.

"I know who you are," she said. Her eyes burned into him like emerald fire. "I was at the funeral, but you left before I could catch you. Full disclosure, I followed you here."

"Really?" asked Jack suspiciously, "Why would a lawyer be following me? You're not going to serve me with papers, are you? Because that would be a crappy move on a day like today, even for a lawyer. Last time I was home was.... December 2019? I'm embarrassed to say, the only time I went out, I got stupidly drunk at Twin Peaks. If it's about the hostess I slapped on the butt, I paid the disorderly conduct fine and court costs."

"I'm not serving you papers," she assured him. "But I'm sorry I missed that. You really don't remember me, do you?"

"Look, I'm drawing a blank here," Jack said, studying her face intently now, wondering who in the world this beautiful lawyer was, who had appeared suddenly on this very dark day. "I am *really* positive if we'd had *ever* met, I would remember you. It's been a long week. My focus is a little off so..."

"I'm sorry," she interrupted, eyes filling with sympathy. "I shouldn't be playing games with you, not today. I'm...."

"How about you let me guess?" Jack interrupted suddenly. "Games can be distracting. This is the first time I've thought about something other than...well, this is the first time in a week I've had something to interest me. So, we've met before, huh?"

"Oh yes," the woman nodded, smiling for the first time. "And it was *not* at Twin Peaks. Would you like a hint? Something to jog your memory?"

"Okay, deal," Jack nodded slowly, "but nothing vague like, 'Your mother went to school with my mother in third grade.'"

"Fair enough," she agreed. She thought it over for several seconds, trying to find just the right balance. "Your senior year at Franklin Road Academy, you dated Bethany Costner," she offered.

Bethany Costner? That was certainly a name from his distant past. He hadn't thought about that she-devil in years. "Franklin Road, 2004," prompted the beautiful lawyer. Then it hit him, and Jack's eyes widened in shock. Beth had a nine-year-old sister, painfully awkward, and painfully freckled, with hair as orange as the sun. Beth had tormented her unmercifully. In truth, the treatment of her little sister was one of the reasons their relationship had soured. As beautiful as Beth had been on the outside, the way she treated her younger sibling was as equally cruel and off-putting. It had become something even a hormonal teenage boy couldn't overlook, even in a stunner like Beth.

"So, he does remember after all," she nodded, seeing the look of disbelief on his face.

"My God," Braedan whispered, "You're Little..." He almost said Little Orphan Annie, Beth's cruel nickname for her younger sister. "You're little Annie Costner?"

"I am," she replied with a dazzling smile.

Jack was suddenly glad he'd taken pity on that awkward little girl and had gone out of his way to treat her like a princess. By the time his stormy, six-month relationship with Beth had ended, he actually spent more time comforting little Orphan Annie, than paying attention to the Rebel's homecoming queen.

"Wow," Jack said. "I mean, wow!" This time he didn't try to disguise his head-to-toe appreciation.

"I'll take that as a compliment," she said, blushing.

"What are you doing this afternoon, Annie Costner?" Braedan was surprised to hear himself ask, impulsively. "You want to go get a cup of coffee or something? For the rest of your life?"

"Slow down," she smiled. "Just because I followed you here, doesn't mean I'm ready to play house."

"Sorry, that was inappropriate," he apologized, quickly. His parents weren't in the ground an hour, and here he was flirting with a red-headed ghost from his past.

"Apology accepted," she nodded. "Just don't call me Annie. That was Beth's nickname. It's Anna."

"Why did you follow me, Anna?" asked Jack curiously. "And why today?"

"When you skipped out of the funeral." She replied. "I didn't know how long you'd be in town. So..."

"So, you followed me instead of picking up a phone?"

" I followed you because I wanted to tell you in person how sorry I am. It's been a long time, Jack. But I still remember how nice you were to me. I've never forgotten you," she admitted, blushing again.

"I'm glad you didn't just call. How about I repay you with dinner?" Jack asked. "We can catch up, talk about how horrible Beth was, maybe?"

"As lovely as *that* sounds," Anna replied, sarcastically, "I already have dinner plans. Tell you what, do you have a pen?"

"Hey, Dave! Let me borrow a pen." Jack said, turning back to find Hitchcock had been watching the entire exchange. He fished a ball-point out of his shirt pocket and tossed in Jack's general direction. Braedan snatched it out of the air and handed it to Anna. She accepted it, then reached into her handbag on the counter and pulled out a business card, writing on the back.

"That's my cell number. After everything that's happened, if you still want coffee, give me a call tomorrow. And, Jack," Anna said, stepping so close to him their bodies almost touched. "I am really sorry about your mom and dad. They were good people." She tucked the pen into the pocket of his jacket, held his gaze for a heartbeat longer with those emerald green eyes, and then turned back to Dave. "Mr. Hitchcock, I actually do need to look for something. May I come back say, around five?"

"We're open until 8PM, Counselor," Dave nodded.

"It was good seeing you again," Anna smiled at Jack, and walked away before he could reply.

"Do you like her?" Dave asked, turning his attention back to Jack.

"I haven't seen Anna Costner in, Jeez, almost fifteen years?" Jack replied quietly. "Man, that was a pleasant surprise!"

"I meant the H&K, Coastie," Dave said.

"Oh. Oh yeah, of course. Is this your lowest price?" Jack asked. The price tag said $2,300. Even for a civilian version of the German carbine, he thought it was a little steep.

"With that Marxist witch Pelosi on full court press for a new ban, after that horrible Dallas mess?" Dave sighed, "Afraid so. But for the Coast Guard? 10% discount with military ID."

"Start the paperwork," Jack said, removing his driver's license and military ID from his wallet and sliding it across the counter. "Can I get 200 rounds, as well?" he asked, as he began to reassemble the German carbine.

Dave picked up the military ID, studied it for a second, and then looked back at Jack. "You're Big Jim and Maryellen's son," he stated. "I should have guessed from all that funeral talk."

"I am," Jack nodded.

Dave slid the IDs back across the table and reached out to shake his hand again. "I was in the...uh...Coast Guard myself once upon a time. Did some SCUD hunting with the 3rd back in Desert Storm... among other things?"

"We do bad things...." Jack said.

"To bad people," Dave finished.

It was the 3rd Special Forces Group unofficial motto. Jack had been a member of 3rd Group, until he was recruited to try out for Delta. "How does twenty-one hundred sound?" Dave asked. "And I will throw in three hundred rounds and a couple of extra magazines?"

"It sounds *really* good," Jack said, sliding the ID back in his wallet. "But you don't have to do that."

"Call it the "*Group*" rate," Dave grinned. "David Hitchcock. Sergeant First Class, retired."

"Wait...you're not *The* David Hitchcock, are you?" asked Jack, surprised.

"What's left of him," Dave laughed. "Though, I didn't know I had a '*the*' in front of my name."

"Small world," Braedan smiled. David Hitchcock was a Desert Storm legend among Special Forces Operators. He was awarded the Distinguished Service Cross and Purple Heart when he lost both legs to a...Jack looked down through the glass topped counter.

"VA treats me well," Hitchcock grinned. "Despite the horror stories. Most people can't even tell I'm a walking, talking *Loo-ten-ANT Day-uhn,"* he finished, in a passable Forrest Gump. "Computer has been acting wonky this morning, Coastie. Finish putting that H & K back together while I see if I can get it rebooted. Do you mind if I give you a bit of advice, Coastie? No extra charge."

"Always willing to listen to old-timers," Jack smiled.

"You're swimming in dangerous water with the lawyer," Dave said. "Miss Costner is quite a looker, I'll give you that, but don't make the mistake of not being able to see beyond those pouty lips and those big uh... green eyes. She's ruthless from what I hear. One year out of law school and already a scourge on Williamson County prosecutors and a bane of the local GOP. Are you up to date on you drown-proofing?"

"I can handle myself," Jack replied, locking the bolt back into place and doing a function check on the H&K before laying it back on the counter.

"Just remember you were warned," David Hitchcock sighed. "I'll get the computer re-booted."

Chapter Two

Dinner

Once Hitchcock had the computer back up and running, he asked Jack question after question, typing in the gigabits of the personal information necessary to purchase the Heckler and Koch carbine. In-between pages, Jack invited Dave to his aunt's "dinner" at seven. He was pleasantly surprised to discover the former Special Forces operator was already on the guest list.

"I was in your mom's Sunday school class," Hitchcock informed him, "Your mom is...was a special lady, and I am truly sorry for your loss. I hate that I didn't go to the funeral. I don't do funerals anymore. I've watched too many people I cared about get put in the ground. My wife was there, but I guess she didn't get a chance to introduce herself."

"I popped smoke before it was over," Jack replied. "I've seen too many people put in the ground myself."

For some reason, finding out David Hitchcock was a student in his mother's Sunday school class was more surprising to Braedan than learning of his invitation to dinner. He just wasn't that accustomed to warriors, even retired ones, going to.... Sunday school. Going through life without both of your legs, he guessed, could change a man. It didn't make David Hitchcock any less of a legend. Whether Dave had become a Bible thumper or not, he'd be delighted to have someone at one of the Braedan dinner parties who wouldn't spend the night asking him stupid questions like, "What's it like to kill someone? Or "How many terrorists have you tortured?"

"I'll probably be the talk of the town because of it," Jack sighed, signing his name on the credit card slip and collecting his brand-new H & K 36D carbine, along with his 300 rounds of 5.56mm.

"Ah, let them talk," Dave shrugged. "Each man mourns in his own way. See you at seven?"

"Looking forward to it," Jack said, reaching out to shake Hitchcock's hand, one last time.

"And seriously, you watch your step with Ms. Costner," Hitchcock advised him again. "She's as liberal as any Harvard lawyer can get. Can I help you find something?" he asked, turning to his next customer.

Jack returned to his parent's home to find his Aunt Kate busy in the kitchen, with a couple of ladies from First Methodist church. After a couple of polite, "Nice to meet you" greetings, he gave his aunt a quick kiss on the cheek. "I met one of mom's Sunday school kids in town. David Hitchcock."

"Dave is a dear," Katrina smiled, continuing to stir a concoction she was mixing up in a tremendous Pyrex bowl. "He was in the army too. Lost both his legs, poor man. Had a rough go for a long time, but he's back on track now."

"He's got one powerful witness," one of the church ladies said.

"Powerful witness, indeed," his aunt nodded.

"Well, I'll leave you ladies, to your gossip," Jack said, wanting to make an escape before Kate could launch into how Dave found Jesus. She was just like his mom. Neither of them ever gave it a rest. "If you need me to open any jars or some other manly chore, I'll be upstairs cleaning my new toy."

"I think we can manage, hon," his aunt smiled sadly. "Dress nice for dinner. No jeans. There are some *very* special people coming tonight."

"I'm sure," Jack sighed, already mentally steeling himself for the Big Jim and Maryellen memorial praise and worship dinner. "Ladies," he excused himself with a slight bow.

As he headed up the stairs, he could hear them laughing quietly in the kitchen. "*Church ladies. What a weird breed they were. Whatever makes them happy...*" Jack thought. "*Me, I have a brand new 36 Delta to play with.*"

Jack spent the afternoon cleaning his new carbine, making sure every little piece was spotless, oiled, and ready for action. When he was finished, he took it to the "bonus room" which had become over the years nothing more than gun storage for the many firearms Big Jim owned. He found an empty space on the wall between a Mossberg 590 pump and Marlin 30/30 lever action rifle. After standing to admire it for a moment, he decided the H & K would be coming back with him to Fort Bragg, despite all the piles of paperwork he'd have to suffer through to get it on base.

Jack stifled a yawn. Realizing that he was still tired from the return flight from Africa and his drive from Fort Bragg, he went back to the guest room and took a nap. When he awoke, he found the time was nearing 6 PM. He brushed his teeth, took another quick shower, and after a moment's thought, he found a pair of clippers and trimmed back his deployment beard. Looking less the operator now and more civilized, he dressed in khaki's and a light blue collared shirt and proceed downstairs. He found the table already set in the grand dining room, with wonderful smells coming from the kitchen. In his dad's study, Jack found his Uncle Sean smoking a cigar and watching CNN.

"Those things will kill you," he said, leaning against the door jamb.

"Everyone has to die of something," Sean Braedan replied, rising from his dad's favorite leather chair. "Come give your uncle a big hug, my boy. We're alone now, no one to gawk."

"How have you...ugh, been?" Jack asked, as he was enveloped in Sean's embrace. His uncle was a good three inches taller and fifty pounds heavier than Jack. Still fit for someone who celebrated his sixtieth birthday, just two months ago. Sean Braedan almost squeezed the breath out of his warrior nephew.

"Good, now that you're back in the states," Sean smiled, holding his nephew at arm's length. "They're Cuban," he said, inclining his head toward the ash tray where his cigar was smoldering. "Want one? Only good thing to come out of the entire Obama administration, as far as I'm concerned."

"Sure," Jack nodded, "Mind if I make myself a cocktail? To enhance the flavor of these fine cigars, of course."

"Pour me one, as well," Sean smiled. "Bourbon...."

"On the rocks," Jack finished. It was the only thing he'd ever seen his uncle drink.

"Until the last one comes home?" Sean asked, accepting his tumbler of *Jim Beam Black.*

"Until the last one comes home," Jack nodded, clicking his glass to his uncle's. It was a traditional Braedan toast.

"Have a seat and tell me what you've been up to," Sean said, clipping off the end one of the Cubans. "Nasty business, at that," he said, inclining his head toward the 50-inch flat screen above the study fireplace as he handed Jack his cigar.

The sound was turned down on the TV and closed caption was scrolling across the bottom of the screen. It was the way Big Jim had watched the news for as long as Jack could remember, and apparently his uncle had the same habit. A network talking head was on split screen with a reporter in Tel Aviv. They were discussing yet another homicide bombing attack in Israel. It was on a bus this time, in downtown Jerusalem. Ever since the Israelis had announced plans to start rebuilding a temple, Jerusalem had been a battlefield. This bombing was particularly lethal. There were 46 confirmed dead, so far. The smoke hadn't even cleared before the IDF began pounding the Hamas military headquarters in Gaza to rubble. Syria had paused their decade old civil war to mass troops along the Israeli border in a show of solidarity. Hezbollah in Lebanon was showing signs of doing the same. Israel responded by placing their army and air force on maximum alert and calling up all reserves.

"Same stuff, different day," Jack shrugged, allowing his uncle to light his cigar with a wooden match. No other flame would do for a quality cigar. Big Jim insisted on it, and Sean agreed.

"I really think the Jews have had enough this time and will burn down Gaza to the ground," Sean replied. Jack knew his uncle didn't mean *"the Jews"* in any derogatory manner. His dad was...well, had been now he supposed, the President of the local chapter of "*Christian Friends of Zion*" in Williamson County, and his Uncle Sean was the treasurer. Against Jack's protests, the group took annual trips to Israel. They never called it Israel, of course; to them it was simply "The Holy Land."

"I don't doubt it, Uncle Sean," Jack agreed. "I really have no idea why they've waited this long. I'm sure it's all about oil until they get their first refinery online next month, and pressure from the US to play nice. Politics." *That last word he said with a tone of barely disguised contempt.* "We did an Op last winter with IDF commandos. Deadly bunch of gunfighters. They are certainly ready and willing. They're just waiting for a green light."

"It's inevitable," Sean sighed. "And coming soon. You look tired," he said, suddenly switching off the TV and turning to face his nephew. "And I don't mean from lack of sleep."

Was it so easy for his uncle to see how much of a mental toll the last few years had taken on him? Jack wondered. *Could he see in his eyes what the Team only discussed over beers in private, that they were losing the will to throw themselves into the meat grinder day after day with still no clear vision on defense from the current administration?* Iraq was lost.... again. Afghanistan hung by a threat. The focus, if you could call it that, from Washington was now on North Korea, Africa, and Eastern Europe while China roamed unopposed in the Pacific.

"I still believe in my country," Jack said quietly, "or...the idea of my country. I just think we've become.... lost."

"Your aunt and I worry about you, son," Sean replied. "Your mom and dad did, as well. You know none of us agreed with the choice you made when you dropped out of college and went into the service, but we respected it."

Jack knew that to be true. His father had almost had a stroke when Jack came home one month into college and announced he had dropped out of Vanderbilt University to join the army, and not just the army, but the infantry. Big Jim had shouted and pounded his fists and raged about, "throwing away his life." On graduation day at Fort Benning, Georgia, however, his father had been on the front row. He had pinned on his airborne jump wings three weeks later and had flown to three different awards ceremonies over the last decade, two at Bragg and the last in Washington D.C., for Jack's Distinguished Service Cross in 2017. Big Jim had cried at that one.

"But...how long are you willing to be a trigger puller for a government that no longer abides by the constitution?" his uncle asked. "I know you can't talk about what you do anymore, but how long are you willing to risk your life and the lives of your men for the globalist agenda?"

"What else can I do, Sean?" Jack whispered, twirling the ice in his empty glass. *That* was precisely why he was so *"tired"* as his uncle put it. What do you do when you realize you have killed dozens...scores...of men over the last decade for a country that was no longer the same one you swore an oath to?

"All a man has to do to change his life," Sean replied, refilling his nephew's tumbler with *Jim Beam*, "to *decide* to change it. Your dad lived by those words."

Katrina Braedan poked her head into the study at that moment and crinkled her nose at the smoke. "You boys have about fifteen minutes to finish those foul things and freshen up. Our guests will start arriving soon."

"Yes, dear," Sean replied.

"Yes, ma'am," Jack echoed.

"Drink up," Uncle Sean winked, re-filling his glass to his nephew's. "I bet we can finish this bottle before your Aunt Kate comes back. Tomorrow, if you're up to it, I have something to show you. Something your dad and I finished last fall. I think it's time you see it."

"What might that be?" Jack inquired, sipping his bourbon.

"Tomorrow," Sean promised. "Tonight, we honor your parents."

At promptly one minute before 7PM, Katrina Braedan had Sean and Jack in tow and posted in the foyer to begin receiving the guests. Not surprisingly, at least not to Jack, the first to ring the doorbell was David Hitchcock, Sergeant First Class, retired. Even a retired Special Forces operator with two artificial legs couldn't abide being one second late hitting his time hack, even if it were for a dinner party. There was a beautiful, olive-skinned woman on his arm, with eyes the color of onyx. She was tall and lithe, with dark hair flecked with grey. She greeted them with a warm smile.

"David. Rebecca," Katrina smiled, giving each a kiss on the cheek. "So glad you could come."

Sean shook Dave's hand and gave his own peck on the cheek to the sergeant's lady.

"Coastie, this is my wife, Rebecca," David said, introducing the dark-eyed beauty.

"I'm Jack," Jack said, taking her hand.

"I am pleased to meet you, Jack," she replied. "Even under these circumstances. I'm so sorry for your loss. Maryellen talked of you so much. I feel like I know you already."

She was definitely not American. She had a Middle Eastern feel about her, but she didn't carry herself like an Arab.

"*Me-ei-fo a-ta, Israel*?" Jack asked. *Where are you from, Israel*? "Did I say that right?"

"Indeed," she replied, smiling with pleasure.

"I told you he'd guess it, Becca," David winked.

"That's about the extent of my Hebrew, I'm afraid," Jack smiled. "Other than can I get another beer?"

"We'll be on the back veranda to start," Katrina informed the pair. "Make yourself at home. Big Jim and Maryellen wouldn't have it any other way."

"See you inside, Jack," David smiled. "We'll see if you can guess which branch of the Mossad, Becca served in."

"I was never in the Mossad," Rebecca insisted.

"Of course not, dear," Dave smiled, kissing her cheek.

The other guests arrived in a steady stream. Some Jack thought he recognized from the funeral and others were completely new to him. He greeted them all cordially as a Braedan was expected to. He accepted the "sorry for your loss", and "thanks for your service" with the standard humility most service men and women had developed over the nearly two decades of continual war...or overseas kinetic contingency operations, as the current administration called it. A rose by any other name was still just as brutal and bloody. The last guest to arrive however, brought a surprised smile to Jack's face, even on this sad day.

"So, *this* is your dinner plans, Annabelle Costner?" he asked, as Anna stepped through their door. If it were possible, she was even more beautiful than when he'd first seen her earlier that afternoon. At *Guns USA,* Anna had looked all dark and mysterious, like the hottest Black Widow ever born. Tonight however, she was every inch a southern belle. It was a warm evening for early April, still in the mid-sixties, and Anna was wearing a bright, flower print sundress, flats, a matching clutch, and carried a light shawl over one arm; in case the evening cooled. No braids tonight. Her flowing auburn hair was combed to a lustrous sheen and draped over her left shoulder. A simple strand of pearls accentuated the smooth, pure, whiteness of her perfect neck. Jack didn't believe in love at first sight, or second, but he found himself barely able to breathe looking at her.

"Welcome Miss Costner, no discussing the town's lawsuit this evening," Sean smiled. "You'll have ample opportunity to badger me next week in front of Judge Wilcox."

"A promise is a promise, Mr. Braedan," Anna laughed softly. "Thank you again, for inviting me, Ms. Braedan."

"You are very welcome, dear. And you simply *must* call me Katrina. Or Kate," Jack's aunt insisted. "Sean speaks so highly of you. Even though you almost gave him a stroke last week."

"Thank you again...Kate," Anna smiled.

"Jack, why don't you show Anna to the veranda," his aunt smiled, innocent as a newborn lamb.

Jack offered her his arm, and she took it smoothly, like he'd escorted her to countless other dinners, on countless warm, spring evenings. "So...why the following and the guessing games this afternoon if you were coming here tonight?" he asked, trying to sound casual. David Hitchcock's warning rang in his head. Beth had been a beauty as well, but a manipulating, soul-less, harpy underneath. He really hoped her little sister hadn't turned out the same.

"I'm sorry about that," Anna said, sounding sincere. "I don't really know why I did it. Truthfully? Seeing you again caught me off guard, I guess."

Jack studied her for telltale signs of lying; yet another skill the Special Forces had taught him over the years to aid in the interrogation of insurgents and general ne'er-do-wells. She met his gaze boldly, her emerald eyes never leaving his. Her smile was genuine and warm, no change of voice inflection. "Lawyers," he sighed, "What if I water boarded you? Would you confess then?"

"You think getting me a little wet will make me talk?" Annabelle Costner smiled. She certainly had a beautiful smile. "Plying me with fine liquor on the other hand...."

Jack smiled back, unable to help himself. "Challenge accepted," he replied, and led her to the veranda and its open bar.

God Bless Methodists. The Braedan family didn't mind you being a little lubricated if you didn't overindulge. It was self-service at the bar, and Jack poured himself a generous helping of bourbon. Anna requested a Vodka and cranberry, Grey Goose if they had it, which they did. With their drinks in hand, the pair joined the mingling guests. David immediately waved them over and they joined the retired Special Forces sergeant and his wife.

"*Shabbat Shalom*," Jack said, greeting the striking Israeli again.

"*Shabbat Shalom*," Rebecca smiled appreciatively, "Technically, the Sabbath ended an hour ago. As a Messianic Jew however, I won't fault a Methodist for not knowing."

"Messianic Jew?" Anna asked. "I'm Anna, by the way. Anna Costner."

"Pleased to meet you," she smiled, "Since the men seemed to have lost their manners, I'm Rebecca, and a Messianic Jew is a Jewish Christian who still follows the Torah," she explained. "Well, most of it anyway."

"You're in enemy territory, Counselor. Are you packing that Sig Sauer?" Dave asked, ignoring his wife's glare. Anna had returned to his store and bought a P226 9mm. "No offense, but I'm kind of surprised to find you at James Braedan's house, even if you've caught his son's eye. Despite my warning."

"So, you warned him about me?" Anna asked with a quiet laugh, touching Jack lightly on the arm. He suddenly felt flushed, and not from the bourbon. "Don't believe everything you hear that comes out of the Williamson County Court House, Mr. Hitchcock. Katrina invited me after I called to offer my condolences."

"Ms. Costner is here in part to learn I'm not the bigoted monster she believes me to be," Uncle Sean said, joining them with his Aunt Kate on his arm.

"Anna is here because she is a wonderful light in a dark world," Katrina smiled, joining them. "That advice you gave the First Methodist Ladies council about rezoning for our daycare was a lifesaver."

"That was supposed to be our little secret," Anna smiled. "You'll ruin my reputation if word gets out that I gave free counsel to a church, Ms. Kate. Apparently, I'm supposed to be some sort of heartless monster," she finished, eyeing David Hitchcock playfully.

Dave cleared his throat and quickly found a curious ice cube in his drink that needed immediate inspection.

"She likes keeping secrets," Jack observed. "I've discovered that much at least, about little Annie Costner today."

"Jack threatened to water-board me later," Anna remarked casually, taking a sip of her drink.

"Jack!" Aunt Kate gasped.

"It's just a special op courting ritual, Kathrine," David said, smiling at Anna for the first time this evening. "They only use it on red-headed lawyers."

"The IDF are experts at waterboarding as well," Rebecca said, eyeing her husband disapprovingly.

"Come on, Kate," Sean laughed. "Let's go mingle. This group plays too rough for us."

After his aunt and uncle had moved off to make other guests welcome, Jack turned the conversation back to Rebecca, asking how they'd met. David was only too happy to change the subject and deflect his wife's ire.

"It was at the end of the mission that cost me both my legs in Desert Storm," David began. "We'd just taken out a SCUD missile site when we got ambushed. They really walloped us, but we took them out as well. It was a real, honest to goodness gunfight. When it was over, I was lying there in the Iraqi desert all blown to crap, with all my other team members' dead, when this band of wandering Bedouin *appeared*."

"One Bedouin," David smiled, kissing Rebecca on the cheek, "spoke perfect English with an Israeli accent and knew enough emergency field surgery to keep me alive until I could be evacuated on one of those secret *Bedouin* helicopters. I woke up a week later in Evat, Israel with no legs and a US State Department flunky wanting to know how the heck I had ended up in an Israeli military hospital, 300 miles from my last reported position.

He was growing somewhat agitated that I couldn't explain myself, when this fiery, young IDF Captain, who looked suspiciously like the *Bedouin* female who treated me in the Iraqi desert, stormed in and practically threw him out of my hospital room. After she tossed him out, she made sure I was comfortable, kissed me on the cheek, and thanked me for what I had done. Those SCUDs were raining bloody...well, they were a problem for Israel at the time, if you remember. Or maybe you don't? You were just a toddler back then. After that, she disappeared without another word."

"My CO showed up the next day with the US Ambassador to Israel, gave me the standard "*don't say anything to anyone*" about those "*Bedouin's*" or how I ended up in an Israeli hospital. A week later, I was in Bethsaida, Maryland. I spent the next two years rehabbing and learning to walk on my new legs. The army retired me, gave me a nice medical pension and I kept my mouth shut like a good solider about those Bedouins. But I never forgot about that non-existent IDF Captain."

"When my confidentiality agreement expired in 2011, I flew to Israel and began asking anyone and everyone who would talk to me about IDF units that may or may not have "*unofficially*" been in a position to help a half dead Special Forces Operator in the Iraqi desert in the Spring of 1991. I was asked to leave twice, quite rudely I might add, and outright threatened once. I was sitting at this outdoor cafe in Jerusalem drinking warm beer, feeling really sorry for myself, and actually about to just give up and fly back to the states when, suddenly, there she was."

"I had to shut him up," Rebecca sighed, "David had *no idea* the...trouble he was causing in, uh, certain departments of the Israeli government."

"She begged me to leave before I got us both permanently...silenced, and I said I'd only go on one condition," Dave grinned. "That she have dinner with me as a way of saying '*thanks for saving my life*.' The rest, as they say, is history."

"We were married two months later," Rebecca smiled, lovingly caressing David's cheek. "We lived in Tel Aviv until I retired."

"From the Mossad?" Jack grinned.

"From the Ministry of Agriculture," Rebecca insisted. "We moved to the states and settled in Tennessee because I love horses..."

"And I love guns," David finished.

"That's Williamson County," Jack nodded.

"That has to be the one of the most romantic stories I have ever heard," Anna said quietly, her emerald eyes misting with tears.

"How.... how did you meet mom?" Jack asked.

"We were a Messianic Jew and a lapsed Catholic," David shrugged. "First Methodist seemed like a good compromise. Maryellen Braedan was the first person to greet us when we walked through the doors."

"We knew instantly we were exactly where God wanted us to be," Rebecca said, concluding the story.

"I know what you mean," Anna agreed quietly, then seeming to realize she's spoken out loud, she glanced quickly at Jack and looked away, blushing furiously.

"Would you like to freshen up before dinner, Anna?" Rebecca asked, coming to her rescue. Apparently, the beautiful Israeli had a habit of rescuing people in distress.

"I would indeed," Miss Costner said, her cheeks glowing crimson.

"If you gentlemen will excuse us," Rebecca said, taking Ann's arm and leading the embarrassed lawyer away.

"That's quite a woman you've found for yourself, Sergeant Hitchcock," Jack remarked as he watched the two ladies weave their way through the crowed veranda.

"Better than I deserve and that's a fact, Coastie." He nodded. "How about we freshen our drinks, and you can *NOT* tell me that it was your bunch who took down Sayeed Mohammed Ali last week."

"Sayeed who?" Jack replied, finishing his tumbler of bourbon.

"Exactly," David laughed. "Freshen your drink and tell me the hypothetical details."

Dinners at the Braedan house were served buffet style, the food laid out with flair and loving care by Katrina and the ladies from First Methodist. As was customary at all Braedan gatherings, the guests gathered in a large circle before the buffet table and held hands for the blessing. It was usually Big Jim who gave it, but...now it seemed the responsibility would be assumed by his brother. Jack bowed his head dutifully and closed his eyes, taking the hand of a gentleman on his right and reaching out with his left to grasp Anna's.

"Abba Father," Uncle Sean began in his rich baritone, "Thanks for the giving us the opportunity to fellowship tonight with friends and loved ones. Even on this day, when we mourn our loss, we know that Big Jim and Maryellen have ended their struggle. We ask that you bless this gathering; bless the hands who have labored to make this possible. We thank you for your kindness to us. We ask that you be with all our brothers and sisters throughout the world who suffer for your sake and give them strength to endure. We humbly thank you, for bringing Big Jim and Maryellen's son safely home, once again. We look forward to the day when all men can live in peace. When they can beat their swords into plowshares and their spears into pruning hooks and learn war no more. Most of all, Lord, we thank you for the mercy you've shown us through the redeeming Blood of Christ, our Savior. It's in Jesus name, we pray. Amen."

"Amen," Jack echoed, with all the other guests.

"Now if y'all don't mind," Sean announced, "Jack, you go first, son. No MREs or rice and flat bread, I'm afraid. But your aunt and these fine ladies have laid out a good spread. Miss Costner, you're an honorable foe and the Braedan's guest tonight, you can follow him if he leaves anything. Everyone else just fall in behind them."

Knowing his aunt was likely watching him like a hawk, Jack collected plate and silverware from the head of the table and passed them to Anna, like a good southern gentleman, before securing his own. He selected the roast beef instead of chicken, and then mashed potatoes with gravy, some southern fried cream corn, and a couple rolls. Anna chose the exact meal, and in equal portions. It pleased him to know she was a woman who wasn't afraid to eat, and he gave her an approving wink.

"What?" Anna asked. "I like good southern food. Is that a crime?"

"I didn't say a word," he smiled.

The pair selected seats near the center of the long, rectangular dinner table. David found a seat to Anna's left and Rebecca sat to Jack's right. The evening flew by, filled with polite conversation, good food, and wine. Uncle Sean regaled them all with golf and hunting anecdotes about Big Jim, while everyone around the table seemed to have a tale of Maryellen's kindness and unexpected sarcastic wit.

David and Anna spent a great deal of the evening in an animated discussion on the 2nd Amendment, each winning and conceding positions until they both agreed it was a complicated subject. By the end of the debate, it was no longer, "Ms. Costner" and "Mr. Hitchcock", but Dave and Anna. Jack fielded questions about the US pulling out of Afghanistan. He avoided the specifics and generally agreed with most of the guests that it was past time to be gone and done with that hard piece of ground. When he could disengage himself from the other guests, he talked to Rebecca about her love of horses; recounting to her the time he'd been invited to participate in a *Buzkash*i match by an Afghan tribe, after he and his team had "*taken care of*" a troublesome warlord on one of his missions.

Halfway through his tale, the entire table had stopped to listen.

"It sounds simple enough," Jack told them. "Grabbing a goat carcass from horseback and flinging it into a circle of rocks, but there were a couple of times I actually feared for my life. I managed to touch the goat once. Apparently, it was a sort of a big deal because after it was over, they adopted me into their tribe and tried to marry me off to one of the elders' daughters."

"That sounds horrid," Kate shuddered.

"Oh, it wasn't so bad. She was a pretty little thing," Jack grinned, winking at Anna.

Before anyone realized it, it was approaching eleven and soon helping hands began clearing away the table and pitching in to clean up. Honored guest or not, Anna dove right in, much to the smiling satisfaction of Aunt Kate. She walked over to Jack and casually remarked, "Beauty, brains, and not afraid of the kitchen. She'll make someone a wonderful wife someday."

Jack chose to ignore his aunt's none too subtle suggestion, of course.

Rebecca and David said their goodnights, with Anna receiving warm parting hugs from both, as if they'd known each other for years. "Why don't you come over for dinner tomorrow?" Rebecca asked. "You and Jack."

"Becca, honey," Dave said taking his lovely wife by the arm. "Don't overstep."

"What?" Rebecca asked, as if wounded. "It's just dinner," she said, kissing Anna on the cheek.

"Coastie, I'm man enough to admit when I'm wrong." He grinned, giving her a quick kiss himself.

Rebecca disengaged herself from David and gave Jack an affectionate hug. "Ask her," she whispered into his ear, "the girl is absolutely smitten with you."

After the Hitchcock's departed, Anna excused herself and went to speak briefly with his Aunt Kate, receiving yet another warm hug and kiss. "Walk me to my car, Coastie?" she asked, returning to take Jack's arm.

"The night is still young, Miss Costner," Jack said, a bit disappointed. He hadn't gotten to spend nearly as much time talking to her as he'd hoped.

"I've had a wonderful evening, Jack. But I've got a brief to finish before I turn in," she smiled.

"About the mosque?" Jack asked, escorting her through the house. "If you want my opinion...."

"If I want *your* opinion, I'll water-board it out of you," Anna smiled.

"You think getting me a little wet scares me, Ms. Costner?" Jack asked, mischievously.

Outside, Anna directed him toward a fire engine red, Nissan 370Z convertible parked at the head of the drive. Jack raised an impressed eyebrow. "It gets me around," Anna replied. "I had a wonderful evening, Jack Braedan."

"It was nice, wasn't it?" Jack said. "It's been an odd sort of day. Seemed so.... surreal is an overused term, but without mom and dad at the dinner...well...I'm glad you were part of it, Anna Costner."

"I always respected your dad, and your mom was a dear," Anna said hesitantly. "I don't know if you know this, but...I talked to your mom occasionally. She used to keep me updated on you...on your... umm, exploits?"

"Did she now?" Jack inquired.

As their conversation lulled, they stood awkwardly beside her car. As Jack tried to think of something to say that would prolong the evening, Anna suddenly stepped close to him and placed her arms on his shoulders. "Would you kiss me if I asked you to, Coastie?" she asked quietly.

"Why, counselor," he smiled, feigning shock, "What kind of man do you take me for?"

"I'm only going to ask one..."

She didn't get to finish. Jack pulled her close and kissed her; tenderly at first, but a fire soon ignited between them and the kiss became passionate. Eventually, she summoned her strength and pushed him to arm's length. "That's quite enough for a first date, Jack Braedan."

"So, this was a date then?" he asked, equally as flushed.

"After a kiss like that?" she smiled, "I'm sure I could convince a jury of your peers. So, are you going to ask me out to dinner at the Hitchcock's or what, Master Sergeant Braedan? Big war hero like you afraid of Little Orphan Annie?"

"You terrify me, Annabelle Costner," Jack admitted truthfully.

"Call me in the morning, Jack," she whispered. Leaning forward, she brushed her lips against his quickly, before pulling away.

Jack sighed and opened her car door.

"Get some sleep, Jack," Anna said, sliding into the sports car while giving him a glimpse of her long, athletic legs. "You look tired."

She gave him a dazzling smile as he closed her door, ending the evening by firing up the powerful engine and pulling out of the drive.

"Fat chance of that," Jack muttered, as he watched her headlights disappear into the night.

Chapter Three

The Event

Jack was awakened by an annoying vibrating sound. He stretched slowly and opened his eyes. He reached over and picked up his iPhone off the nightstand. He had missed half a dozen calls during the night. Major Brant had called three times over the past hour. Wondering what world crisis had transpired for "Big A" to call him so early in the morning the day after he'd put his parents in the ground, he was about to press *Return Call*, until he noticed it wasn't so very early after all. It was almost 0900. He must have been totally wiped. He hadn't slept this late in a decade. Even after a night out pounding beers with the team, he normally never slept much beyond 0600. He wondered if this was how late "*normal*" people slept on a Sunday.

But there had been nothing normal about the last week. Fast roping into the wilds of Yemen one minute, then a week later attending his parent's funeral and leaving before they were put in the ground. Most amazingly of all, had been meeting the grown up and dangerously seductive, Anna Costner, barely an hour later. Thinking of Anna, he remembered the softness of her lips and the feeling that had come over him as he watched her drive away.

"No," he shuddered, trying to banish a thought that began to grow in his mind. That was just *WAY* too terrifying to contemplate. As he lay there pondering why all he could think about was Anna Costner, when his parents weren't even in the ground a day, the message center on his iPhone buzzed again. It informed him that "Julie" had called twice and that there were unread messages waiting in his voicemail.

Good Lord, didn't any of his team realize his parents were dead? They probably only wanted to know how he was doing, but five calls since midnight?

Jack rolled out of bed, found a pair of his jeans on the floor, slipped them on, and stuffed his phone into his back pocket, ignoring the persistent buzz. Barefoot, he went down the stairs and left down the hall to his parents' bedroom. The door was slightly ajar. Wondering what he would find, Jack hesitantly pushed the door open. The room was empty, of course. The bed wasn't made, which was surprising. Maryellen Braedan *never* left an unmade bed behind. If the house had been on fire, she'd have taken care of that before heading for safety. He guessed that even his Aunt Kate hadn't found the strength yet to come in here and "straighten up."

His dad's worn, King James Bible lay open and face up on the nightstand. On impulse, Jack picked it up. It was open to 2 Thessalonians. Big Jim had highlighted a passage and put bold asterisks at either end. *"For this cause, God shall send them a strong delusion, so that they should believe a lie."* His dad had written a single word in the margin. Underlined as well. Aliens? Big Jim was always going on about how extraterrestrials were actually demons in disguise. Jack never paid the talk any mind. God and demons and aliens. They were all equally a fantasy as far as he was concerned.

Holding his dad's Bible in his hands, words came flooding back to him unbidden. He could recall just about every conversation he'd had with his parents when they talked to him about God. They pleaded with him to go to church with them every time he came home. It was one of the reasons he visited so infrequently.

Where had God been when the towers fell? Where was God when Timmy Horn had been blown to bits in Iraq? Where was God then when Will Kovac had died in his arms in Helmand Province, throat shot and choking on his own blood? Where had he been when that drunk had ended the lives of his parents in a fiery crash which didn't even allow one last look of his mother's face? If there was a God, he was certainly nowhere to be found when things got rough.

Plain as day, he heard his dad speaking in his head, *"And ye shall seek me, and find me, when ye shall search for me with all your heart."*

He dropped the Bible, as if he were holding a pit viper.

Jack left his parents' bedroom in a rush and went back down the hall to the kitchen, opened the refrigerator and found a bottle of Aquafina. He downed half the bottle and headed to the front door. In the foyer, he found the alarm set. Aunt Kate must have activated it when she and Uncle Sean left for the night. He punched in the code, disarming the system, and stepped outside. His father's Silver Cadillac Escalade was in the drive. There was an empty space beside it where his mother's white BMW was usually parked. He knew from overheard conversation last night that Maryellen's car, at least the blackened, crumpled thing that remained, was in Cavin's Salvage yard out on Highway 2. The sight of that empty space brought Jack to his knees.

Again, as clear as a bell, he heard a voice in his head, not his dad's this time, but one deeper, full of compassion and authority at the same time. *"Your struggle has never been against flesh and blood, Jack. But against principalities, against the rulers of the darkness of this world, against spiritual wickedness in high places."*

"I'm going crazy, aren't I?" Jack moaned, dropping to his knees. "Jesus, help me."

As soon as he said the words, a calmness flooded over him. Like the calm he felt before stepping off the back ramp of a C-130 into a cold, starry night at 30,000 feet or fast roping into swirling dust seconds before some firefight. But this calm was.... different somehow. It was hard to explain, but his weariness was gone. Vanished. The hole in his heart left by his parent's death was still there, but it had been filled with...something. Purpose maybe? But what purpose?

Another sound slowly intruded upon Jack's calm. So faintly... on the breeze... he could hear, sirens? He looked to the south, toward downtown Franklin five miles away. Smoke clouded the horizon, a lot of smoke. Someone's life was going up in flames. *Welcome to the club*, Jack thought. His iPhone buzzed in his pocket, demanding that he pay it attention. "Big A" was calling yet again.

Jack touched the phone receiver symbol on the screen.

"What?" he asked, snapping though he hadn't meant to.

"Jack!" Major Brant, hissed, equal parts angry and relieved. "Where have you been, man?" He rattled off a string of curses. "Big A" never cursed. "The world has..."

The call dropped off.

Jack looked at the phone in his hand curiously. Four bars. Plenty of reception. He punched *Return call* on "Big A" but was informed by a pleasant voice that, "all circuits were currently busy," and that, "His call could not be completed at this time." "Try again later," the voice advised him. He tried again immediately, but he got the same results.

Curiously, Jack touched the envelope symbol for messages, tapped in his code, and selected *Julie.* After several seconds, it finally went through. The voice on the phone sounded like Staff Sergeant Julian Hesterman, but it obviously couldn't be him because Julie had never sounded so terrified in the four years he'd known him. "Jack! Call me back now!" Julie almost shouted, "The planet has gone all *Twilight Zone*! It's unreal, man! HQ is sending out all kinds of crazy flash traffic! Call me!"

Jack selected the other message from Julie, from 36 minutes ago. "Call me, Jack! Dammit I'm trying, *Mac*!" This apparently to Sergeant First Class Terry "Mad Mac" McDowell. "I gotta go! Call me, man!"

Jack tried Hesterman's number but got the same, sweetly annoying voice that told him his call couldn't be completed.

There was one last message from a 910-area code. 910 was Fort Bragg, North Carolina. Jack selected it, waiting impatiently for the phone to connect. For some unknown reason cell service was crap this morning. He was just about to hang up and try again when he heard a computer generated, disembodied voice that was even more disturbing than Julie Hesterman's uncharacteristic panic. "All leave, passes, and furloughs have been canceled as of 1100 hours Zulu. All service members are ordered to return to duty. If you cannot return to your home station due to the current situation, report to the nearest US military installation within 24 hours. Presidential Directive Charlie Mike Echo 177BV5 is in effect."

Presidential Directive Charlie Mike...What? What the heck was that? Jack wondered. It suddenly occurred to him to turn on the TV. Jack went back into the house to Big Jim's study, found the remote, and turned on the 50-inch flat screen. The Emergency Broadcast Alert filled the picture, and that old, familiar, horribly annoying tone filled the air. After a few agonizing seconds, the tone went away, and a computer-generated voice announced chillingly that "This not a test. A State of Emergency has been declared by the President of the United States. All citizens are advised to stay in their homes and remain calm. Avoid unnecessary travel except to seek emergency medical care. All Fire, Police, Medical personnel, and Emergency Responders report to your station, your medical treatment facility station, the nearest FEMA, or Department of Homeland Security Office. All National Guard personnel are ordered to report to your units. All active-duty personnel report to your unit or the nearest federal military installation. A Presidential announcement will be made at 1PM Eastern Standard Time."

The annoying Emergency Broadcast alert sounded again, and the message began to repeat. Jack glanced at his wristwatch. 1300 Eastern was still about four hours away. His iPhone buzzed in his hand and Jack jumped in surprise.

Julian Hesterman was calling again.

Jack pressed *Answer*.

"Jesus, Jack!" Hesterman cried, "Where have you been?"

"Julie, what's going on?" he asked, "Have we been nuked?"

"Nuked? I don't know! Maybe?" Julie replied, "Listen, I must be quick. Cell service is sketchy and to be honest, I don't know how long they.re gonna leave it up under *Charlie Mike...."*

"What the hell is *Charlie Mike?"* Jack demanded.

"Presidential Directive Charlie Mike Echo, 177.... It doesn't matter! It's nationwide Martial Law, Jack! Now shut up and listen!" In four years, under the worst of circumstances, under fire in Syria and Afghanistan, and twice when Jack thought his entire team was about to buy the farm, Julie Hesterman had never lost his cool, and he had definitely *NEVER* told his Team Chief to shut up. Julie took a deep breath and continued with a measure of self-control.

"Jack, before *Charlie Mike* was declared at about 0100 hours, something freaky happened. EMPs. Maybe from solar flares. I don't know for sure. Grids went down, planes started falling out of the sky. There's a rumor that the President and Air Force One is missing! Everyone is freaked out. I mean everyone....it was on CNN, FOX, even MSNBC! There are blackouts everywhere!"

"Julie, that's...that's crazy."

"It's Mayan Apocalypse for real crazy!" Hesterman interrupted, "It was on the internet too before *Charlie Mike* shut it down. Jack, listen up and listen well. Flash memo from DOD (*Hesterman was speaking of a Flash Priority Memorandum from the Department of Defense*), "It...it says we are all "retaking" our oath at ten hundred hours. Do you understand what I'm telling you, Master Sergeant? At 1001, there's going to be a new boss. With Charlie Mike and martial law declared, I don't think it'll be the constitution this time."

"This is crazy," Jack repeated. Crazy or not, whatever had happened while he slept, the United States of America seemed to have died because of it.

"Jack," Julie said.... then hesitated. An agonizing few seconds of silence passed and Braedan could imagine Hesterman looking around to see if anyone was close enough to hear him. "Me and Mac, maybe a couple of others, we're bugging out. You hear me, Jack?"

"Sweet Jesus," Jack said quietly, realizing the seriousness of what the Delta veteran had just confided in him. Whatever had happened during the night to precipitate a national emergency, Staff Sergeant Julian Hesterman and Sergeant First Class Terrance McDowell, both decorated operators, both Red blooded American heroes dozens of times over, were going AWOL (Absent Without Leave) because of it. They were abandoning their posts because of *Charlie Mike.*

"They've already closed down post," Hesterman said quietly. What he didn't say, was MPs would be guarding the gates, and unless they could slip out through some unwatched section, it might take the use of force to get off Fort Bragg.

"I understand," Jack said quietly. "Be careful, Julie. You know where I am, brother."

"So does Big Sister, don't forget that," Julie advised. Big Sister was the nickname his team had christened the new Secretary of Homeland Security. What Staff Sergeant Hesterman was implying was maybe not today, maybe not in 72 hours, but someday, someone would check to see why Master Sergeant Jack Braedan had not returned to duty, as ordered by Presidential Directive. "I love you, Jack. See you on the Drop Zone."

"Stay safe, brother," Jack replied. But Hesterman was already gone.

Jack looked numbly at the iPhone in his hand, stunned by this sudden turn of events. The Emergency Broadcast Alert was repeating itself again. Some worldwide calamity had occurred overnight while he slept. Martial Law was underway. Two men he trusted with his life, men he loved closer than brothers, were going AWOL. Mad Mac McDowell was the most by-the-letter, squared away warrior that Jack had ever served with. As Delta Team Intelligence Chief, Mad Mac was hardwired in to the latest and greatest intelligence as any man he knew. If he was "bugging out," Jack thought maybe he needed to ground, as well.

First things first however, he needed to check on Uncle Sean and Aunt Kate. He tried them on his iPhone, but service was down again apparently. He decided instantly to go check on them in person.

Jack went back to his room and quickly finished dressing, putting on a tan, multi-pocketed, military style shirt, thick socks, and a pair of sturdy hiking boots. He had no idea what awaited him once he stepped outside the safety of his front door, so operating under the motto of "*Better to expect trouble and not find it than to let trouble find you unprepared*," he next headed to the "bonus room." There, Jack slid his arms into a leather, dual slotted, shoulder holster. He selected a pair of Springfield 1911, 45 caliber, semi-automatic pistols to fill it, made sure they were loaded, and put two extra magazines in the back pocket of his jeans. He also selected a Mossberg 590, 12-gauge pump shotgun, which was modified with a collapsible, AR-15 style stock with pistol grip a forend grip on the pump action.

Like all shotguns in the Braedan arsenal, the Mossberg had its barrel plug removed to allow the loading of six shells instead of three. Jack loaded the shotgun with six Winchester, PDX1 Defense rounds; a nasty shell that contained a three-ounce rifled slug, backed up by three double-aught pellets. He stuffed a dozen more of the defense rounds in various pockets of his shirt. Ready for anything short of a full-scale invasion by communist China, Jack headed for the door.

He fired up his Jeep and was a mile down Route 11, when his iPhone buzzed again. He looked at the unfamiliar number on the screen for a second; almost ignoring it, then it sank in. "Anna?" He asked, picking up.

"Jack! Thank God!" she cried. "Someone is trying to break into my condo! I dialed 911, but every line was busy. I didn't know who else to...."

"Where are you?"

"Laurenwood. C13. It's on Buckworth Avenue."

Jack hadn't been in Franklin in two years, but he knew the place like the back of his hand. Buckworth was only a few miles away. "I'll be there in two, maybe three minutes!"

"Hurry! Please!" There wasn't a single trace of the confident lawyer from last night in her voice. "I'm upstairs. The door won't hold much...."

The call dropped.

Jack stepped on the accelerator and pushed the Jeep to 90 mph.

About a mile from the city limits, he passed a large colonial burning merrily on Parker Ranch Road. It was the Meier place. One of Franklin's most well know residents, the guy wrote Christian self-help books if Jack recalled correctly. There were no firefighters anywhere in sight. If they were engaged at some other location, by the time they were finished it would be too late. The roof of the million-dollar home was only minutes from collapse.

Jack almost became a part of the surreal landscape when a White Volkswagen Jetta came screaming out of Vera Valley Drive, barely missing him. The Jetta never even slowed down. He wanted to pull over on the shoulder of 96 to let his heart rate slow, but it had been at least two minutes since Anna had called. A City of Franklin Police cruiser passed him in the other direction, doing at least one hundred miles per hour headed out of town, with siren wailing and lights flashing. Unless the Franklin PD was now hiring gangs of red bandana wearing Latino teenagers to patrol the streets, it was safe to assume the cruiser had been stolen. Jack moved the Mossberg pump to the dash where it would be readily available (and clearly visible) and drove on.

Exactly three minutes and twelve seconds after Anna's call, Jack wheeled into Laurenwood Condominiums, rising on two wheels as he turned off Buckworth Avenue. He found C13 easy enough. Anna's Nissan was parked out front. The front door to the condo was open. Jack jumped out, Mossberg in hand, checked to ensure there was a round in the chamber and moved the shotgun's safety to fire.

The doorknob to Anna's condo had been smashed to ruin. The door itself was scarred and battered like someone had beaten it with a hammer, and the frame was splintered in two places where duel dead bolts had finally given way. Jack entered muzzle first, sweeping the hallway, then clearing the living room, all as silent as death. Then, he heard a crash from upstairs, like a door being kicked in.

"Where are you, Red?" a rough voice called from upstairs, two others at least, whooped with laughter.

Jack moved quietly up the staircase; butt of the shotgun tucked into his shoulder.

"Come on, Red!" the voice called out again. "We aren't gonna hurt you."

"Much," one of the other voices added gleefully.

There were three rooms at the top of the stairs: one on either side of the hallway, one facing him. Only the door on the right side was open. He heard pounding from that room. "Open up, dammit!" the voice demanded. "Before I get mad!"

"Yeah! Open up, we got something for ya!" another joined in.

Jack moved silently to the door and took a quick look inside; three men. The one pounding on the closet door had a large caliber handgun. His backup had a serrated edged hunting knife. A third man was rummaging through a dresser, tossing out clothes. He'd laid his handgun on the bed. "Oooowe! Look what I found, Daryl," that one said, holding up a pair of black, lace panties. "Can we make her put these on before we do her?"

Jack took a calming breath and then stepped into the doorway. Door Beater must have sensed movement because he wheeled to meet him. Jack Braedan was barely a week removed from a forced entry raid in the mountains of Yemen. He didn't hesitate. He put a PDX1 round just above his sternum. The force of the 12-gauge round threw the man backwards and punched a fist-sized hole out his back, spraying the wall behind him with red gore. The Mossberg was deafening in the enclosed room. Jack's ringing ears barely registered Knife Guy's scream, as he turned and quickly put another 12-gauge round in his chest. Jack swung the muzzle of the Mossberg to Dresser Looter. He dropped the lace panties he was holding, as the front of his jeans turned dark with urine. He looked at the bed where his discarded pistol lay. It was maybe five feet away.

Jack could see him thinking, considering the distance. The muzzle of the 12-gauge pointed at him must have looked as big as the old civil war cannon out in front of the Franklin Municipal Court house. Dresser Looter decided not to chance it. He slowly raised his hands and gave Jack a "*what the hell, we were only having fun*," grin. On any other day, under any other circumstances, that would have ended it. Jack would have found something to tie up the scum bag and called the police. But the world had changed in the last eight hours, and obviously not for the better. Dresser Looter's eyes widened when he saw his death written on Jack's face. Before he could open his mouth to plead for his life, Braeden pulled the trigger again and put a PDX1 round in his chest.

"Anna?" he said loudly, taking three shells out of his shirt pocket and reloading the pump.

"Jack! Thank God!" The doorknob to the closest began to turn slowly.

"No!" Jack ordered. "You keep that door shut until I check the rest of the house. Don't move. You hear me?"

"Yes," came her shaken reply.

Jack cleared the rest of the condo quickly, then returned to Anna's bedroom. He didn't know what type of metal Annabelle Costner was made of, ruthless lawyer or not. But...he didn't think any reasonable person, unaccustomed to violence, would react calmly to the mess he'd just made with the Mossberg. "Anna, I'm going to need you keep your eyes closed when I open the door, okay?"

"Okay."

"You do as I say now." Her bedroom was a slaughterhouse. He placed the Mossberg against the wall. "I'm going to open the door, okay?"

"Okay."

He opened the door slowly. Anna was crouched on the floor, dressed only in a white tee shirt and panties, her arms wrapped around shapely legs. She'd tied a belt around the doorknob and had been using it to keep it shut against the best efforts of Door Beater to reach her. "You okay?" he asked, offering her his hand.

She took it, allowing him to pull her to her feet. As soon as she was out of the closet, Anna threw her arms around his neck. Jack held her tight, smoothing her hair and whispered soft, calming, nonsense. "It's going to be okay," he assured her as she sobbed into his shoulder. Barely eight hours into "*The Event*" as everyone would soon be calling today, Jack could not know how wrong he was. He lifted her effortlessly and carried her into the hallway. Lowering her to the floor, he sat beside her and held her as she cried it out.

Slowly, Anna regained her composure. She looked up at Jack and he took her face between his strong hands, wiping tears off her cheeks with his thumbs. Even disheveled and eyes red from crying, Anna Costner was a beauty.

"Look at me, Anna." Her emerald eyes met his. "Nothing is the same as it was when you went to bed. I don't know what's happened yet, but I'm betting it will be a long, long time before anyone comes to check this out."

"I don't understand?" she asked, uncomprehending. "What do you mean?"

"I mean, no one is coming. Your neighbors haven't called 911. No patrol car is speeding here to investigate shots fired. We can just sit right here and wait, but no one is coming to take our statements. Forensics isn't going to come gather evidence, so I won't end up in prison. The coroner's office isn't going to come with body bags. Something bad happened last night. Martial Law has been declared and it appears to be '*every man for himself*.' I'm...I'm going to ask you to let me do something that'll make your lawyers' skin crawl."

"What...what is that?" she asked.

"I made a real mess there, and in a few hours, it'll only get worse. In a few days, it's going to be *bad*. Do you still have family in Franklin, somewhere to stay?" he asked.

"Beth lives in Atlanta," Anna replied. "Dad took a job in Utah with Shell Oil after mom left him two years ago. Mom.... I don't know where she is. The Med maybe?" She said the last with just the slightest hitch in her voice.

"Friends?"

"I lost contact with all my high school friends," she shook her head. "Since I moved back from college all I've done is work, eat and sleep. What's going on, Jack?" Anna asked. "I woke up to the emergency broadcast blaring and barely finished peeing before those.... before I called you."

"I don't know, Anna. I really don't," Jack admitted. "Martial law has been declared. There seems to be...well, I don't know, to be a lot of blackouts around the world."

"Blackouts?" she asked. "What do you mean blackouts?"

"I don't know," Jack sighed. "Nuke EMPs would be my guess. I'd tell you more if I could. Look, how about you go wash your face? I'll get you some clothes, and we can talk about this somewhere away from three dead bodies. Okay?" he stood and offered her his hand.

"Okay," she nodded, taking a deep breath. He helped her to her feet. "Thank you for coming, Jack. I don't know how long I could have...."

"Later," he said, reaching up to brush the hair from her face, "When you're not in the same house with them, you can tell me what happened. Go on now. I won't be long."

Anna nodded, and somehow resisting the urge to a peek inside her bedroom, she turned without another word and disappeared down the hall.

Jack went to work quickly. She may be forced to bug out right now, but Anna would want to come back eventually. Jack opened her bedroom window and punched out the screen. Looking below he found a common back yard shared by three other condos. He didn't know if anyone was at home in the little quad, but he wasn't going to leave the three bodies stinking up Anna's room. One at a time, Door Banger, Dresser Looter and Knife Guy's limp bodies were lifted and pushed unceremoniously out the window. He took the comforter from her bed and wiped up as much blood as he could off the walls and hardwood floor, then tossed it out the window as well. The .44 magnum he stuffed in the back of his jeans. The 9mm from the bed went in his right front pocket. The knife he wiped clean of any prints, and it followed its former owner out the window.

Jack found a nylon, overnight bag in the closet where Anna had been hiding and began stuffing it full of jeans and sensible, functional blouses. He tossed in a pair a pair of running shoes, then threw the bag on the bed and began adding t-shirts, socks, panties, and bras from her dresser. When he'd stuffed it full, he placed the bag in the hallway then picked out another pair of comfortable looking jeans, a light, pullover sweater, thick socks, and a sturdy pair of hiking shoes.

Collecting everything, he knocked softly on the bathroom door. When Anna opened it, Jack caught his breath involuntarily. Her face was scrubbed fresh and clean, and her hair was pulled back in a ponytail. Maryellen Braeden and the good ladies of First Methodist Church would have shockingly described her as "half naked," but she seemed not to be the least bit concerned.

"Get dressed," Jack said, doing his best to avoid looking at her as he handed her the clothes and bag. "Put whatever needs you have from the bathroom in this bag."

"Thank you," Anna said, accepting the bundle from his arms and closed the door.

While she dressed, Jack went back to her bedroom and retrieved the Mossberg. The room was as clean as it was going to get without hot water, bleach, and a good scrubbing. It wasn't long until Anna poked her head in the door. She was dressed and carrying her overnight bag like she was headed on a trip. Looking at her, you'd never guess she was minutes removed from an assault attempt that resulted in three dead bodies lying on her bedroom floor.

"Can I get my purse and my phone?" Anna asked.

"I put your iPhone in the bag," Jack nodded. "Get your purse but be quick."

Her only reaction at entering the hastily cleaned slaughterhouse that had been her bedroom, was a briefly raised eyebrow. "Where.... where are we going, Jack?" she asked, walking over to the nightstand by her bed and securing her handbag. Dresser Looter had left it undisturbed, more concerning with rummaging through her underwear drawer.

"You can come with me to start," he suggested. "If that's okay? I was headed to check on Uncle Sean and Aunt Kate when you called."

"Your aunt and uncle live on the other side of town," she said. "But it's Sunday, Jack. If the world has truly gone mad as you say, they'll be at the church."

"Think so?" he asked.

"Your iPhone working? Give them a call."

"I've tried," Jack said. He tried again. It went straight to voicemail.

"Here," he said, handing her the 9mm in his pocket. "Look, I don't know what's going on yet, but I'd not leave it out of arms reach for a while," Jack advised.

"I left it on the coffee table last night," she said, sheepishly chambering a round in the 9mm pistol, before stuffing the Sig Sauer in the back waistband of her jeans. "Spent seven hundred dollars when I went back to *Guns USA* yesterday and I leave it on the coffee table. Stupid! So? The church first? If they aren't there, we go to their house," Anna said, pulling the strap of her travel bag over her shoulder.

Jack and Anna headed downstairs. He went to her kitchen without asking and grabbed a couple bottles of water from the refrigerator. Stress dehydrates you. Anna would be craving fluids later when she calmed down. Outside it was quiet. There were no gawkers. No one had come out to investigate the sound of the shotgun blasts that would have carried throughout the condos. If anyone was curious, they had the good sense to remain inside their homes and watch through the safety of curtained windows, behind closed and locked doors.

Anna had the keys to the Nissan out, but Jack stopped her with a light hand on her shoulder. "We'll come back for your car after we check on Sean and Kate. I promise. Right now... right now I think we'll be safer if we stay together. Okay?"

The look she gave him said she understood what he really meant was *she'd* be safer if she stayed with him, but Anna appreciated the fact he didn't say it. "Okay," she nodded.

Jack opened the passenger side door of the Jeep for her, and Anna tossed in her bag as she climbed inside. Back out on the street, Jack drove slowly. After years of traveling up and down the dangerous roadways of Afghanistan, he'd learned to drive and be constantly alert for trouble. There were no IEDs lying in wait for them, to be sure, but most people out and about seemed to have a dazed look on their faces. Others had the look of troublemakers like Anna's uninvited guests. Everyone else seemed to be following the advice of the emergency broadcast message and staying inside. As soon as he found his aunt and uncle, Jack knew the best thing to do was take them home and do the same. At least for a few days, until things settled down. Then he'd decide if he was going back to Bragg.

He stopped at the red light on the corner of 11th Street and West Main out of habit, then realizing any cop out right now would have bigger problems than writing him a traffic ticket, he looked both ways and drove on. Anna was silent in the passenger seat, staring out the window blankly at the passing houses.

"I had to do it," Jack said, breaking the silence.

"I know," Anna nodded, turning to look at him. "Have I thanked you yet? I don't remember. After I dialed 911 and it was down, I just didn't...I didn't know who else to call."

"Did...did you know them?" he asked.

"The big one was Daryl Franks," Anna said quietly. "Long story short. Even I couldn't get that piece of filth out of the charges against him. Threats were made. He was released yesterday which is why I bought this pistol. Turn left up here."

Jack turned left on to 3rd Street. He could see the spire of First Methodist Church, two blocks down. Anna didn't seem ready or willing to elaborate further, so he didn't press. As they pulled into the parking lot of the church, just minutes later, he almost told her to wait for him in the Jeep, but decided on "Stay close to me," instead. He put the Jeep in park, checked to make sure there was a round in the chamber of the Mossberg, then climbed out. He waited for Anna to join him. She held the 9mm at low ready, like she'd been practicing storming a church all her life. Jack nodded in appreciation, and then motioned for her to follow him.

The front door of the church was unlocked. Jack pushed it open slowly, sweeping the vestibule with the muzzle of the shotgun like he'd done hundreds of times before in far off lands. Doing so, while entering a Methodist church in the US, however, was a first.

On a normal Sunday morning, the First Methodist sanctuary would have held two hundred worshipers. This morning, there was maybe six people in the pews and one lone man down front by the alter. He was on his knees, praying maybe? When one of the parishioners' noticed Jack was carrying a shotgun, she screamed and bolted for the side exit. The others followed. Except for the man down front. He turned to look at them and slowly got to his feet. Even one hundred feet away, the interior only lit by burning candles on the ledge of stain glass windows, Jack could see the man had been crying.

"If you are going to shoot me, go ahead," the man said, turning his head to look at them wearily. "I'm ready."

The man, a boy really, couldn't have been older than twenty. He was dressed in a white cotton shirt, khaki slacks, and brown loafers. Jack lowered the Mossberg as he approached. "I'm not going to shoot you," he replied reassuringly. "I'm looking for Sean and Kate Braedan. Do you know them? I'm their nephew, Jack."

"You're Jack Braedan?" the young man asked, standing to face them. "Your mom talked about you all the time. I'm so sorry for your loss. She was an angel."

"Yes, I know," he nodded. "Sean and Kate...are they here?"

"No, Jack," the young man replied sadly. "They're gone. They've been taken."

"Taken?" Jack asked, alarmed "What do you mean, taken?"

"Picked up in the night after all this started. So, I've heard," he replied. "A lot of parishioners along with them. *"And he was given power for a short time to make war with the saints,"* he said, apparently quoting scripture. Tears started rolling anew down the young man's cheeks.

"I'm sorry, Lord," the young man said, turning to address the huge, golden cross hanging behind the choir loft. "The pastor saw this day approaching. *He saw*! But I didn't believe! I believe now, Lord." He fell on his knees at the alter and began crying again, his shoulder's shaking silently. "I'll stand firm to the end!"

"Are...are you okay?" Anna said, stepping around Jack to kneel at his side. She laid the 9mm awkwardly on the alter and placed a comforting hand on his shoulder.

"I'll be all right," he nodded, wiping tears from his eyes as he regained his composure. "As well as anyone will be for the next seven years."

"Look, ummm...." Jack began.

"I'm Jeremiah Graham," the young man said, standing again and turning to him. "I was...no, I still am the youth minister here." He offered Jack his hand and he shook it reflexively.

"Look, Jeremiah," Jack continued, "I've got to find Sean and Aunt Kate. Why in God's name would someone take them in the middle of the night? Who took them? Do you know?"

"Locals most likely," Jeremiah said. "Could have been state or Federal I suppose. Sean Braedan is an important man."

"Why on earth would anyone take Uncle Sean and Aunt Kate?" Jack demanded.

"Because they will be a threat to the new order," Jeremiah said sadly.

"What new order?" asked Jack.

"The one that will form out of this chaos," Jeremiah explained. "The police and..."

"Police," Jack nodded. "That's where we'll start."

"And do you think if Franklin PD has them, they'll let *you* leave?" Jeremiah asked. "You're military, take a second and think this through. Shouldn't you be headed back to base? You show up armed, demanding to see your family, you'll probably end up "*detained*" as well. Or dead."

"Look Jeremiah, I don't know what's going on, but why in God's name would Sean and Kate be picked up by the police?" he demanded.

"For the sake of God's name is exactly why they are a threat," Jeremiah explained calmly. "Something happened last night to send the world into chaos, and steps will be taken to bring it quickly under control. Harsh steps. Those steps will include silencing and rounding up Christians. Not TV fakes, or hypocrites, or "*good people"*, but washed in the Blood, honest to God, born again Christians. Without the salt, the world will lose its flavor soon."

"Look, Jeremiah," Jack said uneasily, "we can debate this religious stuff some other time. Right now..."

"The debating is over," the young man interrupted. "It is time to choose a side. My advice to you if you'll take it, is to go home and wait, and watch. Soon, maybe not tonight, maybe not tomorrow, but very soon, the government is going to present a very logical *sounding* reason why thousands, maybe millions of not just people, but *Christians*, have been rounded up." Jeremiah promised. "And those same people who rounded them up, well...as soon as that logical explanation starts to wear thin, they are going to do everything in their power to shut people up who know what's really going on, who really know what's about to happen."

"Jeremiah," Anna began, "What is happening? Why... why weren't you..."

"Why wasn't I taken?" he asked. Jeremiah sighed and then quoted scripture once more. "*They will appear to have a godly life, but they will not let its power change them.*' I was a fake Christian. I admit that freely now, Lord!" He said, turning back to the cross, before turning to face her once more. "I will make you a deal, Miss..."

"I'm Anna, Anna Costner."

"You watch and listen," Jeremiah said, "If everything I just said doesn't come to pass, you can forget we ever had this conversation. Everything will settle down in a few days, Sean and Kate will be released, and everyone can go on living their lives as best they can in this old world. But.... if what I said *does* happen, you both come back and I will give you my testimony and you will hear the truth, and the truth will make you free. Deal?"

"Jeremiah," Jack began again. "I can't just go home and wait while Aunt Kate is in danger."

"If what I think is happening is really happening, she is beyond your help," the young man said sadly, turning to him. "Even Ms. Costner won't be able to free them. But they *will* be coming back again. They will be coming back with Christ in about seven years, in power and glory, and Big Jim and your dear mother will be with them. I've seen Big Jim's Bible. He had all this stuff underlined," Jeremiah said confidently. "Go home and read it. Deal?"

"Okay, deal," Anna nodded.

"Anna, this kid is...." Jack began.

"Crazy?" the young man smiled. "*The wisdom of this world is foolishness in God's sight*. Crazy would be me telling you I know *exactly* what's going to happen in the future. Crazy is also dragging Christians out of their beds in the middle of the night in the United States of America. I'll make you the same deal, Jack. Go home, watch, and listen and read for the next few days. Then you tell me which is crazier. What is happening in the world, or what's underlined in Big Jim's Bible?"

"Okay, Jeremiah," Jack agreed, just to shut him up. This religious stuff had always managed to rub him the wrong way. Things were chaotic right now, sure. Crazy even. But believing some 2,000-year-old book knew what was happening?

That was insane.

"Give me your number," Jeremiah said, "If I hear anything about Sean and Kate, I'll give you a call."

That Jack Braedan did willingly.

Chapter Four

Charlie Mike

"Do you think he will be okay?" Anna asked as they climbed back into the Jeep and pulled away from First Methodist. "We should have asked him to come with us."

"The kid's whacked if you ask me," Jack sighed. "And we couldn't force him to come with us."

"Like you did with me?" she asked.

At first, Jack didn't answer. She had no family in the area. She'd just had three intruders shot dead in her bedroom. Both were good enough reasons for him to *"ask"* her to come with him. The truth, however, was as soon as he realized it was Anna calling him and she was in danger, he wanted... no, he knew he *needed* to protect her.

"I didn't force you, Anna," he admitted quietly. "Besides, that was...different."

"Why? Because I'm a helpless woman?" she asked, going on the defensive quickly.

"I didn't say that?" Jack sighed. "You're not helpless."

"But the woman part?" she asked hotly.

"I'm sorry Anna, but yes. You were in trouble. I just shot three men in your bedroom. I didn't think you should be left alone to deal with it, so sue me. And you're an excellent kisser."

Good Lord! Why in the world had he said that?

"I'm not going to sue you," Anna finally replied. "You saved me from.... well, you saved me. Thank you. Again. And...for the record...you're a pretty good kisser yourself." She blushed furiously.

"*What on earth are we doing*?" Jack wondered. The world was spiraling out of control and going to hell in a hand basket, and here they were flirting like high school kids! Although, he was *really* beginning to enjoy seeing her blush, it was pure insanity while on the hunt for his potentially missing aunt and uncle. Plus...he didn't need the distraction of thinking about kissing the lovely Miss Costner while they were out on the streets with danger maybe lurking at every turn. *Damn*! He was doing it again!

Luckily, Anna changed the subject. "Ummm, I don't know if it's in your plans, but can we check on Rebecca and David as well? After your Aunt Kate and Uncle Sean, I mean?"

He hadn't even thought about the Hitchcocks, but they ran in the same crowd as Sean and Kate! "I, ummm... don't suppose you know where they live?" asked Jack.

Anna unbuckled her seat belt and leaned over into the back seat to rummage through her bag for her phone. Jack did his best to keep his eyes on the road. Unsuccessfully. Even as the world was descending into madness, he couldn't keep his eyes off Anna Costner. What was wrong with him? Jack literally shook himself.

"What?" she asked, returning to her seat, and resecuring the safety belt.

"Nothing," he replied, while thinking, *eyes of the road!* "Is it working?"

"No," Anna said after a minute of trying to get her iPhone to connect to the internet.

"Phone booth?" he said hopefully.

"When was the last time you saw a phone booth, Jack Braedan?" she asked incredulously.

"*Guns USA*? It's right up the road. Maybe someone will be there who knows where they live. Then, Uncle Sean's?"

It only took a minute for the pair to drive the few blocks. There was very little traffic on the streets of Franklin. The only other vehicle they saw was a speeding police cruiser, lights flashing and sirens wailing, as it shot across the intersection of 3rd and Vine. It flew by so fast; Jack couldn't see whether it was occupied by real cops or another group of joyriding thugs.

Guns USA was not going to be of any help. It was currently being looted. Jack stopped the Jeep at the entrance of the parking lot. They watched as several men carried out armloads of weapons through the shattered glass of the front doors and loaded them into the back of a late model Ford pickup. From the looks of things, the Emergency Broadcast signal seemed to be keeping most folks at home, while at the same time releasing troublemakers into the streets. When a pair of the looters pointed toward the Jeep and started their way, Jack decided it was time to get going. He shifted the Jeep into reverse and stepped on the accelerator with so much force, he left a cloud of white smoke behind. David and Rebecca Hitchcock were part of those "Born Again" believers Jeremiah mentioned. If he and Rebecca weren't *taken,* as Jeremiah called it, the former Green Beret and Mossad agent were just going to have to fend for themselves for the time being.

"Anyone else you want to check on?" Jack asked, as they sped away.

"No one I'm willing to risk my life over," Anna replied. "I know that sounds cold, but no. Just Sean and Kate's, to make sure they aren't there, then I think we should just get my car and get out of town."

"Agreed, counselor," he nodded.

He had Anna try their number again while he drove. He wasn't surprised when it went to voicemail. Uncle Sean lived in an obscenely big house just off McColllen Lane behind an iron security gate and a six-foot-tall stone wall. When they got there, they noticed that the security gate was standing wide open. The front door to their home was open as well. Not forced or battered in like Anna's had been, but standing wide open, nonetheless.

They swept through the house, Jack with his Mossberg and Anna with her 9mm, like they'd been clearing mansions as a two-man hit squad for years. Even on edge as he was, Jack couldn't help but admire this amazing young woman. There was more to Anna Costner than emerald green eyes and fiery auburn hair.

The house was empty.

"Let's get my car and go, Jack," Anna whispered in the eerily empty house. "I don't know what's going on, but I'll feel safer out of town. And this empty house is giving me the creeps."

Jack could read it in her eyes. As much strength as Anna was showing on this day, she was nearing a breaking point. The hunt for Aunt Kate would have to wait. If there was anyone who could handle himself in a world gone mad, it was Sean Braedan. He'd just have to trust that his uncle could handle whatever was happening for the time being, until he had made sure Anna was safe.

Back at the Laurenwood Condos, everything was still quiet. Jack made Anna wait in the Jeep while he checked around the 370Z. Nothing seemed out of place. No one was lurking in the shadows waiting to pounce or hiding in the cramped back seat of the Nissan. He motioned for her, and she hurried over to her car to unlock it with the keyless entry. Jack handed her one of his 1911s and two spare magazines.

"Two is twice as good as one," he explained, when she raised a questioning eyebrow. "You stay on my bumper, Anna. You don't stop for anything or anyone, clear?"

"Okay," she nodded.

"I mean *anything,"* Jack emphasized again, thinking about that cruiser with the Latino gang members tearing around Williamson County. "If we get separated, you keep going to the house and you get inside and lock the doors. The alarm code is 0405. 0405 got it?"

"0405. I got it," Anna nodded.

"Okay," Jack said, opening the door for her. "On my bumper, Anna."

"Okay!" she said, rolling her emerald eyes at him. "Let's go already."

"Sorry," he sighed.

Jack waited until she had the 370Z engine started and saw reverse lights before climbing back into the Jeep. He turned left on Buckhold and left again on Highway 96 West, keeping one eye on the Nissan and one eye on the road in front of him. He had to admit, she did a decent job staying on his tail. He pushed it to 70 miles per hour on a straight stretch as soon as they left the city limits. Anna was never more than two or three vehicle lengths behind him. They made it back to the Braedan home in less than five minutes.

Jack was relieved when both vehicles pulled through the electronic gate leading up to the house and it was closing behind them. He didn't really know what they'd have done if that cruiser full of *Vatos* had decided to set up a check point, blocking the highway out of town. Luckily, they hadn't seemed to have thought that far ahead yet. He regretted not taking the Heckler & Koch for extra firepower. He wouldn't be making that mistake again the next time he ventured into town. He pressed the automatic garage opener, as they pulled up to the house and motioned for Anna to take the space on the left. As soon as things settled down a bit, he'd move Big Jim's Cadillac out of the driveway and around back, out of sight. No sense advertising someone was home.

They entered the house through the garage. Jack had left the television on in his dad's study. He could still here the same emergency broadcast message repeating as they walked down the hall. Although it seemed like it had been many hours since he'd left to look for his aunt and uncle, it was still a few minutes before 11AM. The president wouldn't be on for another hour yet.

"You haven't eaten since last night, have you?" asked Jack, laying the Mossberg on the kitchen table. "Put that bag down anywhere and I'll make us something to eat. If you're hungry, that is."

"I know my way around a kitchen," Anna said to him. "I am a woman after all. Surely you have some sort of *man* stuff you could be doing other than cooking for little old me?" She finished sarcastically.

"I guess I do," Jack sighed. She wasn't going to let his earlier remark go anytime soon. "There should be eggs in the fridge. Should be some left-over roast..."

"I got this," Anna assured him. "Go patrol the perimeter or something and leave me alone."

"Okay," Jack nodded, knowing he was going to have to fix this quick.

Jack found spare keys for his dad's Caddy in the study and moved the Escalade to the back of the house. That done, he took a quick walk down the drive to make sure the front gate was still secured, and then headed back inside. Delicious smells were coming from the kitchen, but he left Anna to her business and headed to the bonus room. He selected a Bushmaster AR-15 off the wall. It was compact, lightweight, and easy to use. He loaded a thirty round magazine and chambered a round. He did the same for his new H&K. After searching for a couple minutes, he found a nylon holster for Anna's 9mm and headed back downstairs.

Back in the kitchen, Anna had set out plates and silverware in the breakfast nook and was busy over the stove, adding shredded cheese to a big skillet of scrambled eggs.

"I brought you something," he said, leaning the carbine against the wall by the kitchen door.

"Better not be flowers," Anna said, looking to see what he'd brought. "Oh!" she said before giving the eggs a couple of stirs and adding a pinch more salt. "Jack, I'm sorry for..."

"Apology accepted. And I'm sorry too. Rule number one. Nothing we say in the next 24 hours can be used against us in a court of law. Rule number two...we always go armed from now on until we figure out what's going on. Or I decide we don't need to anymore."

"So, is that rifle for me?" she asked.

"It's light and easy to fire," he nodded. "Perfect for..."

"For a woman?" Anna asked, but she smiled when she said it.

"For home defense," he replied. She was relentless.

"Is that holster for me too? Could you put it on me? These eggs are about 60 seconds from being perfect."

Jack took the 9mm from the waist band of Anna's jeans. His hands shook slightly, as he finally managed to clip the Sig Sauer and holster back in place. Jack scowled at his uncharacteristic timidity. Less than twenty-four hours ago, he hadn't even thought about Annabelle Costner in a decade. Now, he couldn't come within two feet of her without his heart racing or look in her direction without thinking about that single kiss from the previous evening. Or how soft her lips had been, or the way her eyes danced when she laughed, or....

"Ummm, I need to get the eggs off the stove," Anna said quietly.

"Oh!" Jack stated in surprise, when he realized he'd been standing there with his hands resting casually on her hips. "Sorry."

"Go sit down," she ordered.

Jack obediently took a seat in the breakfast nook and Anna brought over the eggs, hot off the stove, and scooped him out a generous portion. She soon returned with buttered toast, some of the leftover roast from last night's dinner, chopped and mixed with sautéed onions, and a tall glass of milk. When she'd dished herself out a similar share and took her seat, Anna picked up her fork and prepared to dig in. Purely out of habit, because he was seated for a meal at a Braedan table, Jack reached across the table with both hands palms up, and motioned with a "come on" gesture that she was supposed to take his hands. He might be a Jesus scoffer with the Team, but you simply *did not* eat at Maryellen Braedan's table before you giving thanks.

"Uh, thanks, Lord," Jack began, "for keeping us safe this morning. I'm not particularly good at asking for things, but if you have the time, could you watch out for Sean and Aunt Kate today, wherever they are...and for David and Rebecca, and for Anna's family too. Watch out for us while.... while we're dealing with this. Amen."

"Oh!" Jack said, almost forgetting the standard line of grace at a Braedan table, "And bless this food Lord, and bless the hands who labored to prepare it. Use it for the nourishment of our bodies and strengthen our bodies in service to you. In Jesus' name, Amen."

He started to pull away, but Anna held on letting him know there was more. "And thank you for sending Jack to save me this morning," She gave his hands a final squeeze. "Amen."

"You won't think I'm a heathen if I make a sandwich, will you?" Anna asked. Without waiting for a reply, she started piling the roast and scrambled eggs on her toast.

"Dealer's choice," he shrugged.

They ate in silence as they both wolfed down the food. Jack hadn't realized he was so hungry. Anna finished her first sandwich quickly and went back for seconds, helping herself to a portion just as large as her first. Jack knew it was probably stress relief. Jack was about to go for seconds himself when he heard the TV in his dad's study suddenly change from the repeated emergency broadcast to an even *more* annoying alarm, then "Stand by for this urgent announcement."

"I almost forgot!" he said, hurriedly placing his dirty plate in the sink and almost sprinting to the study. He found the remote and turned the flat screen up even louder, not wishing to miss a single word. Anna wasn't far behind him. Jack patted the seat beside him on the couch and she joined him, curling her long legs underneath her.

After what seemed like an eternity, the scene finally switched to the White House briefing room. The President's Press Secretary was standing nervously at the podium. Jack couldn't recall his name at the moment, but he remembered him well from his brief visit to DC after the chaos in January. His team had been brought in to advise the new administration's security chief on Delta's domestic threat assessment analysis. He was an annoying, self-important little weasel and didn't care much for Jack's opinion that the real threat was China. He was also flamboyantly gay. Not that Jack particularly cared. But the weasel was more concerned with "*getting to know him better*" than any threat to the President.

"He hit on me once when I went to Washington," Jack confided.

"Hush, here he comes," Anna hissed, slapping his thigh painfully.

"Ladies and Gentlemen," the Press Secretary announced, "The President of the United States."

However, it wasn't the senile old swamp rat America had allegedly voted for in the last election, who stepped to the podium. It was the female, vice president with the most annoying laugh in history. "My fellow Americans," she began, "Last night, at approximately 1 AM Eastern Standard Time, the planet witnessed an... *event* which has resulted in large sections of the world suffering unprecedented power outages. My chief science advisor has informed me multiple observatories around the world witnessed historic waves of CME's, Coronal Mass Ejections. The largest solar flares every recorded. These solar waves acted as bursts of intense electromagnetic energy, interrupting the systems of many things humanity has grown to depend on. One of the more deadly results of this *Event*, was the degradation of flight instrumentation on numerous aircraft in US, Europe, and Asia, causing, it pains me to say, catastrophic instrument failure. Sadly, this resulted in very many deaths. Including, confirmed early this morning, the President, who was returning from an inspection of our missile defense system in Alaska. Air Force One went down in the Canadian Rockies. There were no survivors."

"My God," Anna whispered, reaching out and taking Jack's hand.

"In accordance with Section IV of the 25th Amendment, I have been sworn in as President. As your President, I want to assure you that we are doing everything necessary to bring us safely through this crisis. As a result of these flares, there was a disruption of the operation of power grids in many areas of the world. Currently, there are large population centers without normal access to electricity. This unfortunately means a disruption of refrigeration for food storage, power for homes, and a degraded ability for hospitals and emergency personnel to take normal lifesaving measures resulting from injury or illness.

Here in the United States, this disruption includes a large section of the west coast, reaching from our border with Mexico, up to Southern Canada, and west, as far as the Rocky Mountains. In the Midwest, the affected area begins around the Great Lakes area of Chicago and Detroit, stretching almost down as far south, as St. Louis and east, as far as Cleveland Ohio. Much of the New England and northern Atlantic states have also suffered the outages, from Bangor Maine to Boston and New York City.

If you are listening to me via radio, the internet, or are fortunate enough to have power, rest assured your government is on top of the situation. We already have a plan to restore power to about 25 percent of the affected areas. Sadly, restoring the entire power grid may take weeks, even months, in some cases. But I would like to assure you, our defense capabilities were only minimally damaged, and the United States stands ready to defend itself against any nation that might think to take advantage of this unfortunate event.

"Many other governments worldwide are currently operating under similar...difficulties, because of this...*Event*. The United Kingdom has gone dark across the channel to Paris and south through Spain to Madrid. Many other areas seemed to have suffered only localized bursts of this energy, while others still seem to have been barely affected. Those nations, most notably, India and China just to name two, have already called and graciously offer whatever aid they have available to help us recover from what transpired last night. In two days' time, an emergency session of the UN General Assembly will meet here in Washington to discuss world-wide recovery efforts. The Capitol building will host the General Assembly until power is restored to New York City or a suitable replacement city can be named."

"My fellow Americans, I know many of you are frightened." Jack reached over and took Anna's hand, squeezing it reassuringly as the Vice President...the President continued. "You are frightened. You are worried for your safety. Many state and local governments across our great nation have been affected; some to the point of being no longer able to provide the basic functions of law enforcement and emergency services necessary to promote the general welfare."

"For this reason, it is with profound regret and heavy heart as my first act as President, I have enacted Presidential Directive Charlie Mike Echo 177BV5. The forty-eight contiguous states, as well as the states of Alaska and Hawaii, are now under martial law. For the protection of our citizens, I have federalized all National Guard and activated Army and Naval Reserve Units. They, along with Army, Navy, Marine and Coast Guard, have been placed at the disposal of Rear Admiral

McGinnus, Chairman of the Joint Chiefs of Staff. I have federalized all local law enforcement agencies: county, city, parish, and state, and placed them under the direction of the Secretary of Homeland Security. "

"Only moments ago, I concluded a meeting with the cabinet, members of the Supreme Court, and many key leaders of Congress. It has been recommended by these dedicated public servants, with profound, utmost regret and unspeakable sadness... that because of the extreme and devastating nature of this *Event*... along with the current uncertainty and chaos currently sweeping our great nation... that I regretfully announce the temporary suspension of the constitution, and heretofore, the unassailable and sacred individual rights."

"Until such a time as this country is once again secure and the situation is stabilized, I have directed the Secretary of Homeland Security and Director Fallon of the Federal Bureau of Investigation, to...once again regretfully... detain certain individuals here in the US, who Homeland has deemed a possible hindrance to the re-establishment of good order and discipline of the nation.

"What the hell does she mean by that?" Jack snarled.

"Quiet, Jack," Anna whispered, shakily.

"Certain groups quite frankly have been under observation for some time by the office of Homeland Security. A small, stubborn minority of citizens who have a strict, unrealistic view of certain elements of the constitution, and are unwilling to compromise. Also, certain members of the religious sector, fundamentalists and separatists even, whom Homeland has also been quietly watching."

"She's talking about Christians," Jack snarled incredulously. "About Aunt Kate!"

"It is with great sadness and a heavy heart," she continued, "that I have directed the full force of Homeland Security, the FBI, NSA, and other organizations to begin...detaining a very *small* number of these individuals. It is for their own safety, for good order, and for the security of the country, as we sort out the events of the last few hours. Rest assured they will be treated with dignity and will receive full hearings to determine when and if they should be released back into the world's community. Many other nations in our global community have taken the same steps in dealing with these poor, misguided people who cannot seem to move beyond outdated and obstinate views.

It is with a heavy heart that I must also announce the following, effective immediately: There will be dusk until dawn curfew throughout the land. Effective immediately, to ensure good order and discipline in this troubling time, the private ownership of all handguns and rifles is suspended. In the next forty-eight to seventy-two hours' local sites will be identified by the Department of Homeland Security in cooperation with local authorities, for the turning in, registration, and cataloging, of all weapons. Upon the lifting of this Presidential Directive, all weapons will be returned to their lawful owners should they be determined to be mentally sound and not a threat to the community at large. After one week from today, any person found in possession of any banned weapon will be subject to incarceration without trial until the lifting of martial law.

"To ensure the swift and truthful flow of information during these unprecedented times, and to prevent added chaos with the publishing of reckless and harmful conspiracies and outright lies, the government of the United States is assuming operation of all radio, television, and internet services."

"In order to ensure public safety, freedom of assembly is suspended. There shall be no groups larger than five persons, save immediately family members, gathered in any public place without the written permission of the Department of Homeland Security 72 hours prior to the event, save for FEMA "Safety Centers" that we are even now establishing. This will remain in effect until such time as it is lifted by the National Security Council and the Department of Homeland Security."

Jack muted the sound on the flat screen. Anna had begun to cry softly. He lifted his arm and she slid against him, resting her head on his shoulder as she wept. "Welcome to the New World Order," he said bitterly. "I think I'm gonna throw up."

Jack only paid passing attention to the remaining Presidential pronouncements; more rights taken away in the name of stability and security, and more punishments announced for the citizens who refused to obey. It was the death of the American Republic. No mention was made of the change to the oath of allegiance Julie had warned him about this morning. He imagined that bit of news might have just been too much for the panicked public to handle. Last night America went to bed with a President, and now they had a Marxist dictator.

Anna continued to cry softly, soon slipping her head off his shoulder and into his lap. Jack found a pillow for her to rest her head on and continued to stroke her hair as she lay there. The events of the day, the *Event* itself, had finally overtaken her. Over the last decade he had grown accustomed to dealing with any situation imaginable, but she...she couldn't be much older than twenty-four. He couldn't imagine what she must be going through.

As Anna drifted off to sleep, Jack continued to watch as the new President announced sweeping changes to their way of life. Soon, mercifully, she left the podium and network talking heads began to foolishly trumpet how all these draconian measures were necessary for the survival of the country. When even those sycophants ran out of things to say, the networks finally shifted to their news desks. Jack began watching clips of the devastation caused by the solar flares and convoys of military vehicles, as they rumbled through the streets. It was worldwide chaos as countries struggled to deal with untold number of deaths caused by the catastrophic power outages.

Perhaps most foreboding of all the news footage was the crash of an Air France 757 in Israel. Fate or karma or.... maybe even a fickle God himself, had chosen the jumbo jet in-route from Paris to New Deli, India to drop out of the sky over the city of Jerusalem and crash directly into the Dome of the Rock on the Temple Mount. IDF troops had immediately taken control of the crash site, backed by Merkava tanks, armored personnel carriers, and infantry. The Israelis were fighting pitched battles with rioting Palestinians as bulldozers swept away the rubble of the third holiest site in Islam. Some Iranian Imam, Muhammad Ali bin blah blah blah, was shown ranting about how the Infidels and Zionist had taken the opportunity to destroy the Dome of the Rock under the cover of the international chaos, spitting in the face of all Muslims.

In Syria, Bashere's forces and ISIL embraced each other as brothers once again and were preparing to fight the common Zionist enemy. Mobilizations were occurring in Egypt, Iraq, Lebanon, and Saudi Arabia. All indications were that Israel seemed to be only hours away from launching a pre-emptive attack on her neighbors reminiscent of her actions in the 1967 "Six Day War." Jack's mind flashed back to the conversation he'd had only yesterday with Uncle Sean in this very study. It seemed his uncle had been right. The Middle East was about to burn.

With the government now in control of all public broadcasts, Jack wondered briefly why they were allowing the unedited broadcasts of such dire and disturbing news. Then it occurred to him it would likely only reinforce their position for declaring martial law and the suspension of so many basic rights. Show the populace that the world had gone crazy, and civilization was on the verge of a meltdown, and they would accept any measure, however harsh, to ensure their safety. A previous administration had grown famous for the idea of "*never letting a good crisis go to waste.*" The new one had just been handed perhaps the absolute biggest crisis in the history of mankind and certainly seemed eager to take advantage of this rare opportunity.

Jack turned off the television in disgust. It was someone else's problem now.

Chapter Five

The Letter

As carefully as he could without waking her, Jack slipped from beneath Anna and laid her head back on the couch. She murmured in her sleep, but only stirred and nestled deeper into the pillow. He brushed her auburn hair from her face, marveling briefly at how peaceful she looked after how her day had started. Jack kissed her forehead and went back to the kitchen to clean up the dishes and cookware. He loaded the dishwasher, then took Anna's AR and placed it inside the study, so that it would be near her if she needed it. After hesitating briefly, he went to his parent's room.

He stood in the doorway overwhelmed by the many memories that came flooding back into his mind, as he surveyed the empty room. There was Big Jim teaching him how to shoot his first .22 Marlin, out in the woods behind the house. And his mom's famous Saturday morning blueberry pancakes. Both parents had been in the stands cheering him on, as he played center field for the Franklin High Rebels. His dad's look of anguish and his mom crying, as he boarded the Greyhound bus on the way to basic training at Ft. Benning, Georgia. The strongest memories, strangely, were all the times both formally and during life's little moments, they'd tried their best to instruct him with the Bible.

Crazy or not, Jeremiah Graham's words sprang into is his at that moment. *"Big Jim probably had all this underlined in his Bible,"* he had said. His dad's worn, leather bound King James was laying on the floor where he'd dropped it, earlier that morning. His dad had been the smartest man he knew, and his mother, the kindest and most loving women he could imagine. Maybe, just maybe, there was something to their Bible and their religion after all? Jack walked over and picked it up. It was open to the Book of Isaiah, Chapter 9. He read the first verse high-lighted he saw.

"The people that walked in darkness have seen a great light; they that dwell in the land of the shadow of death, upon them the light has shined." Isaiah 9:2 KJV.

Jack took the Bible back to his dad's study. Anna was still sleeping soundly. He poured himself a tumbler of Jim Beam, sat in his dad's big leather chair, turned on the nearby lamp and began to read. Two hours and another tumbler later, Jack was about to take a break and put the Bible down for a while, when a plain white envelope fell into his lap. Examining the envelope, he found a single printed word on the outside.

Jack.

Jack looked up to find his house guest, watching him intently. "Hey, sleepy head," he smiled, marking his spot, and setting the Bible in his lap.

"What is that?" she asked, stretching as she sat up.

"I don't know," he replied, looking at the envelope curiously.

"Well, open it and see," Anna said, rising from the couch and walking over. She motioned for him to make room. The leather chair was big enough for both. Barely. Jack shifted over and she joined him.

It was sealed. Jack slid a finger into the crease and tore it open. Inside, were a couple handwritten pages on plain stationary in Big Jim's bold, authoritative script. The envelope still felt weighted at one end. He opened it and a simple, unmarked key card fell out in his hand. Jack put the key card aside and unfolded the letters. They were his father's words; he could almost hear them audibly as he began to read.

"Out loud, please," Anna murmured, nestling against him.

Son,

If you are reading this, I want you to know that your mother and I love you. I don't know what occasion has prompted you to open this book, but since you've never brought this letter to me, I'm assuming something has happened to us. Your Uncle Sean has either explained the contents of this letter to you, or he is gone as well. Regardless of the circumstance, I want you to know that we all love you very much. Your mom and I have tried over the years to prepare you for this day, but the hardness of your heart always closed us out. I only hope that when you read this, you will finally be open enough to listen to the Holy Spirit and understand.

I have seen this world growing darker over the last several years, filled with wickedness in high places and outright violence and sinister evil hidden in the shadows. But plain enough for wise eyes to see if you know where to look. I used to believe that your mom and I, and other Christians, would be "Raptured" out of this place before things got really bad, but recently the Spirit of God has led me to believe that the Lord, Yahweh, has a job for His people in these dark times, and it's not to be "snatched up" and ferried up to paradise while the world burns. For many, that task will be martyrdom in Jesus' name. For others, it will fall to fighting and endure to the end. The enemy is cunning. Do not be deceived. He is the Father of Lies and was a Liar from the beginning. You will have to look with Eyes of the Spirit and a discerning heart. Lucifer can disguise himself as an angel of light and is also a great copier of the Father's plan. Beware, he will twist things to his own ends.

Tribulation is coming that will rock the Church. Not the stone and mortar buildings, but the "True" Church, the followers of Christ Jesus. I know that I may seem to be rambling, but these are glorious times for those filled with the Spirit. There is a strong delusion coming that if possible, will fool even the elect. Something will happen that is a lie, but people will be unable to discern the truth. You must stand firm until the end and watch with open eyes.

If you read all the verses in my Bible I have highlighted, it will explain in detail how from the beginning of time, how the Lord, God, Yahweh, God of Abraham, Isaac, and Jacob, has spoken words for believers to prepare them for the trial coming upon all the earth before the "Day of the Lord's Wrath."

That is what's coming, son. It's not a New World or new dawn of man or whatever the Enemy will proclaim. The Lord will finally tire of the greed, and lust, and hatred in the heart of man; that all his thoughts are continually evil, and the final chastisement will begin. I am sorry you will have to endure it, son. But endure it you must, if you can, because at the end when the

Lord Jesus returns in Power and Glory and judge the nations and the remnants that still live, He will renew the earth and begin His thousand-year reign. Your mom and I will return with him, riding on White Stallions.

Son, hard times are coming. Some worldwide catastrophe will happen soon that will precipitate a world government and will also lead to the persecution of Christians. I believe in you son and know you have trained for hard times in the last decade. Other than continually praying you'd come to a saving belief in Jesus, I've tried to do some things to help you survive as best I could the coming years ahead of you.

The key card in this envelope will open a door to a sanctuary your Uncle Sean and I have been building in secret these last few years for the Braedan family. If you are reading this, this sanctuary is for you and whomever you chose to join you. The code you will know. I don't trust the world enough to write it down. I pray you find it still secure by the time you read this.

Son, I've done all I can to raise you right, and I hope you know that I love you and your mom loves you too. Above all, Jesus loves you. He loved you so much, He suffered horrible torture and died for you, so that you might have eternal life. Then the Father raised him up again and placed him at His right hand. It's all written down in the Good Book. I've underlined many, many passages that will help you find the Truth if you will let the Holy Spirit lead you.

I'd like to say I'm watching over you now, but that just isn't so. If we have been imprisoned, we are beyond helping you, save through prayer. If we are gone, if we are dead, we are asleep in the Lord, waiting patiently for the Day of the Lord, when judgement will be given to all the earth. My prayer, since the moment that you were born, is that you'd be with us for this glorious Wedding Supper of the Bride, but if you are reading this now, well, you've got one last chance, son. It's still not too late. The hard times ahead will seem more and more like cruel punishment as time goes on, but all the judgments are truthfully just the last call for humanity to finally turn from their evil ways and turn back to the Lord. All you must do to change the course of your life, son, is to "decide" to change.

I love you, son. God bless you and keep you until we meet again. Dad

The letter was dated March 11.¨ It had been written barely a month ago. Along with Big Jim's letter was a briefer message from his mom. Jack read that aloud, as well.

Jack,

This won't be a long letter. Your dad has written down what you need hear to hopefully get a head start on the difficult times ahead. All I am going to say, is that I love you more than life itself. You have been a source of pride to me, since your first breath. I know your path has been a hard one, but I know now, the Lord was using the path you'd chosen to prepare you for what lies ahead.

My dearest son, the Lord Jesus has revealed to me, that you will meet someone soon who will be a comfort to you and a help mate. He didn't reveal to me a name or face, but I believe in my heart I know who He has in mind. Treat her with love and tenderness and respect, son. Love her as Christ loves the Church and she will be the source of strength to you in the hard times ahead.

I love you, Jack,

Mom

Maryellen's letter was dated just seven short days ago. Penned the day of the crash.

Anna's eyes had filled with tears while Jack had been reading, but not tears of frustration or fear or stress this time. Jack put the letters down and shifted in the leather chair to look at her. She met his gaze, unafraid. There was a hope and calmness about her now she had no right to possess after the trails she'd endured today.

"They knew," Anna whispered. "Your parents knew this was coming."

Jack was a detail-oriented warrior. He knew how to gather all the intelligence that was available, analyze data, discard what was irrelevant, and see right through to the heart of a tactical problem. Along with his courage and his confidence in the men around him, it was what made him such an effective team chief. There was little sense wasting energy denying that Big Jim and Maryellen knew something catastrophic was going to happen. Even.... even if somehow his parents had written those letters last night, it would have still been astounding. There was only one conclusion he could draw from this letter and the events of the last 24 hours. Big Jim could take this worn, well studied Bible and see things that were to come.

"Yeah," he admitted. "It certainly looks that way, Anna."

"What are we going to do, Jack?" Anna asked quietly.

"We have a couple hours of daylight left. We could go see if we can find what this key card opens," he said, even though he knew she meant much more than that.

"Or you could read to me," Anna suggested, snuggling against him, laying her head on his shoulder.

Jack turned the Bible to a random page and began to read. "*In the beginning was the Word, and the Word was with God, and the Word was God. The same was in the beginning with God. All things were made by him; and without him was not anything made that was made. In him was life; and the life was the light of men.*"

They sat for the remainder of the afternoon, randomly scanning through the books of the Bible, reading highlighted scripture. When Jack's voice grew weary, Anna took over. As the afternoon grew into evening, they had basically finished two Gospels, half the book of Psalms and a goodly portion of Genesis and Isaiah before they decided to take a break.

"I have more questions now than when we started," Anna sighed. "Do you think Big Jim would want you concentrate reading the New Testament or are there things we will only be able to find the Old Testament?"

"You are asking the wrong person," Jack said. "In case you have forgotten, a few hours ago, I called this stuff crazy. I resisted everything they tried to teach me all these years."

"You had Jim and Maryellen around you your entire life," Anna said. "My family was well, not the best of moral examples."

"I left home when I was nineteen," Jack sighed. "I guess I've been back.... *maybe*...six months total since then."

"Yet you still absorbed *ten times* more religious training than I received," Anna replied. "The extent of *MY* mom and dad's teaching was "*Now I lay me down to sleep.*" I'm ashamed to say the only thing that I'm proud of, regarding my college years, are my grades."

"Then we are in big trouble, Miss Costner," Jack said. "You probably shouldn't look to me for advice on something like this. I sure haven't been too adept at "*turning the other cheek*" in my line of work. I still don't know if I believe what I'm reading."

"Do...do you think maybe we should pray about it?" Anna asked.

"If you want," Jack shrugged.

Anna closed the Bible and placed it on the table. She could remember praying, really praying a total of *twice* in her adult life. Both times were within the last twenty-four hours. Once, in this house as she held Jack's hand while praying for the dinner they had, and the other, as she was locked in a closet, desperately pleading to God that he would help Jack to hurry and save her. She took Jack's hands in her own, partly because that's how the Braedans prayed and it was all that she knew. But also, because she drew strength from holding the hand of the strong, confident man who had rescued her that morning.

"I don't know how to start," Anna admitted sheepishly, blinking back tears.

"All mom and dad ever did was talk to God like they were talking to their best friend," Jack said. "Try that."

"Okay," Anna nodded, closing her eyes.

Jack gave her hands a squeeze of encouragement and closed his, as well.

"God, thanks again for watching out for us, today," Anna began, "Look, we have a problem. We don't know where to start to find the truth. We could use some help. None of this makes sense to me. But I.... we are going to keep trying to understand. Please show us what we need to know. Amen."

"In Jesus' name," Jack said quietly.

"Excuse me?" Anna said.

"That's how you're supposed to finish," he explained. "In Jesus name. *Whatever you ask in My name, that will I do, so that the Father may be glorified in the Son*. Wow! Now, where did *that* come from?" Jack asked, astonished by the words he had just spoken.

"Didn't we just read something about, 'I will cause you to remember...ummm, things?'?" Anna asked, reaching for the Bible again.

"I believe so," Jack nodded slowly. "How about we look that up after supper? I am starving. Even Jesus had to eat, right? I make a killer grilled cheese sandwich?"

"I *am* hungry again," Anna admitted. "Can...can you make grilled cheese for two?"

"You got it," he nodded, sliding out of the chair.

"Call me when it's ready," Anna said, picking the Bible up off the floor and opening again.

"Yes, Counselor," Jack smiled.

Jack couldn't find any American cheddar slices, the stuff of traditional grilled cheese sandwiches, but he did find thinly sliced deli turkey in the refrigerator, and Swiss, plus some freshly baked sourdough bread that apparently had been overlooked during yesterday's dinner party. He buttered the sourdough, heated an electric skillet, and made grilled turkey and Swiss cheese sandwiches with spicy brown mustard. There was a gallon of iced tea remaining in the refrigerator. He sliced up some fresh lemons and added it in.

Anna did not complain.

While they were eating, a barrage of text messages began flowing into both their suddenly active phones. Julie reported he and Mac had crossed the "LD" (the Line of Departure) and were busy reconnoitering a new FOB (Forward Operating Base). He interpreted the messages to mean they had both found their way safely off Fort Bragg and were looking for a place to lay low. Major Brant asked if he was on his way back to Bragg or was heading to Fort Campbell since it was closer to his home. He didn't know quite how to reply to that text. He'd decided sometime during the last few hours, his days in the Army were over. He couldn't lie to the man he'd fought beside for the last two years, but he couldn't reveal he was not on his way back to swear an oath to the new grand potentate. Should he simply ignore it and hope "Big A" took the hint by the desertion of Julie and Mad Mac? He opted to think his reply over for the time being and let "Big A" report whatever the heck he needed to the Squadron.

Jeremiah Graham also texted him a short message saying he had been praying for them all afternoon and that he was looking forward to seeing them soon. That text, he answered quickly, telling the young man that he and Anna both had a lot of questions and that they'd try to come see him, as soon as things settled down.

Anna received one from her boss, telling her until this settled down, not to come into work. If she had some vacation time saved up, it might be a good idea to use some of it until things were clearer. She didn't bother replying. She also received one from both her dad in Utah and her sister Beth in Atlanta. She replied to both telling them that she was safe and would call them just as soon as the phone lines weren't overwhelmed. They didn't ask and she didn't seem to think it necessary to tell either of them, (particularly her big sister) that "safe and sound" was at the home of Jack Braedan.

After the kitchen was cleaned and the dishes were washed, Jack and Anna retired back to the couch in the study. They turned on the TV, but there wasn't any new, real news about the *"Event."* Wild estimates were being made from initial reports that as many a hundred thousand people might be dead or missing already, because of the catastrophe. The network talking heads and their consultant *experts* bemoaned the extent of the crisis and how long it would take to bring things “back to normal.” But one and all praised the new American president and her counterparts worldwide with their quick and sweeping actions to limit the damage and efforts to restore order.

“I think they *knew* this was coming!” Jack said angrily, “I’ve been thinking and if my time-line is correct, they probably started rounding up Christians as soon as this thing began! Maybe even before. They certainly had a plan for this before the *Event*. Nothing this sweeping could have been executed on the fly.”

“But why?” Anna asked.

“Because they are always looking for an excuse to take more and more control?” Jack speculated angrily. “Because the Tin Foil hats were right and it’s all part of a secret plan?”

“Or God’s plan,” Anna suggested. “Turn that thing off and let’s read for a while. I like Psalms. Can we read some more of that?”

Jack retrieved his dad’s Bible from the coffee table and Anna assumed what apparently was becoming her favorite reading position, nestled against him with her head on his shoulder. Jack didn’t know if it was the comforting words of Psalms or the warmth of the beautiful woman snuggled close to him, but he decided reading the Bible wasn’t really that bad after all.

It was nearly 10PM when Jack had had enough. Anna had begun to doze off and he could barely keep his eyes open. “Okay, time to call it a night,” he said, closing the Bible and putting it back on the coffee table. “Come along, Miss Costner.”

Jack helped the mildly protesting young woman to her feet, secured her AR-15, and escorted her to the kitchen. After collecting her bag, he led her upstairs to the other guest room. “There are fresh towels in the bathroom if you want to take a shower. There should be an un-opened toothbrush or two in the cabinet if you didn’t pack your own.”

"Okay," she nodded sleepily. "Thank you, Jack, for everything."

"Okay, the next *Event* rule is you've thanked me enough. By my count, that's at least five times. Are we clear, Miss Costner?"

"Clear, Jack." she nodded.

"I will be just down the hall if you need anything, Anna. Get some sleep. It has been a long day and I have absolutely *no* idea what tomorrow is going to bring."

"Good night, Jack," she replied. Anna seemed to want to say something more, as an awkward silence settled over them. Then she suddenly hugged him tight, resisting the urge to thank him again.

"Well, ummm, I'll be right down the hall," Jack said, reluctantly breaking their embrace. He turned quickly and closed the door behind him. Leaning against the closed door, he sighed heavily. Twenty-four hours ago, the "old Jack" would have coaxed the beautiful woman into sharing his bed. But now, even though he could hardly look at her for longer than five seconds without lustful thoughts popping into his head, and even though his heart raced every time she touched him, all he wanted to do was protect her, and make sure she was safe from harm. This "*Event*" had apparently done more than just turn the world upside down. It had apparently given him some morals. Somewhere, he just *knew* his mother was smiling.

"Secure the house, then take a cold shower," Jack sighed.

After a peek into the hallway to make sure Anna was gone, he went downstairs and made a quick circuit of the first floor, making sure all the doors and windows where locked, and then he set the alarm. He'd have to remind Anna of the code in the morning. Back upstairs, in his own room again, he picked up his discarded clothes and put them away. (Maryellen Braedan would not approve of a disorderly house, regardless if it might be the end of the world.) He then brushed his teeth, took off his shoes, stripped out of his shirt and jeans, and climbed into the shower.

Cold water only.

About an hour later, just on the verge of falling asleep, Jack heard a soft knock on his bedroom door.

"Jack?" Anna opened the door, hesitantly. Silhouetted by the dim light spilling in from the hall, Jack could see she looked pretty much the same as he'd found her hiding in her closet this morning; dressed only in tee shirt and panties.

"Is everything okay?" he asked, sitting up, instantly alert.

"Can I, ummm, can I sleep with you?" Anna asked, her voice barely above a whisper. "I just.... I don't want to be alone tonight," she said, walking into the room before he could reply.

"You're not going to make this easy on me, are you, God?" Jack asked silently, looking up toward the heavens. Jack wondered briefly what would happen if he said no, then flipped back the covers. As she climbed in to join him, he slid from underneath the bed sheet putting it between them. Even in the dim light he could see her looking at him curiously.

"That's the only way this is going to work, Miss Costner," he said admitted quietly. "I'm not as strong willed as you seem to think I am."

"Jack Braedan," Anna said, lifting his arm and sliding close so she could lay her head on his chest, "you are without a doubt the most chivalrous southern gentleman I have ever met. Would you kiss me again if I asked you?"

"Given the circumstances, I.... uh, really don't think that would be a very good idea."

Even though he couldn't see her face, Jack could feel her smiling. "Are you okay?" she asked, laying a perfect hand on this chest. "Your heart is going a mile a minute."

"Are you serious?" Jack sighed wearily.

"Jack, what do you think about...about your mom's letter?"

"What about it?" he asked hesitantly.

"Do you think...could she have been talking about...about me?" she asked quietly.

"Would you *like* to be the helpmate in her letter?" he whispered. He didn't think it possible, but his heart had begun to beat even faster. Anna's hair was as soft as silk and smelled like.... peaches?

"Good night, Jack Braedan," Anna replied snuggling against him, the smile in her voice almost audible.

Anna was asleep in only a few minutes. For Jack, it took much, much longer.

Chapter Six

I know how crazy this sounds

Jack Braedan awoke to a glorious spring morning, with the sun shining through the second story window of his parent's spacious country home. For the briefest of moments, he thought he had dreamed the events of yesterday. Then he rolled over and saw his Mossberg 12-gauge pump resting by the door. The same shotgun he'd used to kill three men, who under the cover of world-wide chaos, had been planning to assault a beautiful young woman with fiery auburn hair and emerald greens eyes. That same young woman, who with the pull of a trigger, had become the center of his existence now that Maryellen and Big Jim were gone, and his aunt and uncle were missing. The same young woman who had left her scent lingering on the pillow beside him and made his heart race even now by merely thinking about her.

"A red-headed, liberal lawyer, really?" Jack sighed wearily, looking up at the ceiling. "Mom said you never laid a burden on someone bigger than they could handle," he muttered. "I hope she was right."

Jack rose, dressed in jeans and a tee shirt, brushed his teeth, and headed downstairs. Anna was cooking breakfast, like him dressed in jeans and a t-shirt, her AR-15 slung across her back. The sight of the "*red-headed, liberal lawyer*" stopped him in his tracks. She was without a doubt, one of the most beautiful women he'd ever met. "Hey," he said, leaning against the door jam, admiring the view.

"Hey yourself," Anna replied.

She scooped a skillet full of steaming scrambled eggs onto a serving plate. "This is the last of the eggs, I'm afraid. Unless there is a secret stash I couldn't find, we need to think about what we're going to do..."

Jack walked over and took the skillet from Anna, setting it down on an oven mitt. Lifting her arms, he unslung her rifle, and hung its carry strap across one of the kitchen chairs. She stood there, regarding him curiously. He lifted her arms, placing them around his neck, and gently pulled her close. "Would you kiss me if I asked you to, Annabelle Costner?" he said, studying her face intently.

Anna's breath quickened at his touch, the pupils of her emerald eyes dilating. "Ask me," she whispered.

"Would you kiss me, Annabelle Costner?"

She did.

"Mmmm," she murmured into his neck, much, much later it seemed. "Now *that* is the way to start the morning."

"I think we'll make that *Event* Rule Number 4," Jack said huskily into her ear, continuing to hold her close.

"Definitely," she sighed.

"Event Rule Number Five, however," Jack said. "Is that you stay in your own bed from now on."

Jack broke their embrace reluctantly and held her at arm's length. "I am not as strong as you think I am, Ms. Costner."

"You don't get to make all the rules, Jack Braeden," Anna teased. "*Event* Rule Number 5," she said, taking his hands and moving them down to her hips. "I sleep wherever I please. I'm a grown woman. If...and that's a very big if, I choose to sleep in your bed again..."

"Anna?"

"If I choose..."

"Anna," he insisted, growing serious.

"Yes?"

He exhaled heavily, then words seem to come in a rush. "Look, for most of my adult life, I have treated women as conquests, not as people," Jack admitted shamefully. "If I told you how many one-night stands that I've had, how many beds I've visited...well, let's just say there's a word for me in Dad's Bible and it's not saint. Truthfully, I haven't done very much in my life that could be considered moral; certainly not by any Braedan standards, and definitely not by God's. But that person is gone. Sometime over the last two days, you killed him. The new Jack Braedan is not going to spoil...this, whatever *this* is becoming by rushing into something we might regret later, just because the world has been flushed down the toilet."

"Regret?" she asked, with a wounded look.

"Anna, I'm serious," Jack insisted. "Relationships started under stress rarely..."

"What kind of woman do you think I am, Jack Braedan?" Anna interrupted. "Do...do you think I just *throw* myself at every man who breezes through my life?"

"Uh....no?"

"You are damn right, no!" she said, her temper flaring. "Jack, I admit I am scared. God in heaven, I'm so scared! You killed three men in my bedroom yesterday. The world has gone totally and horribly crazy. But...this...this began for me long *before* yesterday." Now her words were coming in a rush and couldn't be stopped. It was like a levy had broken and words just came flooding out. "Jack, I know how crazy this sounds, but I...I have been in love with you since the moment Beth brought you home." She finished in a rush, blushing furiously.

Jack's obvious pleasure at this admission seemed to infuriate her. "Jack Braedan, don't you *dare* laugh at me!"

"Laugh at you?" Jack said, picking her up and swinging her around. "I wouldn't *dream* of it!" He sat her on her back feet again and pulled her close. "I think I'd like another kiss."

"I most certainly *will not* kiss you again," Anna huffed, trying to push away.

"*Event* Rule Number 6," Jack announced. "If a person admits they love you, they *have* to kiss you."

"You don't make all the rules," Anna reminded him sternly, but her struggles ceased.

"I guess if you were to take it back," Jack said, smiling, "you can make a different rule."

Instead of taking it back, Anna kissed him again.

"What are we going to do, Jack?" she asked, her head resting on his shoulder.

"Well, we're probably going to have to microwave the eggs for sure...."

"Jack!" Anna said, trying to pull away again.

"Okay. Okay." Jack breathed deeply. What happened next happened so fast, he had no idea he was doing it until it was over. Once second he was standing and the next he was one knee in front of her. "Annabelle Costner. Will you marry me?" he asked, taking her hand. *What in the world had possessed him to say that*? He heard himself say the words, but it was like someone else had spoken them.

"What?" she whispered. "Jack...you can't, you can't be serious?"

"I have only loved you for one day, not fourteen years," he admitted. "And yeah, I know how crazy that just sounded, but...but I do love you. And I *am* serious."

"Jack, I...I don't know what to say," Anna replied.

"Say yes, Anna," he said, his voice containing much more confidence than his fluttering heart felt. "I don't know what tomorrow, or even the next twelve hours, will bring in this new world, but I know I want you by my side whatever comes. I can't, I won't be able to do this without you."

"Jack," she whispered. "Just because your mom wrote some letter..."

"It's not *just* the letter," Jack admitted. "There are no coincidences in life. I man up at the funeral and tough out at the receiving line, and we still meet. Sure, but I don't go to *Guns USA* and we never have our...moment. You still came to Aunt Kate's dinner, and maybe we still hit it off, but we never start down the path that takes me to your bedroom yesterday morning. I know it. And I know, this...this right now, this is right."

"Jack..."

"Look, you brought this on yourself by telling me you loved me, Anna Costner," he said softly. "Say yes. Say yes, and I *promise* you, you will *always* be the most important thing on this earth to me. Say yes and I promise I will always..."

"Yes," Anna whispered, reaching down to caress his cheek. "Yes Jack Braedan, I will marry you."

"Whew," Jack smiled, relief and terror flooding over him at the same time. "That could have turned out *really* awkward. Would you kiss me again, if I asked, Miss Costner?"

"*Event* Rule Number 7," Anna said, leaning forward and wrapping her arms around his neck. "You can kiss me whenever you want."

The scrambled eggs, forgotten on the kitchen table, began to grow cold.

***

By mutual consent, the pair soon decided they would have to suspend exercising Rule Number 6 and 7 or return upstairs to consummate their newly professed love. Also, by mutual consent, both decided there would be no consummation until after their vows were professed before God. Lastly, again by mutual consent, although neither could imagine how it would be possible, both Jack and Anna agreed that should happen at the first opportunity. In the uncertain world after the *Event*, there was no need for unnecessary delay.

When they sat down to eat, after microwaving the eggs, of course, Anna pulled her chair as close as she could get to Jack's, apparently deciding that something even as a small as the breakfast table wasn't going to separate them this morning. After the kitchen was cleaned and the dishes put away, Jack and Anna went to the study and turned on the television.

Jack was only mildly surprised to discover that the "Event" was not the lead story. A full-scale war had erupted in the Middle East. Israel had launched its threatened pre-emptive strike during the night. Although met by fierce resistance, by dawn IDF forces had secured the West Bank and Gaza Strip, and pushed 20 miles in every direction from the Israeli border. They were retaking the Sinai, and armored columns were rolling through Jordan after Israel revealed a non-aggression Treaty with King Abdullah. They were pushing at breath-taking speed towards the borders of Iraq and Saudi Arabia and showed no signs of slowing.

The Israeli Air Force had conducted devastating bombing runs over the cities of Cairo, Egypt, and Beirut, Lebanon. In Damascus, Syria, IDF commandos had apparently struck two major ammunitions storage sites. Whatever had been left of the city after its civil war with al-Qaida and ISIS had been reduced to smoldering rubble by the secondary explosions. The Arab League was calling for an emergency meeting of the UN Security Council; forces were massing in Saudi Arabia to prepare for a counterattack and in Iraq the citizens and what remained of the American-trained Iraqi army had risen in full scale, bloody revolt against ISIS fledgling Caliphate. Most troubling of all, a nuclear explosion seemed to have occurred in Natanz, Iran; whether from an Israeli missile strike or from some horrible accident at their Uranium enrichment facility, no one seemed to know for sure.

"Turn it off, Jack," Anna whispered, her voice trembling. "I don't know how much more of this I can handle."

"How about we pray," Jack said, turning off the TV. "And after that we...well, we just see what happens?"

"Yes, to both," Anna nodded excitedly, taking his hands, and bowing her head. "Heavenly Father," Anna began, "thank you so much for this day...."

At the end of their lengthy prayer, Jack's iPhone buzzed. It was Jeremiah Graham. National Guard troops had rolled into town just after dark and were occupying Franklin, conducting patrols, and hastily constructing “safety camps” to house all the people they were rounding up. Most importantly, he had seen Sean and Kate. Only a glimpse, but he had seen them. They were at a camp set up on the athletic field of Renaissance High School. David and Rebecca were there also.

“Jack, what are we going to do,” Anna asked worriedly.

“We are going to go get my Aunt and Uncle and the Hitchcock’s,” Jack replied with steel in his voice. “No one does this to “Blackjack” Braedan’s family and friends.”

“Where you go, I go,” Anna nodded, caressing his cheek.

“Let’s get tooled up then,” Jack nodded, “and I’ll brief you on my plan.”

“Tooled up” as Jack called it, meant he took her upstairs and they searched through a trunk until he found a couple of old OCP (Operational Camouflage Pattern) uniforms and enough name tapes and patches to pass in a pinch, then sent Anna off to dress while he shaved and trimmed his hair, then dressed. When she came back, he was relatively pleased. She was a tall, athletic woman, and though his uniform was a little big on her, she filled it out nicely. She had on a pair of civilian hiking boots that were almost passable as military issue.

“So, you’re going to outrank me, huh?” Anna asked, eyeing him suspiciously, as he put the Velcro Sergeant First Class rank on her chest. “You look different, by the way. I liked your beard.”

“Soldiers in the states don’t have beards.” he explained, “Tie that beautiful hair up in a bun. E-7’s don’t weary ponytails, even in today’s army.” Even with her hair in a bun, the old maroon beret he found for her was a little big. “It wouldn’t pass an in-ranks inspection, but you’ll do.” He nodded.

To finish “tooling up” Jack showed Anna how to clear and load her AR, then his H&K as well. “Blackjack” Braedan didn’t usually carry a weapon into combat until it was thoroughly vetted, but he figured he’d bought the 36D for a reason, and this might be it. He also strapped on the Springfield 1911s he'd carried yesterday. Anna would carry her Sig Sauer, as well. Both also carried several magazines of extra ammo.

On an impulse, Jack got the keys for his dad's silver Cadillac Escalade, deciding to leave his Jeep parked inside the garage. Jack showed Anna how to set the security alarm; though he really didn't expect anyone at Vector Security would be monitoring. But if the alarm was tripped, it might scare off intruders.

Their short journey to Franklin was uneventful. It seemed they were the only people on the road, with most choosing to obey the order, to avoid unnecessary travel. At the intersection of Highway 96 and Old Charlotte Pike, they passed a City of Franklin Police Cruiser. It was burning merrily in the ditch beside the road. Jack's experienced eye could tell it had been shot to pieces by a heavy caliber weapon. There were two bodies, at least they looked like bodies, still inside and one lying in the grass by the road. Jack couldn't be certain, but it looked like one of the young Latinos from the day before. The body was riddled with bullets and unmoving.

Not much more than a mile further down the highway, Jack saw what had neutralized the cruiser. Blocking the highway at the intersection of Boyd Mill Avenue and Carlisle Lane sat a Desert tan, Bradley Fighting Vehicle, and an armored Humvee, with a 50-caliber machine gun mounted in the turret. Both vehicles swung their weapons systems toward the Escalade, as it approached. Jack knew the ROE; the Rules of Engagement, most units had operated by in Iraq and Afghanistan. He hoped they were even stricter on American soil. He slowed and pulled to a stop 50 meters short of the checkpoint. Any closer and the Escalade risked being engaged with 25 millimeter HE (High Explosive) rounds from the Bradley's M242 Bushmaster automatic cannon or 50 caliber armor piercing bullets from the heavy machine gun mounted on the Humvee.

"Jack?" Anna asked nervously.

"Probably the National Guard that Jeremiah reported," he said, straining to see if he could find unit identifying marks on the vehicles. "The nearest regular army post is Ft. Campbell in Clarksville and they don't have armor." Jack knew most National Guard units located in Hometown USA were company sized or smaller. That meant for a Cavalry or Infantry unit; the only units in the state of Tennessee equipped with Bradley Fighting Vehicles, there were likely only around 100 troops and maybe 20 to 30 vehicles in the area. The Tennessee Cavalry had last deployed to Iraq in 2010 or so. It was more than likely several of those troops up ahead had seen combat.

"What do we do?" Anna asked.

"Wait for instructions. Don't act threatening." He replied.

"But that's a *tank*, Jack, how could we be threatening?"

He wasn't given the time or opportunity to explain the fundamental differences between a Bradley and a tank, or to expound upon the lethality of VBIEDs (Vehicle Born Improvised Explosive Devices) to Anna before a soldier in body armor and ACH helmet stepped from the protection of the vehicles with a bull horn.

"Stay right there!" the soldier commanded. He turned back to the vehicles, as if someone had spoken to him. A team of three other men appeared from the back of the Bradley. All three were armed with M4 carbines and wearing body armor. One of the soldiers cuffed the bullhorn guy on the back of his helmet. The soldier nodded like he realized his mistake and put the bullhorn back to his mouth. "Ummm, turn off your engine, exit your vehicle and ummm, walk forward slowly."

"What do we do, Jack?"

"Exactly what he said," Jack sighed. "If we tried to run, that Bradley would rip us to shreds. Leave the rifles. Keep your pistol holstered. Don't do anything unless I say. Let me do the talking, okay? Stick to the plan."

"You got it, Sergeant," Anna said quietly.

"Don't be afraid, okay?" Jack said, taking both 1911s from his holster and making sure a round was in the chamber before putting them back again.

"Okay." She nodded nervously, doing the same with her Sig.

"It's going to be fine," Jack promised.

"Jack," she said, grabbing his hand as he went to open the driver's side door, "Can we pray first?"

"Of course," he nodded.

"Heavenly Father," Anna said, closing her eyes and bowing her head. "Watch over us. Keep us safe. Banish our fears. Let us pass by these men without any trouble. Let us find our family and friends and take them safely home. In Jesus' name. Amen."

"You're getting pretty good at that," Jack said, squeezing her hand reassuringly. "Ready?"

"Ready," Anna nodded. "I love you, Jack."

"Rule Number 6," he said, offering her his cheek.

She kissed him on the cheek, with an exasperated sigh.

"You owe me a real one when we're finished here," he smiled. "Shall we?"

They both exited slowly and walked forward toward the checkpoint with hands clearly visible. Jack knew they were taking a calculated risk, leaving their rifles in the Escalade, but they would likely have been gunned down before they made it five feet if they were carrying them. At least, if things turned ugly, they'd have their pistols to try and defend themselves.

They approached within twenty-five yards of the checkpoint before one of the soldiers shouted, "Weapons!"

Three M4 carbine rifles were instantly trained on them.

"Stop right there!" Bullhorn ordered.

The apparent team leader motioned two of the troops forward. They kept their weapons trained on Jack and Anna, as they approached. Bullhorn strapped his...bullhorn around his neck and raised his weapon, as well, following the team leader forward. All three of the soldiers looked young, in their early twenties maybe. The team leader, a staff sergeant, was the oldest of the group, maybe just a couple of years younger than Jack. He had the 278th Armored Cavalry Unit patch on both his right and left sleeve, signifying he at least had been deployed before.

"Well, well," the nearest soldier said, eyeing Anna appreciatively. He was an E-4, a Specialist, with cold eyes and a hard face. "You're certainly a looker, aren't you, Airborne? You don't have any concealed weapons, do you? Cover me while I search her, Tommy," He slung his AR and stepped toward Anna.

"Specialist," Jack said calmly, "Don't lay a hand on the sergeant. It's too early in the morning to get your ass kicked." His tone was as calm and as non-threatening as someone else would say, "*Nice weather we're having today, huh?*" But the look in Jack's eyes stopped the soldier in his tracks.

He immediately pulled the Berretta 9mm on his hip and trained it on Jack, "Ain't nobody told you to talk dirt bag! I bet you aren't even SF!"

"Staff Sergeant," Jack said, ignoring the soldier and addressing his team leader in the same calm tone, "If he touches Sergeant Braedan, I'll drop him where he stands."

"I've had enough of your mouth!" the soldier shouted, "Get on your knees!"

Jack turned to face him again. He'd taken a step closer. His finger was in the trigger well, but Jack could see the selector lever of his pistol was still on safe. There was absolutely no way Jack was going to get on his knees and let this punk specialist disarm him and then be free to lift a finger to Anna. He just needed to take one step closer.

"Specialist, I'm going to tell you one more time..."

"Specialist Dean," the staff sergeant warned sternly, suddenly alarmed.

"I said on your knees you dumb son of a...."

Jack struck without warning, gabbing the barrel of the soldier's pistol, and ripping it from his hand, at the same time snapping out with the heel of his left palm to connect with the bridge of the man's nose. As he dropped like a rock, Jack raised his captured weapon above his head and dropped to his knees in the almost universal sign of surrender.

Everyone began shouting at once.

"Drop it!"

"Drop the weapon!"

"Drop it now!"

"Hey!" Anna shouted. Three M4s started swinging back and forth between Jack and Anna. He took a quick glance out of the corner of his eye and saw she had her 9 mm pointed at the head of the staff sergeant. He didn't think it was possible that he could love her more than at this very instant.

"Soldier," the Staff Sergeant said, clicking his selector lever to fire and pointing his M4 at Anna, "I need you to drop that weapon *right* NOW!"

Things were getting out of control. It would only take one twitch, one wrong move, and people would start dying. *"Jesus, help us,"* Jack prayed silently. Then he noticed the name tape on the Staff Sergeant's body armor, and he knew the way out of this mess.

"Horn?" Jack said calmly. "You wouldn't be related to Tim Horn, would you?"

"What?" the staff sergeant asked, keeping his weapon trained on Anna but now looking at Jack.

"Sergeant Timothy Horn," Jack said, voice as calm as the beautiful spring morning around them. "Killed in Ramallah in 2011?"

The Staff Sergeant's weapon left Anna and was now aimed at him, though it was beginning to lower. "Tim was..."

"Your brother," Jack nodded. "I can see him in you." Jack released the M9 with his right hand slowly, palm outward, in the universal sign of *"Hey, everything is fine"* then slowly brought the pistol down and hit the magazine release catch. He caught the magazine and laid it on the ground. "It's Allen, right?" Jack asked, as he pulled back the slide and checked the chamber. It was empty. Dean hadn't even been locked and loaded. He made sure on selector switch on safe and slowly lowered it to the ground.

"I'm going to reach into my back pocket and get my ID, okay?" Jack continued. Standing slowly, again with his right palm facing out to show it was empty, he reached into the back pocket of his pants and pulled out his wallet. "I served with Tim in 3rd Ranger Bat," Jack said, meaning the 3rd Battalion, 75th Ranger Regiment. "I'm Master Sergeant Jack Braedan," he said flipping open his wallet to his show military ID card.

He held it out, offering it to the soldiers. Staff Sergeant Horn motioned with his head and the Bullhorn guy, Private First-Class Donovan by his name tape and rank, stepped forward and took it from him, then moved back and showed it to Horn.

Staff Sergeant Horn studied the ID for a second, then looked up at Jack. "Tim had a tattoo."

"Scariest winged demon I ever saw," Jack nodded. "He got it in Savannah in '08. We were drunk as Irish priests. He used to say that Rangers might be on his right and left..."

"But the Devil had his back," Horn finished. He flipped his M4 back on safe and lowered his weapon to low ready. "You saved Tim's life in the Shinkay Valley in '08," Horn said, handing Jack his wallet.

"And he saved mine a few weeks later," Jack shrugged.

"Jesus, Master Sergeant, we coulda' killed you." Sergeant Horn said, unsnapping the chin strap of his ACH and pushing his helmet back on his head to wipe sweat off his brow.

"Could have, but didn't," Jack replied. "I was hoping that right sleeve patch meant you could keep your cool."

"Yeah, but these fools," Horn grinned, "Tommy, go see if he broke Brian's nose."

"Ummm, Sarge?"

"Sergeant, would you mind lowering that pistol?" Horn asked, turning to look at Anna. "You're scaring my troopers. And I'll need to see your ID, as well."

"It's okay," Jack said, turning to Anna. She did look scary, he had to admit. Anna lowered her Sig Sauer but didn't put it away. Good girl. It was now or never. He prayed quickly and began to implement part one of his plan.

"Staff Sergeant," Jack began, "This is my wife, Sergeant First Class Bella Braedan. 108th Intelligence Company. She's an Intel spook at Bragg. We flew up for my parent's funeral a few days ago. We were scheduled to fly back yesterday but.... things got complicated."

"That's an understatement," Horn snorted.

"Part of that, complication, is Sergeant First Class Braedan's bags were lost. Fat chance getting them back now, but her ID was in her checked bag." It was a bold lie but told with conviction. Even so, Jack could instantly see the doubt in Sergeant Horn's eyes. ID in her bags? That had been the sketchiest part of this ruse, but he'd said it now and there was no sense back-tracking.

Horn eyed Anna for a few tense seconds, then finally shrugged. "Master Sergeant, what were you two thinking coming up on my checkpoint strapped like this?" he asked.

"I saw those same *Vatos* yesterday," Jack said. "It isn't safe on the roads. You're the ones that shot them up, right?

"About twenty minutes ago," Horn nodded. "That's where we had our checkpoint originally. They tried to run it. We followed the ROE."

"I'm sure you did," Jack shrugged.

"Couldn't sit there and watch them cook," Horn explained. "So, we fell back here."

"It's a good spot," Jack nodded.

"What are you doing out on the road, Master Sergeant?" Horn asked again. "The ummm, President has declared Martial Law, because.... because of the *Event*. Nothing but emergency traffic is supposed to be moving."

It was time for part two.

"Bella, Sergeant First Class Braedan that is, got a message from 101st Headquarters this morning, as we were about to leave for Ft. Campbell. Some former green beret was picked up during the sweeps. His wife is reported to be some sort of Israeli agent. We've been told to collect them. So, Belle, Sergeant First Class Braedan, and I can escort them back to Campbell for interrogation."

"Don't suppose you have names? And orders?" Sergeant Horn asked with a raised eye-brow.

"David Hitchcock," Anna replied. "His wife's name is Rebecca. No orders, written ones anyway. Just a verbal command to go get them from some NSA jerk in Campbell named Peretti."

Peretti? It was all Jack could do to not laugh. Anna could lie on her feet even better than he could. Red-headed lawyers!

"You mean Dave from *Guns USA*?" one of the soldiers asked.

"I have no idea where he works," Anna shrugged. "Just who he is and where we are supposed to take them. How do you know this Hitchcock?"

"Sarge....," Donovan replied. "Dave is a Churcher. One of those Jesus freaks. But a cool dude. I bet they are at the compound down by the high school."

"Look, it doesn't matter," Horn said. "I can't let you go looking for him. We're clearing the town. There's been a lot of craziness going down in Franklin since the *Event*. Even though this area wasn't hit, folks are running wild. We were at drill when we were ordered to come here. Knife Company has been doing patrols and securing the area for 2100 yesterday."

"Look, Allen, can I call you Allen?" Jack asked pleasantly. "You have your orders, and we have ours. Yours is the checkpoint, which you're executing to the letter. And I'll say so in my debrief. Mine is to get Hitchcock and the Israeli to Campbell."

"We've also been told Sean and Kate Braedan may be with them." Anna added.

"And who told you that?" Horn asked.

"A...who was it," Anna hesitated, pretending to search her memory. "Ah yes, Jeremiah Graham?"

"You mean Jerry Graham?" Donovan asked. "He's the youth minister down at First Methodist," the Franklin native informed Horn, "but he's cool as well, I mean, he's not a *real* Bible thumper."

"That must be him," Anna nodded.

"I saw him this morning right before we moved out," Donovan said. "He was passing out bottles of water to the ummm, detainees."

"Look, I'm sorry, Sergeants, I really am," Horn apologized. "24 hours, maybe 48 and we should have the town completely secured."

"Two days is not acceptable, Sergeant Horn," Anna replied sternly.

"Hey Sarge, what if, well, looks like we may have to take Brian, I mean, Specialist Dean to the medic," PFC Donovan said. "We could take their Caddy. The Aid Station is right down the street from the holding area."

"Could you?" Anna asked hopefully.

"I.... don't know if we could do that, Sergeant," Horn said hesitantly.

"That's probably above the Staff Sergeant's call," Jack said.

"But two *days,* Jack?" Anna huffed. "I mean, Peretti isn't going to be pleased. And I don't think we want to displease the NSA given our present situation."

"How about it, Sarge?" Donovan asked. "We load Brian up in their Caddy and take him to the Aid Station? That way you still got two vehicles on the Check Point. I could ride with them. You know, to be seen so the company would know they were cleared? Does it have a sunroof?" he asked, turning to Jack.

"It does, indeed," Jack nodded. PFC Donovan was being extremely helpful. More helpful than he ought to be toward someone who had just coldcocked his one of his squad members. Jack could only imagine a higher power was at work. This getting right with the Lord was cool, he decided.

"Specialist Dean does need to get to the doc," said another trooper; PV2 Hoyte according to his name tape. "I don't think he broke his nose," Hoyte said, smiling at Jack, "but he hit him a pretty hard lick." He grinned and held out his hand. His palm was bloody where he'd attempted to patch up his comrade.

"I'm sorry about that, Sergeant Horn," Jack said, and meant it.

"Ah, Hell," Horn shrugged. "He needed a good whack. I've wanted to do that myself since yesterday. I'm sorry if he offended you...Sergeant Braedan," she said addressing Anna. "I should have been quicker to reel him in."

"You let us complete our mission, and all will be forgiven," Anna said, flashing a dazzling smile at Horn. She had a smile that could melt an iceberg. It melted any resistance that Horn had remaining.

"Tommy, help PFC Donovan load Dean in their Cadillac," Horn nodded.

"Thank you so much, Sergeant," Anna smiled. She even; honest to goodness, batted her eye lashes at him. It was all Jack could do to keep from bursting out laughing. Anna shot him a look that promised retribution later and it was gone in an instant.

"Ummm, you're welcome," Horn smiled sheepishly. "Look, I need to call this in to Black 6."

"Uh, Staff Sergeant...we have a couple of long guns in the SUV," Jack said. "Is that going to be a problem?"

"What are you doing rolling around with.... never mind," Horn sighed. "I'll call it in. National Emergency. You're a Master Sergeant on secret orders from the NSA. I'll send Sergeant Weaver with you for a little extra rank, and Donovan will stay here. Hey, Weaver!" he shouted, turning back to the Humvee.

"Yeah, Sarge?" the 50 Cal gunner asked.

"Get the Bravo out of the back of the Bradley. You're going with these Spec Ops folks into town," Horn ordered.

"Check and a Rog," Weaver nodded, placing the .50 caliber machine gun on safe and climbing down out of the Humvee turret.

Donovan was disappointed when he found out he wouldn't be riding with them into town, but he cheered up when Anna hugged him and gave him a kiss on the cheek for all his help. He grinned stupidly, staring at her with moon-eyes, until Staff Sergeant Horn gave him a whack on the back of his ACH. Apparently, that was their normal mode of communication. Sergeant Weaver climbed into the Escalade, standing on the back seat, placing the M240 Bravo (the Squad Automatic Weapon 7.62mm machine gun) out the sunroof. PV2 Hoyte rode in the back where they had lowered the third seat, watching over Specialist Dean, who was just coming around.

"I couldn't reach Black 6 on the radio," Horn informed Sergeant Weaver. "Commo at the TOC must be down again. Be tall up there, let the Troop see you. I don't want any friendly fire taking out my best .50 gunner."

"Check and Rog, Sarge," Weaver nodded, giving the roof a loud pat, signaling he was ready to roll. Jack drove around the checkpoint, waving at Horn.

They passed several dismounted patrols of six to eight men teams on their way into down-town Franklin. With Sergeant Weaver up top riding "security" however, and PV2 Hoyte in the back with the window rolled down waving at soldiers as they passed by, they entered the town without incident.

The National Guard had set up their Command Post in a field behind Renaissance High School on Everbright Avenue. Jack drove right up to the Aid Station, under the direction of Sergeant Weaver up top. A couple of medics helped Private Hoyte unload Specialist Dean, who gave Jack a venomous look, as he was being offloaded from the Cadillac.

"Hoyte, go to the CP and report to Sergeant Stephens and tell him we're taking these Special Ops folks to the detainee pen," Sergeant Weaver ordered. "And see if they have any Gatorade left! Not that lemon lime crap, but the good stuff. Meet us at corner of 11th and 96 by the barbeque place? Will fifteen minutes enough?" he asked, turning to Jack.

"More than enough, I should think," Jack nodded, thinking he and Anna would likely be in handcuffs or dead in less than ten. "Lead on, Sergeant Weaver," Jack said, reaching into the Caddy and securing his H&K. If his "story" about orders and NSA interrogations didn't hold, things were likely to go south quickly.

The detainee "compound" was a hastily constructed collection of several medium, General Purpose tents in an area of perhaps fifty meters square, surrounded by triple-strand concertina wire. At least thirty people were inside, guarded by armed, two-man teams at each corner of the compound, facing inward, weapons at low ready. On the south side of the compound was opening in the wire where two more guards sat a field table under a blue, Tennessee Titans football tail gate tent. It was to the tent that Sergeant Weaver took them.

"Hey, Matt," Sergeant Weaver said, addressing the corporal that stood to meet them. "Got two Special Ops here to collect some of the detainees."

"Orders and IDs?" Corporal Nelson said, holding out his hand.

"Haven't seen any orders," Weaver replied. "Just doing what I'm told. Staff Sergeant Horn said to bring them, so I brought them."

"Orders. Master Sergeant?" Nelson added reluctantly, noticing his rank.

"I don't have any orders, Corporal Nelson," Jack admitted. "None that I can show you. All Sergeant First Class Braedan," he inclined his head toward Anna, "All she got was a phone call. The devil himself knows how it got through, but some NSA ass hat at Campbell ordered us to lay hands on some civilians picked up in the sweeps."

"No orders?" Nelson said, confusion clearly showing on his face. "Ahhhh.... don't think I can release anyone without orders."

"You're not *releasing* them, Corporal," Jack said calmly. "You're remanding them into my custody."

"I need to call the CP," Nelson said, picking up the hand mike of the ASIP radio laying on his table. "Knife X-Ray, this is Corporal Nelson at holding." Silence. "Knife X-Ray, this is Matt, over."

"Frickin commo been jacked up since this goat rope started," Nelson cursed. "Sorry, Sergeant," he added hastily, color on his cheeks as he noticed Anna's disapproving glare. "Luke, go see if the First Sergeant or the CO are at the TOC."

"Top and the Ol Man are at the BUB at Cool Springs," Specialist 'Luke' Fletcher, replied with a shrug.

"Bub?" Anna mouthed silently at Jack.

"Later," Jack said.

"Well, then go and get the LT numb nuts!"

"He's out on patrol," Luke grinned. Apparently, he found Nelson's discomfort amusing.

"Crap!" Nelson swore, slamming the radio hand mike on the table. "This is EWHAM."

"E what?" Anna asked curiously.

"Echelons Way Above Me," Jack explained. "Look, Corporal, we can stand around here all morning waiting for you to make a decision, or...I can take full responsibility for these detainees and send your CO a detailed report on how helpful you were when I get them back to Ft. Campbell for interrogation."

"Son of a..." Nelson muttered. "I'm a mechanic! I'm not trained for this."

"*Corporal* Nelson," Jack emphasized his rank with all the Senior NCO disdain he could muster, "I don't know if you've noticed, but there have been some crazy orders flying around the last 24 hours. Mine says I must collect two civilians, one a former Green Beret and one reported to be an Israeli spy, and the city attorney and his wife, and take them all to Campbell. I don't know about you, but given the current situation, I, for one don't want to get on some NSA jerk's bad side because YOU couldn't grow a pair and make a decision. I might end up behind this wire myself."

"What were their names again?" Corporal Nelson asked Anna.

"David and Rebecca Hitchcock," Anna said. "A Mr. Sean and Mrs. Katrina Braedan, no relation."

"Well, those two at least I know aren't here," Nelson replied. "Trucked up to Nashville an hour ago."

"Why?" Jack inquired, trying to keep the dread out of his voice.

"Hell, I don't know," Nelson whined, "I'm just a Bradley mechanic. But the Fed that came for them, at least had orders. Master Sergeant." He added perfunctorily. Nelson consulted a clip board on his table, finger running down a list of names. "Hitchcock, David E. and Hitchcock, Rebecca. 33 and 34."

"That's them," Anna nodded.

Everyone stood there for what seemed an eternity. With each second that ticked by, Jack could feel his hastily concocted plan falling apart. Looking around the compound, he weighed his options. These two at the gate he could take out easily. Nelson only had a holstered side arm, SPC Fletcher had a side arm as well, again holstered, and there was an M4 leaning against the table, but out of his reach. Maybe he could the take the two at the south corner as well. Then it would be a first-class gunfight. With the command post only a block away, even with Anna as back up, it didn't look good. *"Jesus help us,"* Jack prayed again silently. What had he been thinking to drag Anna into this?

"Well, don't just sit there, Luke, go get them!" Nelson ordered, suddenly.

Specialist Fletcher returned a couple of minutes later, his side arm pointed at Dave; being support slightly by Rebecca.

"This them?" Jack Braedan asked, praying with all his heart that Dave and Rebecca wouldn't say something to screw this up.

"How should I know?" Nelson muttered.

"It's them," Luke smiled.

"I don't suppose you have any flex cuffs," Jack inquired. "I can't have them riding all the way to Ft. Campbell unsecured."

"Those I have," Nelson said, finally being presented with something he could handle. Reaching under the field table, he retrieved two pair of thick, plastic zip cuffs and handed them to Jack.

"Hold out your hands," Jack instructed the pair firmly, as he walked over to them. Dave sported a nasty bruise on his right eye and a knot the size of a golf ball just below his hair line. He leaned in close as he put the flex cuffs on and whispered. "Keep quiet and we may just get out of here alive."

"You okay?" asked Jack, barely loud enough to be heard as he stepped to Rebecca and put the flex cuffs on her. Rebecca nodded, looking unharmed but tired, and thoroughly perplexed to see them. She raised an eyebrow and tilted her head at Anna, who was doing her best to look menacing with her hands resting on the rifle slung across her chest. "She's taking you in for questioning," Jack whispered with a quick wink.

"No talking you two," Jack ordered loudly as he put a hand on each of their shoulders and escorted them to the other waiting "Sergeant" Braedan.

"Ummm...Master Sergeant, I need you to sign for them," Corporal Nelson instructed.

"Get me the Standard Form 1167," Jack ordered.

Nelson gave him a blank look. He'd never heard of Standard Form 1167. It was understandable considering Jack had just invented it on the spot. "Hell, just give me a sheet of paper corporal," Jack muttered. Nelson took the sheet with the Hitchcock's names on it, flipped it over and handed it to Braeden. Jack signed his name so illegibly a pharmacist couldn't have deciphered it.

"Don't forget to send back that report, Master Sergeant," Nelson said.

"The instant I get to Fort Campbell," Jack promised.

Back at the Escalade, Jack opened the rear door and flipped up the back seat. Helping the thoroughly relieved Hitchcocks into the vehicle. Anna climbed into the back with them. "Take up you're post, Sergeant Weaver," he said to the gunner. He climbed into the driver's seat and turned to face the back. "Sergeant Braedan watch those two, they look dangerous," he smiled. "Which way to pick up Private Hoyte?" he asked Weaver.

"Take a left at the end of the street, then a right at Willow," the trooper said, firing up a cigarette. Now all they had to do was get out of town before their luck ran out.

Chapter Seven

Strong Delusion

"Because they received not the love of the truth, that they might be saved, for this cause, God shall send them a strong delusion, so that they should believe a lie."

2 Thessalonians 2:10-11

On the corner of 11th Avenue and Highway 96 at BB's Barbeque, they found a very distressed PV2 Hoyte. "Master Sergeant, we have to go!" he said, as soon as he climbed in the Cadillac, "You need to get moving, and don't slow down until you get us back to the checkpoint. Take 11th Avenue and then turn left on Boyd Mill Road,"

"What's going on?" asked Jack, pulling out onto 11th, and stepping on the gas as soon as they'd closed their doors.

"You want the bad news or the bad news?" Hoyte asked.

"Start with the bad news, I guess," Jack said, turning left on Boyd.

"Dean was mouthing off in the Aid Station," Hoyte explained. "Talking smack about the Green Beret that assaulted him. Before I left the TOC, I also heard radio traffic from holding asking for clarification about two detainees that he'd just picked up. I suppose this is them, huh? I give it five, maybe ten minutes tops before a NET call goes out to stop a Silver Cadillac Escalade for questioning."

"And you're telling me this because..." Jack inquired.

"Take a right here," Weaver instructed from above, "Then bear left. He's telling you because, hell, you're Master Sergeant "Blackjack" Braedan. Franklin's hometown hero. You have a damn display case in the courthouse."

"Blackjack" Braedan was the reason I joined the Guard." PVT Hoyte grinned.

Anna reached over the back seat and patted his cheek tenderly.

"Won't ummm, won't you get into trouble when they find out you helped us get out of Franklin?" Jack inquired.

"Master Sergeant," Hoyte said, "In a couple of hours, you popping Dean on the nose and running off with a couple of Jesus lovers will be the least of command's worries."

"The other bad news?" asked Jack, wondering what could so trivialize an AWOL Master Sergeant striking a specialist at a check point during martial law and escaping with two prisoners.

"Flash traffic over the command net while I was in the TOC," Hoyte said hesitantly.

"Yeah?"

"Well, ummm, Squadron XO, Saber 5, was on the net ordering a Yellow Tight Air status, for some unidentified aircraft that landed on the freaking capital lawn in DC," Hoyte said.

"What do you mean...unidentified aircraft?" Jack said, turning to look at Hoyte.

"I mean, well, ummm..."

"Spit it out, Hoyte!" Sergeant Weaver ordered.

"Unidentified aircraft," Hoyte explained. "That's all it said."

"Jack! Watch the road!" Anna cried.

Jack jerked the wheel of the Escalade to the right a split second before he ran it into a ditch and lost control completely. "You're messing with me, right?" he asked, looking at the Private incredulously.

"Do I look like I'm messing with you, Master Sergeant?" Hoyte asked. He didn't. In fact, he looked like he was scared out of his wits.

"Jack, what...what's going?" Anna asked, looking as scared as Private Hoyte.

"Well, what's going on is," he said, accelerating the Escalade to 70 miles per hour, "we're dropping Sergeant Weaver and Private Hoyte at the checkpoint and getting us all home, as quick as we can."

After about three quarters of a mile, Boyd Mill Avenue intersected with Highway 96. Jack turned left and pushed the Cadillac to eighty. A mile further and they slowed down as they approached the checkpoint. The armored Humvee still had its .50 caliber machine trained to the West, covering the road, with the Bradley and its 25mm cannon; equipped with FLIR (Forward Looking InfraRed) sights and its Commander's Independent Viewer scanning the sky. It also had its TOW launcher raised.

Inside the launcher were a pair of TOW 2B (Tubed Launched Optically Tracked Wire guided) missiles. Each missile had a thirteen-pound, high explosive warhead used to defeat the most sophisticated armored vehicles in the world. The 2B had a reported range of almost 4,000 meters; 12,000 feet. About fifty yards to the left of the Bradley, a pair of soldiers were setting up an FGM-148 Javelin missile. The Javelin had an 11-pound war head and a range of almost 5,000 meters. Where the TOW had to be held on target the entire time it was in flight and was painfully slow, the Javelin was a "fire and forget" missile that flew at about Mach 1.7; roughly a thousand miles per hour. What that firepower could do against supposed unidentified aircraft, was anyone's guess. But it looked like Staff Sergeant Horn's soldiers at least, were taking the report very seriously.

Staff Sergeant Horn met them as they stopped the Cadillac about ten yards behind the Bradley. "Weaver, get back on your .50 Cal," he ordered. "Hoyte, help Donovan set up a second Javelin."

"Unidentified aircraft, huh?" asked Jack, rolling down the window.

"After the last two days? Seems about right," Horn shrugged.

"You know your guns are facing west, right?" Jack informed him. "DC is the opposite direction."

"West is my sector. You know the military, Master Sergeant. They say scan your sector; I scan my sector. Even if it's the opposite direction. I'm also supposed to be stopping a silver Escalade if it comes this way and hold its occupants for questioning." Horn informed him.

"So, I've heard," Jack replied.

He studied the occupants of the back seat for a long heartbeat, then sighed. "Good thing I haven't seen it then. Master Sergeant, you be careful going home. Ma'am," he said, inclining his head toward Anna.

"Thanks," Jack said, offering Horn his hand. "And *technically,* I suppose it's just Jack now."

"Not going back, huh?" Horn guessed.

"Not after today. Not outside a body bag, at least," Jack shrugged.

"Can't say that I blame you," Horn nodded. "Guard hasn't had to take the new oath yet. Suppose we will get around to it eventually. I don't know what I'm going to do when the time comes, but if anyone asks, I never saw you...Jack. For Tim's sake," he said quietly.

"And Dean?"

"Who knows what he saw or thought he saw?" Horn grinned. "His memory is probably a little foggy from the concussion he got when he mouthed off to a Master Sergeant of the United States Army on official business in Franklin. At least, that's what he told me he was doing after the little, misunderstanding got straighten out."

"That's not going to fly for long," Jack said.

"It'll work long enough," Horn shrugged. "What you may or may not have done after we let you pass our checkpoint, with an armed escort, well...not my problem. Anyway, in another hour we could be fighting commies or aliens or ice giants from Jotunheim and it'll all be forgotten."

"Thank you, Sergeant Horn," Anna said from the back seat.

"You're welcome...Ms. Costner," Horn ginned. "Next time you try something like this," he said to Jack, "don't bring the prettiest lawyer in Middle Tennessee with you. Deal?"

"Deal," Jack promised.

"Watch out for little green men," Horn advised, "and don't be making any trips to town for a while. I'll send word or come myself and let you know when things are settling down."

"You're a good man, Staff Sergeant," Jack said, reaching out to shake his hand again.

"My brother was a good man," Horn replied solemnly, "I'm just trying to fill his boots."

As soon as they pulled away from the check point, Jack reached into his front pocket and pulled out a Gerber folding knife. "Anna, why don't you cut loose our prisoners."

"Sweet Jesus!" Dave exclaimed. "That was some real James Bond stuff! You really *ARE* a secret agent man!"

"More like Mossad," Rebecca laughed, full of relief. "Thank you, Jack. And, your language, David Hitchcock?"

"Sorry, Love," he apologized. "But, Jack? Really? Walking right up to the guard HQ bold as a ten-dollar Fayetteville umm.... I mean, Jack, you have a big pair. Big BRASS ones. James Bond's got nothing on you, my man."

"Dave, Sean and Aunt Kate, where'd they take them?" Jack asked, and the mood was instantly somber.

"I don't know, Son," Dave said sadly. "They kept us separated. They've been ferrying folks in and out of that compound all morning. I don't even know what the hell it is or what's going on. Two sheriff's deputies came knocking on our door about 3AM, the day before yesterday, and said we needed to come in for "questioning." About what I asked? He rattled off some bull shhhh.... stuff about national security. I said show me a warrant. And....

"That's how you got the shiner, right?"

"He surprised me," Dave muttered. "Woke up in that two-bit Nazi camp, about an hour later with one heck of a headache. Good thing I put my wheels on and got dressed before I answered the door, or you'd have rescued a naked cripple. Luckily, Becca was asleep, or they'd be dead."

"Jack, what is going on?" Rebecca asked.

"We're here," Jack announced, pulling to gate the of his parent's house. "Let's go inside and get you something to eat and drink, and then we'll explain what we know."

Jack and Anna led the Hitchcocks into the kitchen. While throwing together some sandwiches and drinks, Jack began to recount the events of the last two days. David and Rebecca sat silent for almost an hour, as he and Anna told them everything about the last 48 hours.

"The President is really dead?" asked David.

"A plane really crashed into the Dome of the Rock?" Rebecca asked.

"Yeah," Jack nodded. "The Middle East is in flames. IDF seems to be kicking everyone's butt, as well."

"Think it's the Psalm 83 war?" Rebecca asked, turning to her husband.

"Now, hon, let's not get that argument started," David sighed.

"Psalm 83 war? What's that?" Jack wanted to know.

"It's one of the few things Becca and I disagree on," Hitchcock replied. "She believes the current state of Israel is the gathering spoken of in Ezekiel, I however, think..."

"We forgot about the aircraft!" Anna exclaimed, jumping to her feet.

Everyone sprang from the kitchen table and followed her into Big Jim's study.

Anna turned on the TV, motioned for Jack to take the love seat and she sat in his lap. The Hitchcocks took the couch.

"What in God's name is that?" Dave asked.

"Turn up the sound, Jack," Anna whispered, entwining her arm around him.

"Yeah, turn it up," Dave seconded.

"Yes," the TV anchor said, undisguised wonder in his voice. "What you're seeing on your screens is real. It's not an illusion."

What they were seeing on the screen was beyond belief. Sitting on the south lawn of the White House in Washington DC...well, hovering, perhaps ten feet above the lawn, was some sort of inverted...pyramid... perhaps fifty meters in height and about the same measurement across at its "base." It was made of some silvery, metallic substance so polished it reflected the area around it almost like a mirror. The only thing that Jack could mentally compare it with was the "Bean" in Millennial Park in Chicago, Illinois. Of course, otherwise it looked nothing like that iconic landmark. It looked like nothing on this earth!

"No one saw the...well, the craft arrive," the news anchor explained. "It just suddenly appeared. It is well known that since 9/11 the White House has installed some of the most sophisticated air defense systems in the world, but sources report that all those systems simply well...failed, as soon as the craft landed. The film you are about to see was taken by an amateur videographer and is now the exclusive property of CNN."

The TV switched to a shaking feed of the craft, then panned to three black SUVs, as they came roaring onto the south lawn. Secret Service Agents spilled out and aimed automatic weapons at the craft. Then, the new President emerged from the center SUV and a...well, door opened in the front of the craft and a silver ramp extended from the opening like liquid metal. It was only seconds later that a well-dressed man appeared, flanked by two tall...otherworldly figures. That was the simplest description. Both were at least two feet taller than the man in the center, had white hair flowing down to their shoulders, sharp, angular features, with pale lips and eyes like black ice. Stranger still, they were dressed in sleek, grey suits that could have been tailored at the finest shop in Milan, Italy.

"Is that..." Dave began.

"Yes," the news anchor said almost on cue. "The man who emerged from the craft is indeed Apollus Cassini, Prime Minister of Italy and current President of the European Union. My sources report that not fifteen minutes before the craft arrived, Prime Minister Cassini placed an urgent phone call to the President and requested to speak at the coming UN assembly being held in the Washington tomorrow. My sources also report it was confirmed Cassini placed the call from his Presidential Office in Brussels, Belgium. Speculation abounds as to why the leader of the European Union arrived soon after in this craft, accompanied by well...dare I say it, visitors from another world?"

"Do you think it's him, Becca?" Dave asked.

"Could be, although lately I have been leaning toward someone totally different," she replied. "It's the *other* thing, that David and I have...debates about."

"Could be who?" asked Jack.

"Jack, what do you think is going on?" David Hitchcock asked, taking the remote and switching off the sound.

"Hey, I wanted to hear this," Anna protested.

"This is more important," Dave replied.

"More important than an alien spacecraft on the White House lawn?" Anna asked incredulously.

"Yes," Hitchcock replied simply. "Well, Jack? What are you seeing?"

"Truthfully, Dave, I have no idea," Jack sighed. "My mind is on overload right now."

"Then tell me what you think has happened in the last couple of days, then." Dave suggested. "Based just on your experiences."

"I *think* our country and a large portion of the world has been thrown for a loop by these solar flares. I *think*, despite what the new Madame President has said about the government being on top of things, it's something we'll be a very long time recovering from. As far as this *detainment* of Christians, I *know* those bastards had a plan formulated to round up.... opposition...long before yesterday and they *may* have even begun the process before the solar flares started. I *think* basically that we're dead as a constitutional republic and probably finished as a world power. I mean, we still have the nukes and the largest navy in the world, but with the West Coast, the Mid-West and the Northeast in the dark, for God knows how long, we are finished economically." Jack finished.

"Based on what you've told me has happened these last couple of days, I agree," Dave nodded. "Now, would you like to know why?"

"I would *love* to know why," Jack sighed, reaching out to Anna's hand.

"Then put on your tinfoil hats and hang on," Dave grinned. "For the last couple of years, Rebecca, and I, along with your parents, your Uncle Sean and Kate, and a few other members of the First Methodist, have been meeting twice a week to study prophecy. We've been matching current events with things that were predicted in the Bible 2,000 years ago. We were all in agreement that for those events to come to fruition, the United States would have to be removed as a world power. You are absolutely right, by the way. Based on what you said has happened and what my own eyes have seen, we are done as the world's leading superpower. And the world *abhors* a vacuum."

"So, someone has to take our place?" Jack asked.

"He's quick," Dave grinned at Anna. "Yeah, someone has to take our place."

"The Beast?" Anna said.

"Have you been wiring tapping our meetings, Counselor?" Dave smiled.

"No, "she replied. "We've been doing some of our own research the last couple of days."

"The Beast?" Jack inquired.

"The Beast, sitting at the head of a One World Government." Dave nodded. The anti-Christ. The Son of Perdition. He has a lot of names. An important clue in identifying the Beast is in Daniel. Read me, Daniel 9:27. Would you?"

"Anna, hand me dad's Bible," Jack said. "Thanks, hon." He flipped through it quickly. Two days ago, he wouldn't have had a clue where to find the book of Daniel, but that was two days ago. Jack found it quickly.

"He will confirm a covenant with many for one 'seven.' In the middle of the 'seven' he will put an end to sacrifice and offering. And at the temple he will set up an abomination that causes desolation, until the decreed is poured out on him."

"And what does that mean to you," Dave asked.

"I'm afraid, that I'm a little confused." Jack admitted.

"'Sevens' are known as a unit of measure for the Jews. Any seven. A week. Seven years," Rebecca explained. "One week, seven years. Earlier in chapter 9, Israel was given seventy 'sevens,' 490 years after the rebuilding of Jerusalem to put an end to sin. It took 49 years to rebuild after the decree from Cyrus. Seven 'sevens.' Then came sixty-two 'sevens.' Yeshua was crucified exactly 482 years after the Temple was rebuilt."

"And the rest?" Braeden asked.

"That interrupted the 490 years for Israel. Since then, we have been living in the "time of the Gentiles." David explained. "There is one "week" one 'seven' still remaining. Most scholars agree that the last 'seven' begins when the First Beast signs a "covenant," a peace treaty with Israel."

"The people of the prince to come," Rebecca. "They laid siege to Jerusalem and destroyed the Jewish Temple in 70 AD."

"The Roman Empire did that," Jack replied. "That much I *do* know."

"And the Roman Empire had its capital..."

"In Rome," Jack answered.

"Which is now the capital of...."

"Italy, of course...."

"I think Cassini may be the Prince to Come," Dave said, pointing at the television. "And one of the Beasts of Revelation."

CNN was again replaying the arrival of Cassini on the alien craft. The camera shot "froze" on Cassini, as the news anchor basically "gushed" praises on the man. The Prime Minister was a handsome man in his early forties. Handsome wasn't really the word for it. He could have easily been a Hollywood movie star. His bearing literally oozed confidence and authority. He wasn't merely the figure head leader of the European Union; he was an actual *leader*. The EU had prospered more under Cassini than at any time, since its original founding in the early 50's. There wasn't a person more respected in the world at the moment. He was an economic wizard. He'd solved the Greek and Irish debt crisis and had strengthened the Euro until it was the most sought-after currency on the market. His foreign policy prowess was also without question. He'd settled the Crimea conflict between Russia and the Ukraine. He'd been instrumental in hammering out an agreement between China and Japan over the disputed island in the China Sea. Most recently he had spent many hours meeting with the leaders of Israel and the Arab League, searching for a long-term solution to the Palestinian dilemma.

He was in short, an international rock star among world leaders.

"He's been a breath of fresh air in the world of politics, hasn't he?" Dave suggested.

"Yeah, he's been that" Jack admitted.

"Just what the world has been longing for, huh?" Dave prodded. "Someone who actually *does* things, instead of just talking about them."

"You could say that" Jack nodded.

"I believe he might also be an agent, straight from the pits of Hell," Dave said ominously.

"What do you see, Anna?" asked Rebbeca. "Look at him. I mean *really* look. Not with your worldly eyes, but with eyes opened by the Spirit. I can see it in you, you know. You've changed since dinner the other night. I know you can do this."

"I.... I don't know," Anna answered hesitantly. "I see, well, I *feel*...darkness? Look at him, he's so perfect, and so beautiful. We read it just this last night, Jack! In Corinthians, I think. The Devil disguises himself as an angel of light. Look at that man, I mean, *really* look. And not with admiration and respect, but...but with eyes filled with the Spirit!"

"My goodness," Rebecca smiled, "You have grown in the last few days."

"Anna, you've really gone all in on this Bible stuff, haven't you?" Jack remarked.

"Jack?" Anna asked quietly, tears beginning to form in her eyes. "You have too, right? If...if not, then I've made a terrible mistake."

'Just tell her she's being silly,' a voice said suddenly in his head. *'Tell her she's a lawyer and needs to use her brain and think and don't let emotion drive her. That man is just a good politician, not some boogeyman predicted by sun stroked, desert prophets.* Immediately, Jack heard another voice in his head. *For our struggle is not against flesh and blood, but against the rulers, against the authorities, against the powers of this dark world and against the spiritual forces of evil in the heavenly realms.* And he thought silently, "Get behind me, Satan!"

"Jack?" Anna said, crying now, and he reached over and pulled her to him.

"Of course, I have, Anna," Jack assured her. "Of course, I have."

"Then look at him, Jack." Anna insisted, crying into his shoulder. "Look with Eyes of the Spirit."

"We've been studying prophecy for years, Jack," Dave informed him. "Watching for signs and examining world events. This man is *beloved* Jack. He's the Beatles and Obama of 2008, all rolled into one. If he only just *asked,* the countries of the West would appoint him Emperor tomorrow. Especially *now*, with alien, well, so-called alien visitors, giving him rides in spaceships. But we'll get back to that shortly. Especially if he could solve this current world crisis and bring an end to this Middle East war. I have a feeling he is about to do just that. Listen to Anna and really *look*."

Jack did as they insisted. The 50-inch-high-definition screen was filled with a screen shot of Cassini as he descended with the two tall aliens flanking him. He looked, and he prayed, *"Lord Jesus, let me see this man for what it really is. Forgive me my weakness. Let me see it with eyes filled with Your Spirit of Truth."* He was handsome; strong and confident.... his charisma was a wonder to behold. He suddenly knew with certainty Dave was right. If he but asked, the world would anoint him ruler. Jack just *"knew"* in his bones, after the last two days the people of this weary planet would fall prostrate without hesitation.

"God help us," he sighed, and held Anna tighter. "What about these aliens? How do they figure in?"

"There are no such thing as extra-terrestrial beings," Rebecca informed him. "Now, extra-dimensional, yes."

"Genesis 6?" Anna asked, sitting up and wiping her eyes.

"You are continuing to amaze me, child," Rebecca beamed proudly. Rebecca and David took turns, explaining to Jack how Genesis, and in greater detail how the books of Enoch, Jubilees and Jasher, recounted how a group of Angel class called "Watchers" fell from grace when they decided to leave their first estate and mate with human women before the flood. Through their forbidden union, a race of Nephilim was created. Giants. Men of renown. Heroes of old, Genesis called them. Their corruption spread throughout the entire earth and was the reason God destroyed the world with Noah's flood. Their DNA remained however, through the line of Ham and his wife. Their bloodline was also responsible for the Sons of Anak mentioned in Exodus. The only way that a reasonable person could reconcile *Yahweh* as a God of love yet would order Joshua and the Israelites to destroy all those tribes in the land of Canaan, down to their women and children, was He needed to wipe out the revived Nephilim bloodline, so it could not contaminate the line of the coming Messiah. Goliath and his brothers were perhaps the last recorded in the bible.

"There's a rumor in the group," Jack said thoughtfully, "a hush-upped mission, of an ODA team encountering a giant in Kandahar Province in '02."

"As it was in the days of Noah," David replied. "So, shall it be at the coming of the Son of Man. Many Christian theologians think it just means people of the earth will be living normal lives, eating, drinking, and marrying...when Jesus returns. But the single most identifying characteristic of the "Days of Noah" was Nephilim corruption of humanity. There's also a theory, with which I agree, that the original Nephilim, the first generation *"sons and daughters"* of the Watchers, were immortal. When they were killed bodily, their souls were left to wander the earth. It's where most *so-called* demon possessions originate; the disembodied spirits of the Nephilim seeking hosts to inhabit. They are also, the source of "alien" abductions and all the genetic experiments reported by abductees. The Nephilim are seeking to manufacture hybrid bodies to inhabit. Bodies without souls, so they can inhabit them more easily. I would say they have succeeded," David finished, pointing at the TV.

Jack and the group watched the television for several minutes in silence. Now that Jack's eyes were opened, he had no idea how anyone could look at Apollus Cassini and not see Darkness disguised as an angel of light. He couldn't look at the so-called "alien visitors", without seeing the evil of their Nephilim inhabited, hybrid host. Would he have been able to see the truth, if Anna and David hadn't begged he look with different eyes and he hadn't prayed for God to let him see in "Spirit and Truth?" Whatever Cassini's purpose was in Washington, whatever message, wise and full of hope his "visitor" benefactors might bring before the UN, he knew that in the end, it would bring only destruction. Of the body AND the soul of the unprepared.

"Anna," he said, taking her hand, "Would you like to go for a ride?"

"A ride?" Her beautiful emerald eyes were still red from crying. "With this going on?" she asked, inclining with her head toward the TV. "What could be more important than..."

"I thought maybe with this Beast revealed and his "*alien*" back up coming to earth," Jack said, taking the remote and shutting off the TV, "now might be a good time to see if we can find the sanctuary that Big Jim's key opens. And I think...I may know where to look. When was the last time you were on a four-wheeler?"

"You know about the Sanctuary?" Dave and Rebecca asked, almost as one.

Chapter Eight

The Sanctuary

"Go into caves in the rocks and holes in the dust before the terror of the Lord and the splendor of God's majesty, when he arises to terrify the earth."

Isaiah 2:19

Jack told them quickly of Big Jim's letter and the key card. Although the pair knew about the sanctuary he spoke, they didn't know its location. When they all agreed now was a good a time as any to go looking for it, he explained to them Event Rule #2. No one goes anywhere unarmed. He led the group to the upstairs "bonus" room. The defacto Braedan armory.

"I think I sold several of these weapons," Dave remarked, lifting a Ruger Mini-30 with collapsible stock off the wall and clearing it.

"I'll take this Galil," Rebecca smiled, doing the same.

"Plenty of ammo for everyone in the closet," Jack smiled.

Jack grabbed a box of 100 5.56mm rounds for his H&K carbine and for Anna's AR-15. A short detour to the kitchen for a few bottles of water and they were off to Big Jim's post steel "shed" out back.

Anna smiled with delight when Jack turned on the overhead lights and revealed a pair of 2015 Honda King Quad 400ASi, painted in Real Tree Camo pattern. Big Jim didn't believe in skimping. The two Honda's were top of the line; powered by fuel-injected 376cc four-stroke, four-valve engines, with heavy-duty front and rear carrying racks, LCD digital instrumentation, and a large 4.2-gallon fuel tank. The beasties topped out at about 60 mph in open terrain and had a range of close to 150 miles on a tank of gas. What more could a former couple of Special Forces operator and their partners ask for, when searching for a hidden sanctuary to shelter them from the end of the world?

Jack was just about to offer to show Anna how to start the four-wheeler, when she slung her rifle across her back, straddled the padded seat, and hit the electronic ignition. The Honda purred to life, and she looked at him over her shoulder. "Well? Are we going or not?"

"I've changed my mind," Dave grinned, patting him on the shoulder. "This one is definitely a keeper."

Jack shook his head and sighed, wondering once again what he'd gotten himself into with this woman.

Jack helped Anna back out of the shed, while Rebecca fired up the other ATV and Dave acted as her ground guide. Apparently, it was the ladies day to drive. After closing the door, he climbed on behind her, and repositioned her AR so it wouldn't dig into his chest.

"Circle around the barn and head through the field in the back," he said into her ear. "There's a trail that enters the woods to the south."

The Braedan family property covered just less than 300 acres in Williamson County, 298 acres to be exact. Of those 298 acres, all but the twenty, encompassing the house, the front yard and the small field surrounding the barn were heavily wooded with oak, cedar, sycamore, and juniper trees. Bynum Creek, even in the driest of seasons, flowed year-round as it meandered through the property from east to west. There were basically just two decent fording spots on the creek that wouldn't force you to ride around soaked to the waist. Jack directed Anna to head to the nearest, only 50 yards south of the barn.

The trail wasn't well maintained, and knee-high fescue rose to slap against the front of the ATV, as Anna drove into the woods. At the fording point, Jack had her slow to almost a crawl through the foot deep, slow-moving creek, then accelerate again once they reached the far bank. It had been many years since he'd been on backwoods of the Braedan's farm, but memories flooded back to him once under the cover of the trees.

While growing up, this land had been Jack's "Hundred Acre Woods," except it wasn't inhabited by Pooh and Piglet and all the gang created in the mind of A.A. Milne, but with Orcs and Dragons and dark, evil things, better imagined by Tolkien, Burroughs, or Robert E. Howard. As a young boy he'd fought countless battles using hand-carved wooden swords against imaginary foes in his very own "Mirkwood" or wilds of "Barsoom." When Big Jim decided it was time for him to "grow up," at age twelve, he bought Jack a .22 Marlin and taught him to hunt squirrel among the tranquility of these same trees. Jack had killed a plump, Eastern Grey, the first time he ever pulled the trigger and since that day, he'd forgotten all about the imaginary denizens of Middle Earth and fantasy, and dedicated himself to projectile weapons, shooting and hunting.

Jack had forgotten how much he loved this place.

Of course, it seemed so much smaller now. The ATVs had ridden for only a few minutes after crossing Bynum Creek, when Jack noticed a side trail heading west that he couldn't recall seeing before. Like the trail they were on now, it wasn't well maintained, but it was a trail he'd never traveled and.... well, it just felt right. After only a second's hesitation, Jack told Anna to head down the trail and the Hitchcock's followed.

After about a hundred yards or so, they came out of the trees and into a clearing; or what passed for a clearing on most of the Braedan property. The area was maybe five acres in size; perhaps two hundred thousand feet square. It had been cleared sometime in the last few years or so, but scattered saplings had grown back in some places, pine and maple and sycamore, some of which were ten feet tall or better. The rest of the clearing was covered in knee-high scrub and field grass. In the center of the clearing, at the end of the trail they were riding, was a dilapidated shed. Jack was immediately suspicious because ten years ago, no shed had been on this part of the property and its current state of disrepair would have taken decades of neglect to accomplish, not just a few years.

"I'm going to be very disappointed if this is Big Jim's sanctuary," Dave said, over the soft idling of the Hondas.

"I'm betting there is more to this place than meets the eye," Jack informed him. "What say we find out?"

They rode the last thirty or so yards and parked at the front of the old shed. Jack swung off the four-wheeler, slung his H & K, and did a slow circuit of the small building, purely out of habit, giving it a thorough inspection. Not finding any immediate signs of danger, he began a closer inspection of the exterior. It was about 20 x 20 feet and wasn't as old as it had appeared at first glance. The wooden planks of its exterior certainly looked forty or fifty years old and gave it the initial "feel" of just some old, abandoned shed, but here and there he could see what looked like much fresher cuts, and saw several places where the nails holding the shed together looked practically new. All these minor discrepancies would have probably been unnoticeable to a cursory glance and remained virtually impossible to spot unless you were *really* looking for something out of place.

There was no lock on the door to the shed, just a simple two by four resting in crudely fabricated brackets on each side. Jack lifted the piece of wood, set it aside and pulled the door open with a squeal of rusty hinges. Inside lay old, uselessly rusted farm tools; a couple of corn scoops, a hay fork with a broken handle, and an old, antique, wooden mule plow that probably had not broken ground since Eisenhower was president. Hanging on one wall was the complimentary mule harness and other sundry items you might have found useful once in the 1940s. There were two corn cribs in the shed, one on either side. The one on the right was filled with moldy hay and scattered mouse droppings. The one on the left was closed and secured with a brown, oxidized American Standard lock that you'd likely need a blow torch to open. That was it.

"What are you hiding in here, Dad?" Jack asked, looking up as if Big Jim might be hanging from the rafters with anticipation to see if his clever son could figure out the mystery.

"Are you *sure* this is where we're supposed to be looking?" Anna asked dubiously.

"This is the only place he could have been talking about," Jack replied, "unless he and Uncle Sean fabricated antique sheds all over these woods. We're missing something. I just haven't found it yet."

Jack gave the interior another detailed, closer inspection, and on his second search of the locked corn crib, noticed that door's left side facing appeared loose. With a little extra effort, the entire door of the crib began to swing upward on pneumatic struts, revealing a metal staircase leading down into the gloom.

"Who wants to go first?" he asked the group.

"It's your farm," Anna replied, eyeing the darkened stairwell skeptically. "Be my guest."

"You've got my back though, right?" Jack teased.

"An Israeli commando wouldn't be scared," Rebecca said casually.

"Who said I was scared?"

"Why are we still standing here?" Anna asked playfully.

Jack narrowed his eyes at her menacingly, but she simply inclined her head toward the dark opening and smiled, "Ladies first."

Jack knew there was likely nothing to be afraid of at the end of this staircase, other than perhaps an odd black widow spider. But years of entering the unknown, with death waiting just around the corner, was a difficult habit to shake off. Purely out of habit, he flipped the safety off the H & K and crept down into the gloom, barrel of the carbine at low ready, constantly scanning, finger outside the trigger well, but ready in an instant to eliminate any threat.

Two steps. Wait. Listen. Let his eyes adjust to the darkness. Two more steps. Wait. Listen.

It took Jack more than a minute to reach the bottom, but the amount of noise he made, wouldn't have aroused a hyper pit bull. It was dark at the bottom, but his sharp, searching eyes, conditioned by years of night missions and countless hours of training under cover of darkness, made out details in the blackness that many "normal" people would have never seen in the gloom. He could make out a door to his front with some sort of keypad lock, low ceiling, and a single breaker switch on the right side of the door. To the left of the door was another, unremarkable, small box that he couldn't quite make out in detail. Without hesitation, he lowered his weapon and reached up with his left hand, flipping the switch to the "On" position.

Overhead, a single bank of fluorescent lights flickered to life.

"All clear. Come on down," Jack called out.

As the rest of the group made their way down, Jack busied himself examining the keypad lock and door. The door itself looked like any standard, industrial type metal door. There was a pull handle, but no knob to turn or thumb release to press. Apparently, either the correct code was all that would open it, or it would require someone from the inside. The small box to the left now was obviously a speaker system. There were the typical slits to talk into and the typical small red button to "push to talk."

"That was absolutely.... creepy." Anna said, reaching the bottom of the staircase. "You didn't make a single noise until you flipped on that light switch. It was like someone just pressed the mute button on you."

"Jack?" He was still inspecting the keypad. *You will know the code*; his dad had written.

"Sorry," Jack said turning to Anna. "Creeping was exactly what I was going for."

"So, what do we have here?" she asked, refusing to take the bait.

"A door?" he shrugged.

"I can *see* it's a door, Jack," Anna muttered. "A door to what? Or where?"

"We're about ten feet underground," Dave announced as he joined them at the bottom of a hidden staircase. "We're standing in front of a securely locked...bunker?" he said. "Big Jim never brought me here, but I'm guessing this is his sanctuary."

"So, open it up," Anna suggested. "You brought the key card. He said you'd know the code."

"Yeaaaah, he did," Jack nodded, looking at the keypad suspiciously. "But I also have an idea how Big Jim thinks."

"Meaning?"

"Meaning," Jack said hesitantly, "if I don't get it right, there may be ummm...well consequences?"

"What sort of...consequences?" Dave asked.

"Good question," Jack replied curiously. "Dad spent a lot of effort to keep this place hidden. I'm betting it won't be a simple 'Wrong guess, try again' if you put the wrong code in this keypad. "

"So, do you want to think about it and come back later?" Anna asked. Apparently, her mind was conjuring up all sorts of ideas for the consequence of guessing wrong.

"No...No, I got this," Jack said, more confidently, reaching into his shirt pocket for the key card. It was a simple, plain white plastic card on the front. No pictures. No letters. Just white plastic. On the back was a standard, magnetic strip just like on any ordinary credit card or bank card. He hesitated for just a second, and then swiped it through the slot.

There was a two inch by three-inch screen above a standard 0-9-digit keypad with a # and * button as well. It came to life and glowed green for just a second then red letters proclaiming "ARMED" appeared and a voice announced ominously, "System Armed. "ARMED" became 60, then the beeping started, and numbers began counting down. 59. 58. 57.

"Do we need to run, 007?" Dave asked, "It'll take these magic legs a little longer to get up than down."

"Jack?" Anna said worriedly.

He thought for a second; then punched in his mom's birthday. 02-18-56. The beeping continued. 53. 52. 51. 50.

"Jack!"

"Hush a second," he insisted, looking at the keypad curiously as the beeping counted off the seconds. What would happened when they reached zero?

Only 30 seconds had passed since he swiped the key card, but it seemed the beeping had been going on for eternity. *"You will know the code."* Big Jim's letter had promised. What number would Jack think important enough for his dad to use as a code only he might guess, to disarm as system protecting a sanctuary built exclusively for him?

"JACK!" Anna said, fear in her voice now as the number on the panel reached 15. 14. 13.

"This or run," Jack said, and silently prayed *"Lord Jesus watch over us,"* then punched in 09112001. After another single "beep" the number "7" disappeared, the keypad announced, "System Disarmed," the screen went blank again, and the steel door popped open about an inch.

"Day that changed America, and my life," Jack said, turning to smile at Anna. "Piece of cake."

"What, what do you think would have happened if you'd have guessed wrong?" Anna asked.

"Who knows," Jack shrugged. "It might have been just a bluff." *'Me,'* he thought silently to himself, *'I'd have put explosives in the ceiling and collapsed the roof on whoever was showing up invited or maybe Chlorine Gas in hidden vents. Or...maybe both?*

"Probably explosives in the ceiling?" Rebecca speculated, looking up at the concrete. "Collapse the roof on uninvited guests?"

"Ministry of Agriculture, huh?" Jack grinned. "Boobie trap a lot of farms in Israel?"

"Yes, as a matter of fact," Rebecca smiled.

"Well, I've punched in the magic code and we're unkilt by Big Jim's security. Shall we continue?" he asked.

"In for a penny, in for a pound," Dave shrugged. "Go ahead, 007."

Jack opened the steel door to find a small room of about 10 feet square. On the left was a wooden four-foot-tall, boxed rack for.... maybe shoes? There were hooks above it. On the right was a gun cabinet, empty now but ready and waiting. At the far end was another door with another keypad locked door. No card swipe this time, just a numbered keypad.

"Jack, look," Anna said, pointing to the wooden rack on the left. On top was a handwritten note and a Honeywell Security System instruction book. The note was from Big Jim, of course and started with, *"Knew you'd guess it, Son."*

The first part of the note convinced Jack that anyone who guessed wrong would never have stepped on the other side of the door. The rest of the note appeared to be a diagram of what they would find on the other side of the next door; a fully stocked, underground living quarters for up to 8 people with enough supplies to survive for several months without restocking.

He handed the instruction book to Dave, while he studied the diagram.

"God bless you, Big Jim," Dave smiled, flipping through the pages of the instruction book.

"Amen," Jack grinned, confidently punching his code into the keypad.

"You'll probably want to change that second code," Dave suggested. "No use making it too easy if you make it past the first door."

"I have another date in mind already," Jack said, then stepped through the door.

Fluorescent lights flickered on by themselves as Jack entered, cued by motion sensors he spotted in the ceiling. What they found was a "cross" shaped common area, with each section of the "cross" perhaps 45 feet long by 10 feet wide. It was finished out just like any home you'd find above ground, but by the dimensions Jack surmised this "sanctuary" was likely built inside standard "SEALAND" shipping containers that every soldier, sailor, and marine would recognize from all those mock "villages" which dotted just about every US installation. They were favorite containers on every coalition FOB and forward base in the Middle East since the War on Terror began and had over the course of years become the favorite of serious preppers, as well.

The floor was covered in a thick, neutral colored, plush carpet. Jack immediately understood the wooden shoe rack in the foyer. That, and the functional but expensive carpet, had Maryellen Braedan's fingerprints all over them. There were a couple of comfortable recliners nearby, so he sat down and removed his boots. Anna did the same with the ghost of a smile; apparently recognizing a woman's touch to this underground bunker as well. In the center of the "cross" was a long, cherry wood conference table with padded swivel chairs.

On the left section of the common area, there was a pair of long, leather couches facing an entertainment center with a 50" flat screen and a desk top computer. Hundreds of Blue Ray disks lined the shelves of the entertainment center. A quick glance revealed classics like "Ben Hur" and "Gone with the Wind," but included recent classics like Lord of the Rings and season series of popular TV shows, DIY videos, plus lots of religious documentaries. Apparently, even in the Apocalypse (or likely *especially* in the Apocalypse) Big Jim realized there would be a need for diversion. The left side ended in another door. This one however, had a standard doorknob.

"We exploring as a group or separately?" asked Jack.

"Group," Rebecca suggested. "Just in case Big Jim has more surprises only you will comprehend."

"Okay group, we're walking...we're walking... And on the left you will find..."

Beyond the door was a living space, not opulent but comfortable, with double beds on either side, a couple of comfortable chairs, clothes lockers, and a reading desk with another desktop computer. The beds had sheets, blankets, and pillows sealed in plastic wrap. How long they'd been waiting was anyone's guess, but when Anna ripped open the seal of the sheets a faint smell of maybe...*Downy Fresh Springtime*...filled the cubical. She looked at Jack and smiled. "I love your mother," she said.

At the end of the living quarters was another door. It opened into a small, but functional lavatory. Jack turned on the water in the sink. It sputtered for a second, then came out in a steady stream. He let it run for a minute then put his hand under the faucet and cupped a small amount, tasting it. Sweet, crisp, and clean. Spring or well water. Not a hint of chlorine, fluoride or any other of the regular government mandated "additives." Above the sink was a fully stocked bathroom medicine cabinet with the normal accompanying items: toothpaste, toothbrushes, deodorant for both male and female, mouthwash, dental floss, and everything you might need for proper hygiene in the "End Times." He turned the water off, and out of curiosity flushed the toilet. Normal. Jack didn't know much about plumbing and water flow, but he did know about gravity. It must have cost his father a small fortune for this set up.

Jack suddenly thought of the TV show *"Preppers"* that had become popular a few years ago. His dad would have flat out ROCKED their prep scale so far. That thought made him shift gears, "Let's go see if we can find a kitchen."

It was outside and to the left of the common area tiled floor; (obviously his mom's touch once again) a huge, functional, stainless-steel sink, and sitting beside it was a four-burner gas oven and stove. Beyond the stove was a refrigerator, empty and warm when opened. But he could hear the motor running and could feel cool air flowing as it began to function normally now that he'd activated the power. On the opposite side of the kitchen were cabinets along the entire wall, stocked with assorted canned and dry goods. Enough food for months, at least!

Just past the kitchen was the dining room. It was simple, but functional and decorated perhaps with an outdoor *Bistro* in mind. Beyond the dining area was another pantry with shelves on both sides. This pantry was full of dry and canned goods, powdered milk, powdered eggs, bags of flour, salt, sugar and other staples, all arranged by category, type, and purchase date. At the end of the pantry section were three doors. One to the left, another to the right, and one in the center marked with a standard "Exit" with emergency lighting.

Opening the left-hand door, Jack whistled in amazement at the shelves of 2.5-gallon water containers on the left, and even more canned and dry goods on the right. With a forty-foot-long container, his rough calculation came to at least 7,800 gallons of water. Yeah, Big Jim would have won *Prepper* of the Year.

Exiting the storeroom and entering the right-hand door, Jack changed his mind. *Prepper* of the Decade, at least! This section had shelves stocked floor to ceiling with 30-pound, horizontal propane tanks. Jack had no idea how long a single tank would last running the gas stove, but if he remembered correctly, one tank usually made it through an entire season of barbequing when he was young. And Big Jim loved to grill out in the summer. At the end of the tanks was a 50-gallon gas water heater, with one of the propane tanks already attached. There would be hot showers during the apocalypse, at least until the propane ran out.

There were several rooms left to explore: back out through the kitchen and on the right side of the front common area. Jack suspected it was another living area and he was correct, but this quarter was meant for a single occupant or perhaps.... two at the most? Unlike the simple lockers and beds, this room looked like any standard master bedroom. Except for the lack of windows, and the narrowness of its width, you'd have never suspected it was ten feet under-ground. It was comfortably furnished and more than just "functional," with a real chest of drawers instead of wall lockers, an oak work desk, and a couple of leather recliners. Because of the narrowness of the room, there was no fixed bed, but a correct "guess" about the cheery finished "box" along right side of the room revealed a queen sized that pulled down from the wall and almost touched the opposite wall when fully extended. Jack tried it out. When deployed, it blocked off access to the door at the end, which most likely opened into the master bath of these quarters.

"I'd say dibs, but Big Jim made this sanctuary for the Braedans," Dave grinned.

Jack stood back in awe at the thought process of his parents, wondering what vision of the future they had glimpsed that prompted Big Jim and Maryellen to prepare such a place. As he stood there, Anna stepped beside him and grasped his hand.

"I must be the luckiest woman on earth." Anna said, her eyes brimming with tears.

"Anna? What's wrong?" Jack tossed his H & K onto the bed and pulled her to him.

"Nothing," Suddenly she was crying into his shoulder. "I...I...wu...was just thu... thinking how blessed I am."

"Hey Becca, let's go see what else we can find," Dave suggested, taking his wife by the hand, and leading her out.

He held her, smoothing her hair, and whispering soothing words until the spell passed. "What brought that on?" He asked, taking her face in his hands, and wiping away her tears. She hadn't cried as far as he could remember since the morning of the Event.

"Jack," Anna breathed deeply. "If I hadn't been assigned that zoning case by my firm, I'd never have faced your uncle in court. Had I not stood up to Sean Braedan because his smug confidence ticked me off, I'd never have met your Aunt Kate. If I had not given her that advice on how to get around the day care zoning, she probably does not invite me to come to your parent's memorial dinner, and...and I'd be dead." The tears started again. "I'd be raped and dead! Or worse!" She started crying again and he pulled her close once more.

"But you're not," he assured her.

"No, no I'm not," Anna admitted, taking a deep breath, and just as quickly as it started, her episode seemed to be back under control. "Instead, while the rest of the world is spiraling into chaos, I've been *rescued* by the bravest, sweetest, man left on the planet. I've been *saved* spiritually, because he had enough honor and self-control not to take advantage of me when I was at my weakest. AND my man has turned out to have parents who built him his own under-ground hide away for when the Devil takes over the world."

"What about the asking you to marry me part?" Jack grinned. "Don't forget about that."

"I haven't forgotten," Anna smiled. "And if you are serious..."

"Of course, I'm serious," Jack assured her, kissing her forehead.

"Then, I have an idea," Anna replied. "If the Hitchcocks will agree."

"You kids okay?" Dave asked, as Jack and Anna rejoined them in the common area. He and Rebecca were seated on the couch, thumbing through books they'd selected off the shelf.

"It was just a little stress relief," Anna said, squeezing Jacks arm. "The last few days finally caught up with me is all. Ummm, David, Rebecca, would you mind doing me a favor?

"Anything you need," Rebecca replied for them both.

"How would you feel about performing a wedding?" Anna asked hesitantly.

"Performing a wedding?" Dave asked, confused. Then it finally hit him. "Wait...you two? You can't be serious. Are you? You practically just met."

"We've lived a lifetime in the last two days," Jack replied. "Look, I know how this sounds but..."

"It sounds crazy is how it sounds," Dave said, shaking his head. "I'm not a minister. There's no marriage certificate. There's...there's..."

"I think it sounds wonderful," Rebecca beamed with delight.

"The question remains," Anna said, laying her head on Jack's shoulder. "Will you do this for us?"

"Adam and Eve didn't have a minister. Or a marriage certificate." Rebecca replied.

"This isn't Genesis," David countered.

"No, it's Revelations," Jack replied. "Apparently."

"All we need are witnesses," Anna said. "Someone to certify our covenant before God. Either you agree or I get Jack to take me back to town and we have Jeremiah Graham do it. But we're doing this today, one way or another."

"Of course, we'll be your witnesses," Rebecca said, moving over to hug them both. "Stand up, David Hitchcock," she said, turning back to her husband. "And tuck in your shirt. You're going to perform a wedding."

It was a mix of traditional and improvisation. Rebecca Hitchcock was the maid of honor and witness. David Hitchcock, Sergeant First Class Retired, gave away the bride and acted as the lay minister. He fumbled through the traditional "we are gathered here today" part, then asked if the pair had anything to say.

"Anna," Jack said, taking both her hands. He hadn't thought about any words to say, he just spoke from his heart. "I have no idea what being a husband is, but if it means I will love you and only you, support you and protect you, give my life for you if I must, and be your shield and your strength, from this day until the last day that I draw breath, I will be your husband. If you will have me."

"Jack," Anna replied, her emerald eyes brimming with tears, "I have no idea what being a wife and helpmate is in this insane world, but if it means I am willing to forsake all others, to love you and only you, to be your light in the darkness, your comfort when all seems lost, and to give my life for you if I must, until time itself is no more, I will be your wife. If you will have me."

"Well, do you?" David asked.

"I do," Jack nodded.

"I do," Anna smiled.

"Good enough for me," David replied. "Now kiss her, before my wife starts blubbering."

They kissed.

"Now, you two want to go consummate your union, or do you want to see what else Rebecca and I have found?" Dave smiled. "I have to say, it's pretty cool."

"I will *not* consummate my wedding with you ten feet away reading, David Hitchcock," Anna said, snatching the book from his hand. *Canning Jams and Jellies*. "Actually, that will come in pretty handy," she said, tossing it back to him.

"Tempting," Jack smiled, "But show us what you've found. We can take care of the details after," he said, kissing his new wife on her cheek.

What David had found was at the far end of the water room; another door leading into another shipping container. Inside there were pipes and 100-gallon metal tanks, along with a big generator at the back, with an array of with switches and controls.

"Best I can tell, this is some sort of solar-hydrogen power system," Dave surmised. "I have no earthly idea where the solar panels might be. I know there are some about four miles from here at the small generating station the greenies talked the city into building back in 2015. But if I remember right all that solar juice is sucked up by Williamson County Power and Electric. Wouldn't surprise me one bit though, if Big Jim somehow had some of it routed to this place. He was on the board of directors at WilCo, after all."

"So basically, this underground bunker of yours has limitless power until the sun quits shining." He finished with a grin. "There's an exit back here too. Later, we'll see where it goes."

"I guess this explains where my college fund went after I dropped out of Vandy," Jack replied.

"If Big Jim were here right now, I'd kiss him square on the mouth," Dave said with admiration. "Sorry, Son." He finished, seeing the pain flash across Jack's face at the mention of his dad.

"It's okay, Dave," Jack said, laying a friendly hand on his shoulder.

"I see Maryellen's touch all over this place, as well," Rebecca said, coming up to give him a compassionate hug. "No use avoiding it. Everything in this sanctuary will remind us of them."

Jack hugged her back, thinking to himself how amazing life was. In barely seventy-two hours he'd buried his parents, found a wife, and became friends with probably the two most capable people outside his team to face this nightmare with him.

"Find anything else?" he asked, giving Rebecca a final squeeze.

"Thought you'd never ask," Dave grinned. "Other than the exits and a couple more bed-room containers, we found a security system."

One of the computers in the common room was on and running. Rebecca had tried it just to see if it was password protected. On the dual monitors were four different sections with pictures on each screen. Looking close, Jack recognized the shack above their heads, the main house, two that had to be different parts of the trail they rode in on, and a couple of other video feeds of the woods.

"Must be security cameras all over this property," Rebecca said. "I've counted thirty-two different feeds so far."

"There won't be anyone sneaking up on this place," Dave remarked. "Looks to me like they activated and started recording as soon as you turned the power on. Which brings to me another point, Jack. The National Guard will figure out pretty quickly who sprang us from that camp, if they don't know already."

"I know," Jack sighed. "I didn't exactly try to hide who I was."

"We probably need to think about moving here soon," Dave suggested. "This place has everything a Tribulation Saint needs, except weapons and clothes. Those you have at the big house. Tomorrow night, Becca and I will slip back into town and grab some of our own stuff. That is, if we're invited, of course?"

"Of course, you are staying here!" Anna exclaimed.

"Of course," Jack agreed.

"Are you sure you want a legless vet and a washed-up Mossad agent hanging around?" Dave asked. "I'm not as young as I used to be."

"Dave, I blew any chance I had of laying low in this town by springing you guys. I'm going to need all the help I can get surviving this thing," Jack said, offering him his hand to seal their friendship.

"Thanks, brother," Dave said, his voice thick with emotion. "You know...you likely saved our lives today? I can't ever repay you for that, but Rebecca and I will certainly try."

"We certainly will," his wife agreed. "Even a *washed-up* Mossad agent can still be useful." The "washed up" part did not escape Dave. He knew he'd pay for that remark later.

"It's settled then," Anna announced. "Tomorrow, I suggest we begin moving into the Sanctuary."

And with that, Big Jim's bunker was officially christened.

"But today is "*My*" wedding day," she finished. "What do you say we close up shop, head back to the house, and celebrate?"

"Celebrate?" David grinned.

"Don't push your luck, Hitchcock," Anna laughed.

Chapter Nine

Your sins are forgiven

"If this group-living thing is going to work, I'm going to have to find a room in the Sanctuary as far away from you two as possible," David remarked casually, as Jack and Anna entered the kitchen together the next morning. "Or get some ear plugs."

Rebecca slapped him hard on the arm almost making him spill his coffee and gave him a disapproving glare.

"What? I'm just saying," he said with a wounded grin.

Anna blushed crimson as she sat down at the table. Jack ignored the bait, pouring himself and his new wife a cup of coffee before taking a seat beside her.

"I'm afraid there is only toast with butter and jam, and coffee for breakfast," Rebecca informed the newlyweds. "That's the last of the food except for canned stuff in the cabinets. We either bring back some supplies from the Sanctuary or begin taking all our meals there."

"Then we'll begin shifting our base of operations right after breakfast." Jack nodded, taking his wife's hand. "Have you already said the blessing?"

"Waiting on the man of the house," Dave replied, taking Rebecca's hand.

Jack bowed his head. The words came easily. He had so much to be thankful for.

It took the better part of the day to ferry all the weapons from the bonus room and everything else they considered valuable in Big Jim and Maryellen's home to the Sanctuary. It was dark by the time they were finished unloading and storing the last load of miscellaneous items: some books, the last few bottles of Jim Beam, and a few other odds and ends from Big Jim's study. Jack joined the group in the common area table and passed out bottles of water.

"Well, I guess that's everything," Jack said, "What do we do now?"

"I've actually been giving this some thought," Dave said, after downing half his bottle. "After we find a place to hide the Escalade and Anna's Z, we... ummm, we burn the house."

"What?" Jack exclaimed, choking on his water. "Burn the house?"

"We've already agreed the National Guard will figure out soon enough it was Jack Braedan of 111 Lighthouse Road who sprang two Jesus Lovers out of the detainee camp. One day they will eventually come looking...sooner rather than later, I'd wager. The best way to convince them we've moved on to a safer location is if they find a smoldering ruin when they come here."

His drastic solution stunned Jack and forced a contemplative silence on the group.

"He's right, Jack," Anna finally agreed, breaking the silence. "Franklin isn't really that big of a city. They'll come to the house soon. Actually, I wish Big Jim had built his sanctuary somewhere other than your family's land."

"They'll come looking," David nodded. "If they find a burned house, they'll poke around a little and look for clues to where we've gone. Once they find a few well-placed, miraculously survived items that suggest we've gone to...I don't know, Canada, they will look for anything they can salvage in the ruins then move on."

"I don't know," Jack countered. "This Sanctuary is great and all, but burn the house? Won't it serve the same purpose if we make it look...abandoned? Like we pulled up stakes in a hurry to search for safer shores?"

"Let me sleep on it," he sighed. "Lighting it up tonight would be seen all the way to Franklin anyway. It might draw them sooner. Not that the smoke won't be seen if we strike a match to it. At the very least, let's make sure we have *everything* we need out of the house. Going all pyro...it's so final."

"We'll decide tomorrow then," Dave nodded. "Look, I know it's a hard thing, but I think it's necessary. Unless we really are bugging out to Canada, I think it's the next best thing."

"I need a drink," Jack sighed.

"Let's turn on the TV and catch up," Anna suggested. "We've not seen an update since yesterday. I am curious to know what Cassini and his pet Nephilim are doing at the UN."

"And what's happening in Israel," Rebecca added.

The four shifted from the common area table to the pair of couches nearby. Jack, as the host and last Braedan, poured them each a tumbler from one of the bottles of bourbon. Spirits were going to be rationed after tonight. As well stocked as Big Jim's study had been, it wouldn't last long. That was one thing the Sanctuary had lacked. Jack supposed that in the tribulation, Big Jim figured booze was one thing that wouldn't be considered a necessity. After passing out their drinks, Jack took a seat next to Anna and turned on the television. The war in the Middle East was the leading story.

A Fox News anchor was currently interviewing a retired US Army Four-Star general. Jack recognized him instantly. At various stages of his career, he'd been CENTCOM commander, the head of NATO, and Chairman of the Joint Chiefs as well. If anyone could be considered an expert in the field of war, it was General Maxwell "Mad Max" Warren. Behind General Warren and the Fox anchor was a map of the battle lines, as they currently stood.

Jack was stunned. Twenty-four hours ago when the group had last checked on the war, Israeli forces had been advancing in three directions and had only pushed maybe fifty miles in some places beyond their borders. If the map behind them was correct, the IDF was in the process of annihilating their Arab foes. Lebanon had fallen. In Syria, the IDF now controlled almost one third of the country, having pushed north beyond Damascus and Hims, as well as to the east to the Iraqi border. Their armored columns had rolled unopposed through Jordan and were a hundred miles into Saudi Arabia. To the south, forces were within sight of the Nile River and within artillery range of Cairo, Egypt and had driven as far as Asyut. In Gaza, they had pushed the Palestinians all the way to the Mediterranean and pounded them until they surrendered unconditionally. There was one tiny pocket of resistance remaining in the West Bank. But that small, battered group was in the process of surrendering to a Jordanian Armored Brigade. King Abdullah was being hailed as a hero by the people of Jordan. Although he was also reviled as a traitor and apostate by the remainder of the Arab world, his secret treaty with Israel had saved his country from destruction. Their rapid advance was being touted as even more successful than the German Wehrmacht's Blitzkrieg of World War II.

In less than 48 hours Israel had almost quadrupled the size of their borders. And their campaign presently showed no signs of slowing.

"Not quite the Covenant Borders yet," Rebecca remarked with wonder, "but astounding, nonetheless."

"Covenant Borders?" Anna asked.

"In the Old Testament," David explained. "God promised Abraham and his descendants a *lot* more land than the UN gave Israel in 1948. Looks like the IDF is trying to claim that promise. It's futile of course, but you can't fault them for trying."

"Your...disagreement with Becca?" asked Jack.

"She thinks her homeland is the Israel of the Bible," David said hesitantly. "I am of the opinion that it's a clever counterfeit. Fabricated by the Illuminati and the Rothchild's simply for the purpose of having a Jewish state to rebuild a temple in. The anti-Christ needs it to proclaim himself to be the Messiah."

"David thinks Israel will not be the *true* Israel," Rebecca remarked confidently. "Until the Messiah returns and grants the land back during His millennial reign. Do you think we'll see it soon, David?"

"Is it Israel, or isn't it?" Anna asked.

"Doesn't really matter in the long run, I suppose," David shrugged, "Cassini will most likely announce very soon a peace treaty between *this* Israel and the Arab world. It will promise Becca's people safety and security, while allowing them to rebuild the Temple in Jerusalem so they can re-establish the daily sacrifice. If it's a seven-year treaty, we'll have our proof that he's one of the Beasts."

"Bibi Netanyahu would take that deal in a second," Jack nodded.

"But what will the Arabs get?" Anna asked.

"Assurance they won't get wiped off the face of the earth?" Rebecca surmised. "And they will get to regroup and prepare for the Gog – Magog invasion."

"If Cassini can stop the Israeli advance," Jack interjected.

"Want to place a bet, Coastie?" David grinned.

"I think I'll hold on to my money, Dave," Jack replied. Dave knew *way* more than he did about what the future held.

"Ah, that paper will be worthless pretty soon anyway," Dave shrugged. "Cassini will be pushing for chips before long. Mark of the Beast."

"Looks like we have a subject for tonight's Bible study," Jack announced.

They sat watching the news for another hour. Mostly battle images of burning Arab tanks, dead infantry, and victorious IDF columns riding through city after city. They updated the Middle East map again and Israel had once again gained ground in all directions. Given a few more days, they would control all land from the Mediterranean and Nile in the east, to the Tigris in the west, the entire Arabian Peninsula to the Arabian Sea, and north to the Turkish border. Jack was just about to suggest they turn off the news and start their study when the Fox news anchor placed a hand to his ear (*the universal studio sign that a producer was talking to him*) and their wait ended.

"General Warren, ladies and gentlemen," he announced, "We are going now to our correspondent in Washington where we've received word the UN Security Council has just concluded a meeting with EU President Cassini and Prince Azalil of the Anunnaki..."

"Prince who of what?" asked Jack.

"Hush, Jack," Anna instructed.

"...the Israeli Ambassador to the UN, Jacob Ehud, and the Ambassadors from Saudi Arabia, Egypt, Turkey and Jordan. Stewart, can you hear me?"

The scene switched to Washington DC outside the United States Capitol building, where the emergency session was being held until New York City could get its power back on. "I hear you, Bob," the correspondent replied. "Bob, there's been nothing officially announced yet, but the emergency session of the Security Council has indeed concluded. Sources say the members were upbeat and relieved, so it appears some sort of cease fire at the very least has been reached. Details are sketchy at the moment, but my sources inform me a deal of historic magnitude was hammered out in a remarkably short time. One can only assume it was Apollus Cassini and Prince Azalil who made the difference. Cassini is a godsend to the world of international politics that's for sure, and our new friends, the Anunnaki. Well, only days ago scientist and dreamers could only speculate that we were not alone in the universe. To have such beings of grace and wisdom come to the world at the hour of our greatest need, we have been truly blessed."

"We have indeed." Bob agreed enthusiastically. "Stewart, did your sources give you any details?"

"Not many Bob," the correspondent replied. "I hate to speculate, but...."

"But you will anyway," Jack muttered.

"Jack...." Anna scolded.

"Sorry," he sighed, kissing her cheek.

"I hate to speculate," the correspondent continued, "but all signs are pointing right now to a cease fire beginning at midnight Eastern Time which would be...oh..."

"0800 hours in Jerusalem," Jack muttered. "Sorry." Another kiss on the cheek.

"About 8AM in the Middle East," Stewart the correspondent replied.

Jack grinned. He was rewarded by an emerald eyed glare.

"One can only assume Bob," the correspondent continued, "but I wouldn't be surprised if the IDF, the Israeli Defense Forces, will be ordered to return to their own borders and Israel will be required to release all prisoners and likely pay some sort of reparations. I can also foresee a War Crimes hearing in the not-too-distant future for this unprovoked attack."

"I'll say it for you, Jack," David volunteered, "One can only assume this brain-dead weasel will be unemployed by this time tomorrow."

Jack grinned and gave Dave a "thumbs up." He still received a disapproving look from his wife.

"Stewart, I hate to interrupt but I'm getting word the President is about to hold a press conference on the steps of the Capitol building." The news anchor informed his audience.

"Right you are, Bob. There has been a flurry of activity visible at the Capitol Building in the last few moments. I would assume...."

"Hate to cut you off Stewart, we're going live now to the steps of the Capitol," the anchor announced.

The scene switched immediately to the Capitol steps. Lights had been erected and to everyone's surprise, the speaker's podium was draped with the UN flag instead of the Seal of the President. The President's Press Secretary stepped to the podium....

"I know! He hit on you. Give it a rest Jack," Anna pre-empted.

"He hit on you?" Dave asked, with a raised eyebrow.

"I'll fill you in later," Jack promised.

"Quiet you two," Rebecca snapped.

"Ladies and gentlemen of the press, the President of the United States of America," the self-important little weasel announced.

"Citizens of America and the world," she began, stepping to the podium. "This is truly an historic day. We have suffered catastrophe and loss, but out of this troubling time a ray of hope has emerged. At this time, I would like to present Prime Minister Apollus Cassini of Italy, President of the European Union. Mister President?" she stepped aside to make way for Cassini. The new

American President's voice could barely contain the disappointment she felt at not being able to make this announcement herself.

EU President stepped to the podium.

"Thank you, Madame President." Cassini nodded. "Thank you, Prince Azalil for allowing me the honor of speaking on behalf of our new friends, the Anunnaki. Thank you as well to the members of the UN Security Council and UN Secretary General for allowing me to be the one to announce this momentous agreement between the UN, the nation of Israel, and the world."

His English was flawless and without accent. It was reported by many that Cassini had an *otherworldly* gift for languages and could speak at least ten fluently. "As my esteemed peer has said, the world has suffered much in the last few days. We as humans are nothing if not resilient. Let me assure everyone listening tonight the governments of the world, with the gracious help of the Anunnaki and in conjunction with the UN, are working diligently with all available resources at our disposal to provide emergency services to the areas affected by the recent solar flares and are working around the clock to restore power and provide all people with the basic necessities needed to live a happy and healthy life."

"What brings us here tonight is the unfortunate conflict raging in the Middle East that was precipitated by the Event. On that issue I, in my own small way, and the other august leaders standing behind me, have worked tirelessly throughout the day. With the guidance and wisdom of Prince Azalil, we have come to a peaceful resolution to the bloodshed between descendants of Abraham. I myself, though I have never spoken of this, have the blood of the Jewish race in my veins. My mother was from the Tribe of Ephraim and the line of the legendary King David. With this knowledge, from my earliest days of public service I have worked diligently to resolve the conflict between warring sons of Abraham. I am humbled therefore, to announce to the world that on this night a historic treaty has been reached that will put an end to all bloodshed in this troubled region. Full details will be provided tomorrow morning after the formal signing of this treaty. I am humbled to tell you tonight that the initial treaty will last for seven years..."

"Behold the Prince," David whispered.

Cassini went on to announce that henceforth, Israel would be assured of its right to exist under the protection of the EU. Jerusalem would be its recognized capital and it had been granted assurances that it could build on the temple mount for the first time in two thousand years. Citizens of the former Palestinian territories who would renounce terrorism would be accepted as full citizens of Israel, with Gaza and the West Bank granted the status of fully participating provinces. What the Arabs were getting out of this deal he didn't reveal at this time, but that their capital cities would not be nuked into the Stone Age by Israel and overrun completely seemed to be their greatest concession.

"Hand me Big Jim's Bible, Anna," Jack said, turning off the television. "What should we expect next, Dave?"

"Let's start in Revelations, Chapter Six?" Rebecca suggested.

"The first seal has been opened," David nodded.

They studied late into the night.

***

Everything was almost ready. Jack and David had finished one final sweep of the house. Jack found two boxes of Cuban cigars that were somehow overlooked the day before. Other than that it had been swept clean and was ready to be sacrificed to the fire in the name of tactical deception. With keys in hand, they were preparing to move Big Jim's Escalade and Anna's Nissan to a place they'd selected just north of Bynum Creek and begin the bonfire, when a HUMVEE pulled up to the gate of the Braeden home.

"Does it look like trouble?" David asked, fingering the safety on his Mini-30 from safe to fire.

Jack reached into the Caddy and secured a pair of Tasco Zip focus 7 x 35 binoculars for a closer look. "Unless I'm mistaken, that's Sergeant Weaver on the .50 Cal."

"Might as well go say hi," David suggested. "If we ignore them or run, they'll just ram the gate."

"They could mow us down with that .50 before we made it ten feet, anyway," Jack agreed. "What the heck. Let's be neighborly."

By the time they reached the gate, Staff Sergeant Horn was standing outside the Humvee waiting for them.

"Guess you didn't get him to Campbell after all, huh?" Alan Horn smiled.

"Engine trouble," Jack shrugged. "We're working on it."

"Well, you better work fast Master Sergeant," Sergeant Horn suggested. "You were on the top of the list at the briefing this morning. A patrol will be coming by no later than 1400. They are bringing all of 2nd platoon. Final prep will begin in less than an hour. If two of the Bradley's hadn't developed ummmm.... engine trouble, they'd be moving already."

"I'm pretty sure we'll be on the road long before then," Jack replied.

"If... I was going to Campbell. I'd take back roads to Dickson instead of 840 and come in from the West. Lots of roadblocks on 65 north." Horn advised him. "But you're not headed to Campbell," he said, looking at the Ruger Mini-30 Jack's *prisoner* from two days ago currently held in his hands. "Don't suppose there's someplace I could, uh, speculate you were heading instead? If I was asked, I mean?"

"Anna's dad is in Utah," Jack shrugged. "Long drive but she really misses him. I hear Vancouver is nice this time of year."

"I think I heard him swearing in Spanish," Sergeant Weaver grinned from the turret of the Hummer, "I bet he's headed to one of those white beaches down in Mexico with those umbrella drinks and pretty Seen-your-Etahs with smoky eyes, loose morals, and hot tempers."

"Care to join us, Sergeant Weaver?" Jack grinned.

"Hot damn, you bet!" Weaver laughed.

"Store that noise Weaver," Sergeant Horn muttered. "I'm not letting you anywhere near Tequila."

"Another time Master Sergeant," Weaver sighed. "Hey, you wouldn't have any smokes would you? Or some Gatorade? Not that lemon lime crap, but the good stuff?"

"Sorry Weaver," Jack replied sadly, "but...if it's okay with Sergeant Horn, and you can wait a couple of minutes, would you settle for some cigars? They're Cuban?"

"Cubans!" Weaver whooped. "You bet. I mean, can we, Sarge?"

"Only if Jack can make it quick," Horn replied. "We're supposed to be out here doing a quick Recon of the place. Should have reported in five minutes ago."

"Two minutes, Alan," Jack promised. "Tops."

"Hey Jack," Horn said as he turned to head back to the house. "This makes us square. You know that, right?"

Jack stepped forward and shook his hand through the gate. "You're a good man Alan. So, am I headed to Canada or Mexico?"

"Place looks deserted to me," Horn replied. "Hell, you could all be on an Anunnaki ship headed to Alpha Centaury as far as I could tell."

***

It was just past noon when Jack finally made his decision. "The house stays," he announced to the group as the stood in the back yard. Dave had a metal, two-gallon gas can in his hand all prepped and ready to go. Everything of practical value has been removed. "In five minutes, I can make it look like we left in a rush. Throw some clothes around. Open all the cabinets. They are basically empty already. Knock over a lamp. There's still stuff inside that a normal person would leave behind if they were in a hurry. Two big flat screens. Paintings. I think the guard will poke around a bit, maybe even check by a couple of times, but sooner or later they'll decide we aren't coming back. Even they won't be here forever. Franklin is small time in the big scheme of things. Sooner or later, we *might* have need of it and putting it to the torch is so final."

"And what about later?" Dave asked. "Big ol' house like this? What if squatters decide you aren't coming back and decide to stake a claim? Do you want someone living so close the Sanctuary? Snooping around in your woods? We can't stay underground forever."

"I'll tackle that problem when and if it happens," Jack announced. "The house stays... At least, for now."

"Your property, Coastie," Dave finally shrugged. "We're just guests. The house stays...for now."

"Thanks," Jack nodded.

"What was I going to do?" Dave smiled. "Bum rush you and toss this like Molotov? Eh, we need the gas, anyway."

"Then, let's get out of here before the Guard shows up. Lunch, anyone?" He asked the group. "I'm buying?"

"How about some freeze-dried Philly cheese steaks?" Anna suggested. She'd been doing an unofficial inventory of the food supplies most of the morning.

"Mmmm, mmm." Jack nodded, "sounds delish."

"Yeah, but you haven't had *my* freeze-dried Philly Cheese," she said, kissing his cheek and mounting the Honda.

"I love you, Anna Braeden," Jack whispered in her ear as he climbed on behind her and put it arms around her waist.

"You owe me one," she smiled, patting his leg.

"I love that I owe you one, as well," he replied.

"I love you too, Jack Braedan," she said, hitting the electronic ignition on the ATV. "We'll exchange payments when we get back to the Sanctuary.

***

"I've been thinking about your plan to go back to your house and collect some things," Jack said, wiping his mouth after finishing his last bite of Philly Cheese. He was sitting on the couch in the common area, watching the computer monitor as the Guard drove a Bradley Fighting Vehicle into his back yard. "I don't think you guys should go by yourself."

"Need to go tonight," David replied. This morning he'd borrowed a change of clothes from Jack, which fit well enough. But Anna and Rebecca, well, they just weren't of compatible size. In height nor proportion.

"What's your plan?" Rebecca asked. Dave's wife was getting a little irritated without a change of clothes for herself, and no one wanted to be around an irritated former Mossad agent longer than was necessary.

"Going to be a half moon tonight. Moon set is around 3AM," Jack replied. "We can tool up and take the ATVs through back woods almost all the way to town. We can ride the bank of Bynum Creek nearly six miles in relatively safety without any lights. Then we take the back streets for the rest of the way. If you know a suitable ORP...that's Objective Rally Point, sweetie," he explained before Anna could ask. He said it informatively, not condescendingly. Anna had a sharp mind. When she questioned him on his all too frequent use of military jargon, it was for a desire to *know* not because it made her feel somehow inferior. "It's a place where you stop short and make sure everything is ready to go before you move forward to your objective."

"Makes sense," she nodded.

"I know just the spot," Dave nodded. "And a pretty good spot for an OP..."

"Observation Post!" Anna smiled, "I know that one from *Lone Survivor!*"

"Met Marcus Luttrell once. Good kid," Dave nodded. "Anyway, the good OP spot where we can stake things out for a bit. Only about 100 yards from the house."

"We watch for a bit," Jack continued. "If it's all clear, then we sneak down quietly. You two break into your own house. Anna and I will be posted outside in over-watch. We should be back before sunrise."

"Wish we had the NVGs that are in my basement," David sighed. "We'll snatch them up and won't have this problem again. There are a couple of other goodies down there you'll appreciate. Having a Federal Firearms license has its advantages. Won't be able to get but a few items this trip, but if it goes off without a hitch we can always go back. Are there any maps in theis place or are we going to do this by memory?"

"I haven't found any yet," Rebecca replied. "But the internet is currently up, slow but up. We can Google Earth it."

"Speaking of technology," Jack said, turning away from the monitor as a fire team stacked up on his back door preparing to storm the house, "have you seen my phone, sweetie?" With the most important people he had left in the world within eyesight almost constantly and doubting that Sean and Kate would ever get a phone call (wherever they were), he hadn't carried it with him in two days. He knew Anna had been in contact with Jeremiah Graham getting updates, so he hadn't bothered.

"Bedroom nightstand," Anna said. "I'll get it, hon. You keep planning our little infiltration. That's the right word, isn't it?"

"We'll make an operator out of you yet, Sergeant Braedan," Jack winked.

"Fifteen voicemails," Anna said, returning quickly. "Mostly from 910 area code. A few from someone called Big A. Couple of texts as well. One from Julie. Who might she be?"

"*Julie* is Staff Sergeant Julian Hesterman. You are the only love of my life, counselor," Jack said, barely able to restrain himself from snatching the phone out of her hand. He deleted all the voicemails then punched up Julie's text. It was from yesterday at 1900. "Trouble outside Chattanooga, swinging south. In-route to Mac's hideaway in Sooner Land if the way is clear. Up for visitors maybe? Like to have you tag along." If they were South of Chattanooga they could be here soon. Jack thought quickly on how to let them know where he was without sending a message in the clear that Big Sister could intercept if she were really listening.

"NGs in the area. Not at T1. Go south till you get wet. 7.62 tracer burnout is decision point. Wait until acknowledged. Welcome to ride it out here. Room for a team."

He hit send hoping Hesterman could decipher the code.

"National Guard here. T1 is obviously the house. South until you get wet is Bynum creek," Anna said, looking over his should. "I'm assuming the tracer burnout thing means some sort of distance? The rest is easy. How big is a team?"

"About five more," Jack nodded. "Not bad Braedan. I just hope Julie is as smart as you."

"I just hope he is as well-mannered as you, if you are inviting him to stay," Anna replied, leaning over to kiss his cheek.

"Members of your team, Jack?" David asked.

"Two of the best," he nodded. "If we can convince them to stay, we might just survive this thing for a while."

"The way the Lord has been arranging things lately, I think we should prepare for our group to grow by a couple more," Rebecca smiled.

They spent the afternoon glued to the computer monitor, watching the National Guard snoop around his house and barn. They sent out a dismounted patrol that swept the woods all the way to Bynum creek. Luckily, they didn't find the fording site and didn't fancy getting wet. Nor did they find the two vehicles they'd hidden on the western edge of the property. Before they pulled out, Jack watched in wonder as Sergeant Weaver looked straight into one of the "hidden" cameras watching them. He smiled and lit up one of the Cuban cigars. Obviously, the cameras were not hidden as well as they could be.

"There's still some good people out there," Anna remarked, squeezing Jack's hand.

With the Guard gone, they spent the rest of the evening pouring over Google Earth and hammering out Jack's basic plan. Jack introduced Anna to TLPs (troop leading procedure) and the value of rehearsing an operation. He also introduced her to PCCs (pre combat checks) and brief backs. David fell right back into operator groove. Rebecca was IDF trained and was usually one step ahead of him. Anna was a fast learner. By the time they were ready to launch at 11PM, Jack was oh....85-90% sure they would pull this off with little difficulty.

Jack had everyone outfitted in OCP camouflage and tooled up by 2245 hours, then went through pre combat checks just as he had with his Delta team countless times before. Dave carried the Mini-30 with two spare magazines. Anna and Rebecca both had ARs. Jack was carrying a Springfield Armory M1A, semi-automatic .308 caliber, with a 10-round magazine and a 4-14 x 56mm Range finding scope. It was zeroed to 500 yards and wasn't a true "night" site, but it still had fairly good light gathering capability with is large objective lenses. There was a contraption on the end of the Springfield's barrel that Rebecca had put together in an hour from PVC pipe, some steel wool, and generous amounts of duct tape, then painted black. She assured him it would be a decent suppressor for two or three shots. When he gave her an incredulous look, she merely patted his cheek and said, "Trust me." All four had side arms, as well.

"I don't care how sneaky you *think* you can be, Anna," Jack found himself saying for perhaps the fiftieth time. "This stuff can't be mastered in a day. You know you don't have to go. We've all done this sort of thing before. We'll be fine."

"You aren't getting out of my sight, Jack Braedan," Anna informed him for perhaps the fiftieth time as well.

"Do it exactly like we practiced, then. Step with the balls of your feet, test each step. Sound travels farther at night. Take it slow and deliberate. Follow me, stop when I stop. Your eyes will adjust quickly. All you have to do is use the binos and be my spotter."

"I'll make you proud." She assured him.

"I know you will," he nodded, pulling her close for a kiss.

"You two aren't going to be doing this while we're on mission, are you?" Dave sighed.

"Okay, I guess we're as ready as we'll ever be if we're going tonight," Jack said, ignoring the remark. "I'll lead. No lights, nice and slow. David, you take over when we get to the city limits. Anyone need to pee? No? Okay, Regulators, let's ride."

The travel down the creek bank was slow and tedious, even with the good illumination they were getting. To Jack, the rumble of the Honda engines was deafening, but he was relatively sure the engine noise would be muffled by the high banks and the surrounding trees. Occasionally, the bank narrowed and they would have to back track a bit and leave the stream bed. Jack would guide them back in as soon as he was able. An hour after midnight, they found themselves at the city limits. David took over and soon they were forced to leave the stream bed for good.

They stuck to the shadow of the woods as much as possible, only occasionally having to detour around fences and into the open fields. Fortunately, the Hitchcock's lived in a sparsely populated area of town and when they were forced to travel the streets, they were all but deserted. One tense moment occurred when they spotted lights in the distance. They quickly pulled over to relative concealment offered by copse of trees, found the lowest area available, dismounted and laid low. A patrol of two M1151 armored Humvees passed by a few minutes later without stopping.

"Patrol," David whispered. "Things in town must be settling down if they are out in this neighborhood."

Jack didn't know if that was a good sign or bad.

They waited fifteen minutes to ensure the patrol wasn't doubling back, then resumed their journey. They reached his ORP site around 0130 in the morning. They shut down the Hondas, concealed them as best they could, and gathered for a quick check of their gear. "About one hundred yards due east, you'll come to the open field behind my house," David informed them quietly. "Closest neighbors are the Goodwins, about half a mile to the west. They were in Florida when the Event went down. We should be all alone out here."

"I'll take point," Jack said. "Just like we rehearsed. Anna behind me, then you, Dave, and Rebecca on our six. Slow and deliberate. We have plenty of time." The moon was just above the tree line. In a few minutes, the only illumination would be the stars and a lone streetlight about a quarter of a mile away on the corner of Elm and Grisham. "How you are holding up, Lieutenant Dan?"

In the dim light, Jack could see he was tired. They all were, save him. Dave and Rebecca had been out of the game a long time. "I'll manage," Dave grinned wearily.

"Okay. Keep it tight. Keep it quiet. Follow me," Jack whispered.

He moved off slowly, as noiseless as the shadows around him.

About ten yards from the edge of the tree line, Jack gave the group a raised closed fist, the signal to "halt," then open his hand palm down and lowered it to waist level. The three took a knee behind him so quietly he smiled. Jack slipped to the prone and slowly crawled to the edge of the woods. Flipping up the lens covers of his scope; he slowly began to scan the area. Ten minutes later, he rolled to his side and motioned them forward.

"All clear," Jack whispered when David crawled up beside him. "You good?"

"My VA dogs are a little tired," Dave shrugged. "Other than that? I'm good."

Jack checked his watch. 0230. Pretty much on schedule. "Whenever you and Becca are ready, move out."

Dave made two soft clicking sounds and Rebecca appeared beside him silently. She gave him a "thumbs up" and without a word, the pair rose quietly and began to make their way in a low crouch across the open field. Becca was in the lead with her AR sweeping right to left.

Anna crawled up beside Jack and immediately lifted the Tasco binoculars she was carrying to add a second pair of eyes just liked they'd rehearsed. After about thirty seconds, she lowered them again and wiped sweat from her eyes. "You good?" Jack whispered, not taking his eye off the scope. This was Anna's first time on an infiltration. The stress of sneaking about could be very taxing. The Hitchcock's were already at the back steps. Dave was laboring just a bit, but he was right on Rebecca's hip.

"You do stuff like this a lot?" Anna whispered, giving him a quick glance.

"Sometimes we chopper right up to the objective. Most days we walk the entire way," Jack replied, still scanning. He took a heartbeat to focus on Dave as he climbed the back steps. With a gloved hand, he punched out the lower pane of door glass. Anna's shocked intake of breath informed him she now believed him about sound traveling farther at night. Two seconds later, Dave and Rebecca were inside their house.

Jack watched the almost imperceptible red glow of their pen lights reflecting off the glass of the kitchen widows. They disappeared for a few seconds then Jack saw a glow in the upper floor window on the right side of the house. Rebecca was upstairs gathering clothes. Another glow in the small window at ground level informed him that David was in the basement collecting "goodies."

Jack checked his watch again. 0300. "Okay, they have ten more minutes then...ah crap!" he hissed, as headlights appeared, and a black Ford pickup pulled into their driveway. It drove all the way to the edge of the house and turned off its lights and engine.

"Jack?" Anna whispered, alarm in her voice.

"Maybe just a couple of kids out joy riding," he said hopefully.

"Two men," she said. "One smoking. He passed it to his buddy. Probably not a Marlboro."

Jack quickly adjusted his scope, and the pair sprang into focus. They weren't teenagers like he'd hoped. The driver was burly and bearded. The passenger only slightly smaller. Jack shifted his aim briefly to the second floor. Red glow still visible. Rebecca hadn't heard the truck pull up. Ground floor was dark. David had. Passenger guy flicked the joint out the window and the glow was clearly visible as it landed on the drive with a shower of sparks. Both doors opened simultaneously.

"The driver has a handgun," Anna hissed.

Jack swore softly and flipped off the safety on the Springfield. They weren't men anymore, just targets. Unlucky targets who had decided to check out the house of Dave from *Guns USA* on the wrong night. Jack put the cross hairs of the scope on Burly guy's head. The man hesitated for a second when he saw the back door open.

"Just turn around and leave," Jack whispered. "It's already been looted."

Burly Guy put both hands on his pistol in a shooter's grip and headed for the steps. Without conscious thought, Jack pulled the butt of the rifle tight into his shoulder and exhaled slowly. A muffled *crack* and the top of Burly Guy's head exploded, showering dark blood on the siding of the house. Anna gasped in shock beside him. Passenger Guy stopped in his tracks, uncomprehending, then slowly turned to face the woods. Jack could clearly see the look of horror on his face. "Sorry, man," Jack said softly and center the cross hairs on his heart. "Wrong place, wrong time."

Crack!

"I'm sorry you had to see that" Jack said softly, scanning the area for other signs of possible trouble.

Anna lay there in stunned silence beside him.

"Babe?" he said turning toward her. Jack knew she was grateful, extremely grateful, for what he'd done to save her from her would be attackers, but actually *seeing* him kill? He feared she now believed she'd married a monster. "Anna?"

Anna turned to look at him and he almost sighed with relief when he saw neither disgust nor horror in her eyes, only sorrow. "I'm okay Jack," she whispered. "It's just...I've never seen... I've never..." Tears welled up in her eyes.

Jack lay down the rifle and pulled her to him. "It's not easy for me, you know," he said. "It never is. But I always know if I don't pull the trigger, it could be me or *my* friends that don't make it home. I know that's not a reason some people would agree with, and I know I'm going to have to answer to God for every one of them someday. But until I do, you and my friends come first."

Anna hugged him tightly. After a moment she moved away, wiped the tears from her eyes, and picked up the binos. "Here they come," she said softly. Her inner strength continued to amaze him.

Rebecca and David exited the house, both with stuffed nylon bags on their backs and weapons raised and ready. David hesitated for only an instant after seeing the bodies of the two men, then breaking right, weapon covering their truck, he quickly moved to clear it, then the corner of the house. Rebecca knelt briefly to check for a pulse on the second man Jack had shot. There was no reason to check the first. She then cleared the other side of the house. Both peeled back when no further threats could be found and headed back to the wood line.

Jack and Anna moved from the prone and took up kneeling positions as they approached.

"Knew there was a reason I brought you along, Coastie," David said, as they joined them. He was breathing heavily. This night was beginning to take its toll on the former Operator.

"Get everything you need?" Jack asked.

"Good bit," David grinned. "One trip isn't going to fit in a duffle bag."

"I can make do for now," Rebecca agreed. "I'd like to check on Chzek and Ketzev, my horses, but we probably should get moving. They should be fine for a few more days."

"Yeah, about getting a move on," Jack said. "I think it'd be best if we get rid of the bodies. I don't want some Guard patrol finding them stinking up your back yard and decide you haven't gone in search of safer shores."

"We don't have time, and to be honest I don't have the energy to bury them," David said, embarrassed by the last part.

"Not talking about burying them," Jack explained. "Becca and I will load them up in the bed of their truck and drive it a few miles down the road toward the creek. Leave it in a field where it'll be easily spotted. You and Anna pick us up on the Hondas and we *di di mau* back to the Sanctuary. Won't take an extra five minutes and there's no trace of what happened here."

"Becca is worn out. I'll help you," Anna suggested. She *knew* her husband had picked Rebecca because she was IDF and Mossad and hadn't batted so much as an eyelash at the two men he'd killed. She also knew he was doing it so to protect her from a close-up view of what he'd done, but the days of being protected from the world had ended. It was time she stepped up and pulled her weight as more than just another pair of eyes.

"Anna," Jack began to protest, "You don't...."

"We're a team now, Jack," she interrupted, standing. "Aren't we?" Without another word she stood and headed out across the field.

"Better catch up with her Jack, or she'll do it herself," David grinned. "Told you she was a keeper. Come on, Becca, let's get the ATVs."

Jack did the heavy lifting, taking the first man by the arms. To her credit, Anna didn't hesitate but grabbed his legs without flinching. The second man, the head shot, she didn't look at directly. Jack couldn't blame her. He was a mess. By the time they tossed him into the back of the pickup, the front of Jack's shirt and his pants were covered in blood and brain matter. Jack found a hose by the back door, turned on the water and washed off the biggest chunks, then turned the hose on the siding of the house and sprayed it down until all the blood was gone. He stuffed a bit of dirt into the bullet hole in the siding, wiped his hands and nodded.

Anna was waiting for him in the cab of the truck. As soon as he was in, she started the engine and backed out of the driveway. Lights out, they drove about a mile and a half from the Hitchcock's, and she pulled the truck into a field on the opposite side of the road. David and Rebecca had been pacing them in the wood line on the northern side and pulled to within twenty yards of the road to wait. On impulse, Jack opened the glove compartment, searched until he found a pen, then wrote something on the truck's registration then got out and tossed it in the truck bed.

"Looters," he replied, when Anna gave him a questioning look, and they headed for the ATVs.

David dismounted and climbed on behind Rebecca. The two bags were tied to the rear cargo rack. Anna waited for Jack to assume the driver's seat, then climbed on behind him, wrapping her arms around him and laying her head on his shoulder. Jack pulled out in the lead, and they turned back to the wood line. They soon arrived at Bynum creek and headed home.

They rode in silence, Anna drifting in and out of sleep. It had been a long day. It was dawn, by the time they reached the point where they needed to leave the creek bank and travel the rest of the way to the Sanctuary through the woods. Jack shut of the Honda's engine, patted Anna's leg, then helped her dismount.

"Why are we stopping, Coastie?" David asked, "We're almost home."

"I need you to do something for me, David," he said. "If you're willing."

"Anything you need, Jack," he nodded. "You've saved my life, twice in the last week."

"I want you to baptize me," Jack said, taking off the Springfield rifle and leaning it against the Honda. "It's not the River Jordan," he said, wading out into the creek, "but I think mom and dad would be pleased to have me do it here." The water was only shin deep where he dropped to his knees. Not deep enough for an emersion, but Methodist were sprinklers after all.

"I've spent the last week reading, praying, and *believing*," he said to the group as they watched him, "but I've not confessed with my mouth. After tonight, I think it's time. Past time, in fact. I've killed, lied, and drank until I've passed out. I've blasphemed God and ridiculed good people. I'm broken. I can't live another day without forgiveness. I'll fall short, I know. But I'll get back up. With Jesus's help."

Anna waded out into the creek and knelt beside him, tears streaming down her cheeks "I want to be baptized with my husband," she said and took his hand. "I've lied in court. I've cheated on my taxes. I've scoffed as well, hated my mother, and envied my sister. I've lain with men outside of marriage. I'm broken and I want to be whole again."

Both David and Rebecca had tears in their eyes now as well but were smiling as they waded out to them. David laid a hand on each of their shoulders. "Do you admit that you've sinned and fallen short of God's will and there's nothing you can do on your own to make yourself clean?" he asked.

"I do," Jack nodded. Tears were on his own cheeks now.

"I do," Anna nodded, sobbing softly.

"Do you believe that Yeshua is the only begotten Son of *Yahweh,* God of Abraham, Isaac, and Jacob?" Rebecca asked, "That He suffered, bled, and died and rose again from the dead on the third day as an atonement for your sins?"

"I do," Jack and Anna said together.

"Do you accept Him now into your hearts and take Him as your Savior?" David asked. "And ask the Holy Spirit, the indwelling Presence of the Father, to come into your hearts and be your guide, your comforter, and your strength?"

"I do," they both replied again.

"Jack Braedan," David said, reaching down into the creek and cupping a handful of water, "I baptize you in the name of the Father," he said, letting the water pour on Jack's head, "and the Son, and the Holy Spirit." He rested his hands-on Jack's head for a heartbeat, then moved to Anna.

"Anna Braedan," he repeated, dipping his hands into the creek, then letting the water pour down her head. "I baptize you in the name of the Father, the Son, and the Holy Spirit."

Rebecca took David's hand, as they each laid a hand on the head of Jack and Anna. "Father," David said, lifting his eyes up to the rising sun. "We come before Your throne as sinners, sinners made righteous in your sight, not by our own power, but by the power of the redeeming blood of Christ Jesus. Jack and Anna have asked to be forgiven of their sins and accepted into the body of believers. You loved them when they were sinners, Lord, loved them enough to come to earth and die for their sins. We humbly pray You will watch over them and give them strength in the days to come. Give them the nmjstrength to endure until the end if it be your will. Or to die as martyrs in your service with the praise of your name on their lips. In the precious name of Jesus, we pray. Amen."

"Amen," Rebecca smiled.

"Jack and Anna Braedan, where are your accusers?" David asked.

"There are none," Rebecca replied.

"Your sins have been forgiven," David said. "Rise and sin no more."

Rebecca and David helped them to their feet and wrapped their arms around them in a loving embrace. The four stood in the creek, hugging, crying, and laughing, as the sun rose over the tree line to shine down on a new day.

Chapter Ten

Sword of David

And there went out another horse that was red: and power was given to him that sat thereon to take peace from the earth, and that they should kill one another: and there was given unto him a great sword.

Revelation of Saint John 6:4

"Where could they be?" Jack asked in frustration. He stood in the Sanctuary kitchen scrambling up some powered eggs. He really did miss fresh eggs. "It's been a week since Julie's last text!" He complained, adding a dash more Tony Chachere's, hoping Anna wouldn't see.

"His phone could be dead, or his service cut off. Not everyone had the foresight to pay Verizon for the next six months like you had us do. I'm surprised anyone still has cell service after the assassination of the president. Have faith, Jack." Anna said, patting his cheek with an oven mitt covered hand. "Keep praying. Things *must* be settling down in Franklin. They'll be here soon."

"That's enough seasoning, by the way," she said disapprovingly, moving him out of the way with a slight touch of her hand so she could remove the pan of biscuits from the oven. Anna had been getting rather good at biscuit making, after the disaster of her first batch. She was confident she'd finally figured out the correct portions of the dry milk mix and correct consistency for the powdered butter. These actually looked like real biscuits.

Jack had been praying for God to grant him patience and to take away his worry about Julie and Mac. They were experienced operators, men that he'd helped train until they were as skilled and deadly as he. It had still been a week though. It was still hard to grasp the fact that the 200 miles that could have been traveled in only a few hours before the Event might take weeks now. They could be on foot now for all he knew, injured even. Dead or captured. Jack immediately rebuked these thoughts and prayed once again for patience, and for the safety of his friends.

"Jack! Anna!" Dave called excitedly from the common area. "Come here! You've got to see this!"

"No, David Hitchcock," Anna called back. "You turn that off and let's eat breakfast in peace while it's hot for once. You know Jack's eggs are terrible reheated! I like your beard, by the way," she smiled, kissing his cheek before moving the biscuits to a serving plate."

Jack had been letting it grow back again, since rescuing the Hitchcock's.

"Now, David!"

"Yes, mother!" David sighed, "Becca! Breakfast!"

In short order, the table was set and the four were holding hands, giving thanks for their meal and all of life's blessings.

"Okay, David," Anna said, as the last of their meal was finished. "I know it's killing you. Clean up can wait, go turn on the TV so we can see what's gotten you all excited.

They made their way to the media room of the Sanctuary and took seats as David turned on the TV. Global News Network, which had only a week ago been CNN, was at that very moment recapping the top story of the morning. David refused to acknowledge Anna's smug smile.

"In a stunning announcement made from EU headquarters in Brussels just moments ago," the GNN anchor announced, "an agreement for a new world governing body has been formed to deal with the continuing world crisis, replacing the ineffectual and now disbanded United Nations. We're going to take you live to Brussels and GNN field correspondent, Hans Van der Berg. Hans?"

"Thank you, Roger," Van der Berg said, acknowledging the anchor. "As you well know, this plan, which was proposed by Prince Azalil immediately following the EU/UN/Israeli Peace Treaty, was virtually all but dead until two days ago... when the new President of the United States was assassinated in a terrorist attack by the underground, radical Christian group *Army of God*. Until her Vice President assumed power in compliance with the American constitution and quickly allowed the talks to go forward. On the heels of the tragic plane crash that took the lives of both the Australian and Japanese's Prime Ministers, all opposition to the proposed 10 Zone World Council seems to have disappeared."

"On the map coming up on your screen...Do we have it? Yes...you can see the 10 World Zones. If you look closely in Zone 7 which comprises most of the Middle East, along with Egypt and Iran, you will notice a section of blue which is the current borders of Israel after their stunning military victories barely a week past. Israel and its currently occupied land will fall under Zone 2 which comprises the majority of Western Europe, along with Iceland and Greenland. Inclusion of Israel in Zone 7 almost brought a quick end to the Seven Year Treaty only days ago hammered out by EU President Cassini."

"Speaking of President Cassini," Van der Berg continued. "my sources tell me, and this has yet to be confirmed, mind you..."

"Of course," GNN replied.

"...my sources inform me President Cassini will soon have a new title. Chairman General of the World Zone Council."

"I could not think of a better choice in this time of crisis," the GNN anchor agreed gravely, turning to look directly at the camera and seemingly into every home reachable by the GNN feed. "As WZC Chairmen General, Cassini with guidance from Prince Azalil of course, will sit at the head of the world council and be the deciding vote on world affairs in the unlikely event of a council stalemate," Van der Burg informed the audience.

"He has indeed been a blessing to the world in these troubling times," the GNN anchor assured everyone. "It is somewhat ironic," he continued, "that this would not likely have been possible except for the terrorist attack on President Harris by radical Christians, who only this morning were identified by the NSA as the *Army of God*. Their recent propaganda was opposed to the new world government and the presence of the Anunnaki. The President, correct me if I am wrong, was the leading voice in disagreement to the formation of the WZC?"

"The gods can indeed take tragedy and turn it to...." Van der Berg nodded. "

"Who's this *Army of God* group?" Jack asked the room as he used the remote to mute the sound. "Some fabricated scapegoat or a real organization?"

"Most likely both," Rebecca replied, rising from her seat to move to the computer table. She began typing quickly into the keyboard, running a query on several search engines at once. Computer wizardry was just another of the petite Israeli's talents. Only yesterday, when Jack had expressed worry about all their computer activity being detected and giving away the location of the Sanctuary, she'd admitted some "*small skill*" with computers and assured him their IP address was had been rerouted and was bouncing around the network until the original source became hopelessly lost. "From my brief stay in the Information Technology Division at the Ministry of Agriculture," she'd smiled, when Jack asked how she'd learned that particular trick.

"Makes perfect sense," Jack had shrugged. He no longer asked Becca if she knew how to do something, he just assumed.

"I think it's safe to assume they are a real group," David said. "Probably started out like our Bible study at First Methodist but branched off into preparation to oppose the One World Government, instead of looking for the appearance of it through prophecy like we did. Kind of surprised we've never heard of them before they assassinated the President..."

"Allegedly," Anna replied. Despite everything, she was still a lawyer.

"*Allegedly* assassinated," David sighed. "I'd venture to say if they *allegedly* whacked her, they were misled into doing it by the NWO to throw off suspicion of Cassini's hands in the matter."

"Here we are," Rebecca announced, turning the monitor so they could all see. "There were a couple with the same name," she informed them. "The most famous was organized back in the 80's, bombed one abortion clinic, never took root, and developed only a few followers. This one is the most recent. Started in 2012. I'd say they are our likely, *alleged* suspects."

"Pretty good web site," Jack observed. He had experience doing research on terrorist groups like the al-Asqa Brigade, Hezbollah, and other radical Islamist. Usually, their web pages weren't so polished. "Stylish home page. Lots of video links. PDF how-to manuals."

"Everything a Tribulation Saint could want to know about fighting the anti-Christ," David agreed. "Do they have "Contact us" or "How to join" tab?"

"Thinking of signing up?" Rebecca asked.

"I'm thinking that although Big Jim designed this place to ride out the Tribulation," David said, "he never expected it to be occupied by half a Special Forces operator, a Mossad agent, and a vigilante lawyer. Looks to me like we have a nice, secure base and the foundation of a pretty darn good Franklin Chapter. I mean when your friends Julie and Mac show up, that is. There's a lot of good Christians right down the road who would appreciate someone fighting for them."

Jack could see the two women pondering his suggestion, Rebecca especially. He really hadn't given much thought to the future other than protecting his own inner circle. With his reading he knew he'd probably die a martyr during the coming years, most likely by decapitation. But the Bible didn't specifically instruct him to die meekly, waiting in some line for his head to be chopped off.

"Hit that contact us button, Becca," Jack said, leaning down over her shoulder. "You know, just for curiosity's sake," he said, turning to smile at David.

When they all agreed they'd composed a message suitably vague enough to conceal their identities but sufficiently specific enough to build a case for their addition to the cause, they hit the send button.

"See if you can figure out where this website originates, Becca," Jack said, assuming she was already considering the idea. "I'm going to clean up the breakfast dishes and take a shower."

"I'll give you a hand," Anna said.

"Pretty small in there, but I think we can make it work," Jack shrugged.

"I meant with the dishes," Anna replied.

"Oh," Jack said, disappointed.

"Well," she said hesitantly, then smiled, "I *do* need a shower."

"Newlyweds," David muttered, "are so sickening."

Jack returned half an hour later, Anna following him drying her auburn locks with a towel.

"Thirty minutes," Dave sighed, looking at his watch. "At the rate you two are going we'll be out of water in a month."

"We followed the five-minute water rule," Jack grinned. "So, what's the word, Becca?"

"These guys are good," Rebecca replied. "But not *that* good. I've narrowed it down to a town near Charlotte, North Carolina, or a big ranch in East Texas. But check this out. We have a reply to our email already."

"Already?" he asked surprised, leaning down for a look. "Show me."

Rebecca pulled it up.

Intrigued. Further details. The return email read.

"Reply with this," Jack suggested. "Did you assassinate the president?"

A response came in less than a minute.

If you think we are stupid enough to do that, we don't need you. We needed that self-important fool to delay the world zone council.

"Good answer," David smiled.

"Type that," Jack instructed.

Next step?

"What's our next step?" asked Jack.

Rebecca began typing. "*How do we know we can trust you? We are in hiding. Too much detail and we risk being compromised.*"

"I imagine we could say the same." Almost an immediate reply. *"You've already tried to find us, as we've already tried to find you. We aren't in East Texas by the way."*

"They're in East Texas," Rebecca smiled confidently.

Next step? The *Army of God* repeated.

"Type, we have a detainee camp close by in Middle Tennessee with…. How many are in there?" asked Jack.

"Fifty, maybe," David guessed. "But that's almost a week ago."

"Fifty souls as of seven days ago," Jack continued. "Intel" *…and by Intel he meant Jeremiah Graham…*" says they will be moved soon. Are you close enough to help?"

"Not in less than two weeks. Sources in area are tracking possible small group in the town of Franklin," came their reply. *"Suggest you seek help from them if you need to move quickly."*

"They've been at this for a while," Rebecca said, impressed. "I won't underestimate them again."

"Type," Jack instructed. "No joy, East Texas. That'd be us."

"You think that's wise?" Rebecca asked.

"If they are the government, they just gave us a heads up they are on to us," Jack replied. "I think they are legit. Type it."

"Then if you must move quickly, all we can offer are our prayers."

"Tell them we'll take them," Jack said. "Tell them we look forward to working together in the future and will be praying for their safety, as well. Sign it *Sword of David,* Your Brothers and Sister in Christ."

"I like that," Dave grinned.

"I thought you might," Jack replied, patting his shoulder.

"Put on the full Armor of God, Sword of David," their new ally replied. *"This fight is not against flesh and blood alone but against principalities, powers, and wickedness in high places."*

"That was interesting," Anna remarked. "What do we do now?"

"Talking with East Texas has made me a little restless," Jack said, "We've been cooped up in here for a week and with the water monitor over there, I just can't keep taking showers. What do you say, *Sword of David*, feel up to doing a little reconnaissance? If we are serious about helping the detainees and The *Army of God* can't help, I guess there's only one person who can give us what we need."

***

"He's agreed to help," Jack announced to the group when he finished texting Jeremiah Graham. "After I apologized *AGAIN* for not making the Sunday service, and after I apologized for not telling him about our baptism. And...after I scolded him for being too reckless. You know his sermon was from Daniel 8? Sounded like he wrote the news script for today."

"That young man is just asking for trouble," David muttered.

"Yes," Rebecca nodded. "He's speaking the truth, and that will certainly get you in trouble. Although it's something this world needs to hear shouted from the rooftops."

"Yeah, I know," David conceded, grudgingly.

"So, what did he say?" Anna asked.

"He said that this is the best opportunity we are likely to get if we want to free them. The Guard has left town except for one lone squad," Jack informed them. "Trouble in Birmingham. Probably those food riots we saw on the web. It's only the one squad and a rotating detail of two city cops watching the compound. That's the good news."

"Let's hear it," David sighed.

"They are definitely moving the remaining detainees to a more secure camp in West Tennessee in the next day or two," Jack said. "I think we should move now, like tonight. Look, I know it's just the four of us," he continued before anyone could voice objections. "Without the *Army of God* for help we'll be outnumbered, but the entire squad can't be on duty 24/7. I'll take us four against any six or eight."

"We pretty well know the layout. Dave, you and Rebecca were in there for more than a day. I'm sure they've likely made improvements, but maybe not. Jeremiah says they are lackadaisical in their security since the rest of the Guard left. It's a bunch of church people after all. They certainly won't be expecting it."

"Yeah," David said, "because no one would be that stupid."

"I prefer bold," Jack smiled.

"It's bold, alright," Rebecca admitted.

"So...here's the thing," Anna said. "What do we do with them, when we get them out?"

Jack was pleased she said when, not if. "We can't bring them all here, obviously. I guess we'll just have to trust God to take care of them. Look, I don't have all the answers. I just know if they are shipped off like Sean and Kate, they'll disappear. What they do after we get them out is up to them, and to God."

"So, what's your plan 007? Walk up bold as brass and say you're picking them up for transfer?" David asked. "That's only likely to work once."

"I'm glad you asked," Jack smiled. Getting a piece of paper and pen out of the computer table drawer, he began to make a rough sketch. "Jeremiah says the night shift the guards are here, and the police are usually here...."

"Where is he?" David asked anxiously. "He said to meet him here at 0300."

"He's a twenty-year-old kid," Anna whispered. "Cut him a little slack."

"A kid that could also be selling us out," Dave said. "Look, Jeremiah is a good kid, I admit. But the Jeremiah I know didn't take his faith too seriously. Just saying. This is the Tribulation after all. People of weak faith will turn on the true Church."

"Jeremiah has changed!" Anna argued. Though she hadn't known him before this started, she felt she knew the man he'd become the day after the Event.

"We're about to find out," Jack said, looking through the NVGs secured from David's basement. "Here he comes."

Jeremiah was doing his best to be stealthy as he moved from tree to tree along Baker Street. He'd even had the forethought to wear dark clothing. But he was still no soldier. He was making *way* too much noise for Jack's comfort. He let Jeremiah get almost upon them before rising out of the shadows.

"Jesus, help me," Jeremiah hissed, jumping. "Is that you, Jack?"

Jack was dressed all in dark clothing, face painted black. He carried the H&K, with the Mossberg strapped across his back and the Springfield .45's in a shoulder holster. "How you been Jeremiah?"

"Busy doing the Lord's work," he said, a little too loudly, until Jack put a finger to his lips. "Busy doing the Lord's work," he whispered comically.

Jack motioned with his head for Jeremiah to follow and he slipped back into the shadows.

"There they are, just like I said," Jeremiah pointed. "Two police at the entrance. No more than two Guardsman on roving patrol. There..." he said, looking through the NVGs. "On the back side. Takes them about twenty minutes to do a complete circuit of the camp."

"You've been watching them?" David asked quietly.

"Almost every night," Jeremiah admitted. "For a couple of hours at least. What time is it?"

"3:15," Jack said, looking at his watch.

"They changed shifts at midnight," Jeremiah informed them. "Relief will come at 6AM."

"Long time to walk patrol and sit in a chair," Jack smiled. They would be comfortable now, and likely tired halfway through their shift. If they did this quickly and quietly, no one would be the wiser for at least two hours. The *Sword of David* would be back at the Sanctuary before any-one knew they'd been here. "You know the plan everyone. Rebecca and I will take down the Guards on the back side, next trip around. Anna, you have your phone. When we have them secured, we'll text you. You wait five minutes, then go ask those gentlemen for a light. David, as soon, and I mean as soon, as she has the drop on them, you're her back up."

All three nodded. Anna was the only one in the group not dressed for the occasion, wearing only jeans and a tight tee shirt, now that she'd shed her dark jacket. "Check your 9 mil, honey. Make sure it's ready."

"I've checked it, Jack," she assured him. "A dozen times."

"And what do I do?" Jeremiah asked.

"You go home," Jack said, "Get some rest, and show up just before 6AM like you do every morning with coffee for the cops and some food for the detainees. Except today, you'll be running to get the Guard squad leader when you discover what's happened."

"Everyone ready?" asked Jack. "Quick prayer then we move. Jeremiah, do you want to lead?"

Jeremiah's eyes lit up with delight at the offer. "Lord, we come before you with Thanksgiving and ask you to send your angels to protect these fine people...."

"There's my signal," Anna whispered as her phone lit up in the darkness. One short sentence. *'Go. I love you.'* "Wish me luck," she said, after waiting the five minutes Jack had instructed. It was the longest five minutes of her life.

"I'll be right behind you, Counselor," David assured her. "You'll be fine."

Anna took a deep breath, then rose from the shadows and headed toward the two policemen at the gate. They saw her when she stepped into the light of the nearest streetlamp. Her pulse quickened, but she continued on. The two men watched curiously as she stumbled, fumbling through her purse, obviously drunk and obviously unaware they were watching her. She put a cigarette between her lips then continued to rummage through her purse. Anna looked up and pretended to notice them for the first time.

She walked toward them, weaving a little, continuing to search her purse. "Hi," she smiled sweetly, now within ten feet of the policemen. "Either of you boys have a light?"

"Honey," the cop on the right leered, "for you, I'll burn the town."

"Wait a minute," the cop on the left said, suddenly suspicious. "Aren't you..."

"I found it," Anna laughed. "Ooops," She dropped her purse to the ground, and bent to retrieve it. When she came back up, she had the 9mm pointed at them. "Don't move. Don't speal," she said calmly, trying her best to imitate the tone Jack had used on the guardsmen that day at the checkpoint.

"I'd do as the lady says," David advised them, stepping from the shadows with his Mini-30, sweeping back and forth between the two. "Nice and slow, I need you to take those sidearms and put them on the table. Good, now your handcuffs. Ah...slowly there, son! Okay, stay calm and this will be over in a bit. Red, get their cuffs. Be good lads. Stand up and put your hands behind your backs for the lady."

"You know this isn't right," Anna said, snapping the handcuffs tightly on the first policeman. "But maybe it's not your fault. Maybe you're just doing your job," she continued, securing the second. "We all have choices to make in this life. After tonight, I hope you rethink what you'd like to do with the rest of yours."

"Take a seat, guys," David said, motioning with the barrel of his rifle.

Jack and Rebecca appeared half a minute later. "Good job," he grinned. Anna offered her a cheek, and he gave her a quick kiss. "Nothing personal, guys," he continued, reaching into the cargo pocket of his trousers for the duct tape. He quickly wrapped several loops around the first cop then moved to the second.

"Mister," the second policeman said fearfully, "they'll kill us for this."

"What for?" asked Jack, beginning to wrap the duct tape around his mouth. "Getting captured by a tipsy red-head, or being overpowered by at *least* a dozen armed radicals? That's the story I'd tell anyway," Jack finished, patting his shoulder. "Do that thing you did with the guard guys. That was cool," he said, turning to Rebecca.

"With pleasure," she smiled, and both cop's eyes widened in fright. "You're going to take a little nap now, gentlemen," she said, slinging her AR. "Just relax. It'll be okay."

With the two policemen now unconscious, the group went about the camp quickly waking the people inside.

"Go with God." "Go." "Get out of here." They urged the startled prisoners. Most were confused. Some frightened at the sight of the armed intruders with black faces. But it didn't take them long to figure out they were being rescued.

"God bless you." "Thank you." "Where should we go?" were the standard replies.

"Anywhere but here," Jack advised them, knowing most of them would probably get rounded back up within the week. Well...that was up to how resourceful they were, and to the grace of God.

"How long are they going to be out?" Jack asked Rebecca as they regrouped at the entrance.

"Hour?" she shrugged. "Maybe more."

"Would it do any good to pop them again?" he asked.

"Couldn't hurt," she smiled.

As she moved to ensure the policemen would be out until their shift change, Jack picked up the clipboard on the table and flipped over the top sheet. *"Thus, sayeth the Lord,"* he wrote on the paper. *"Let my people go."* Underline. Exclamation point. *The Sword of David.*

"That ought to give them something to think about," David grinned.

"Let's get back to the Sanctuary," Jack said gravely. "In a few hours, we will probably be wanted by the World Zone Council, Zone 4, District 1."

"I really thought we'd make the news," Anna said, her disappointment plain to hear as she turned off the television. "Local, anyway."

"Never took you for a prima donna, Counselor," David laughed, "But then again, you are a lawyer."

"People know, trust me," Jack assured his lovely wife. "That was a text from Jeremiah. We are the talk of the town. He hung around and watched, you know."

"Foolish boy," Rebecca sighed. "Someone really needs to have a talk with him."

"His sermon Sunday is going to be about Gideon, by the way," Jack informed them. "That boy is going to be picked up for questioning about this. Mark my words, he should have come with us.

"He believes what he's doing is God's will." Anna replied.

"But it's gonna make him a martyr," Jack sighed.

"Everyone has their part to play," she assured him, wrapping her arms around his neck.

"We did a righteous thing, last night," Jack announced. "Maybe it will strengthen some to endure until the end."

Anna gave him a kiss...

"What was that for?" he asked, "Not that I minded."

"Rule #7. Kiss whenever you feel like it," she replied, crawling into his lap, and laying her head on his shoulder. "My husband is the *Sword of David.*"

"*We* are the *Sword of David*," he said softly. "Your husband is the one who probably just added you to the TBI's most wanted list."

***

"Jack, activity at the house!" Anna announced excitedly.

It was dusk on the third day since their raid on the compound. They had fallen into a routine since then: breakfast, prayer, and Bible study, watch the news, lunch, more news, supper, then more Bible study, prayer, and then off to bed again. They took shifts throughout the day monitoring the security cameras, except during prayer. Until this moment, all had been a quiet routine.

"What is it?" asked Jack, coming from the kitchen where he'd been washing the supper dishes.

"I saw a brief glimpse of a two people down at the gate," she replied. "A man and a woman. I think? At least one was slim and at least a foot shorter. Hard to tell, she was supporting him. Injured, maybe?"

The gate had been down since the Guard rammed it with a Bradley Fighting Vehicle that day they'd come looking for him. In retrospect, he was a bit surprised there hadn't been more visitors looking to loot the house. They'd gone back to the Hitchcock's two days after their initial run to collect their two horses, Strength and Speed, and found their place ransacked and the horses gone. All but the basement, which was a double bolted steel door. That trip had resulted in two SAWS, 5.56mm Squad Automatic Machine Guns and 10,000 rounds, along with an assortment of other goodies. Maybe available houses to loot were running dry in Franklin, and the Braedan home and residents farther out of town were just now beginning to get on people's radar.

"Looters?" he asked. "Or squatters?"

"The one didn't look in any shape to loot," Anna observed. "We'll know soon enough if they are taking up residence. Wait.... See? There! Coming around the west side."

"Zoom in a little," Jack instructed.

Anna typed in commands for camera two to zoom, then focus.

"David! Gear up!" Jack shouted. "Let's get the Hondas!"

"What is it?" asked Hitchcock, joining them at the monitor.

"I don't know who the woman is, but that's Julie!" he replied. "Watch us on the monitor, Anna," he instructed his wife.

"I'm coming with you," she argued.

"Won't be room on the return trip," Jack said, kissing her cheek. "Meet us at the shed with Becca. We'll need help getting him down. He looks to be in bad shape. Becca! Get some medical supplies!"

"On it, Jack," she nodded.

Jack and David came speeding out of the wood line, the headlights of the ATVs fixing the pair about halfway across the field, behind the house. When the woman saw them, she dropped Julie, who collapsed to the ground, and she fumbled with a pistol holstered on her hip, pointing at them as they slid to a stop about ten yards away.

"Stay back!" she yelled. Her voice was shaking. "I'll shoot if I have to!"

"Miss," Jack said, dismounting and raising his hands. "I'm Jack, Jack Braedan. That's my friend, Julie."

"Thank God," she said. The woman dropped to her knees, exhaustion and relief flooding through her.

"What happened?" asked Jack, hurrying to Julie's side. His pulse was weak. Even in the dim light, Jack could see he was pale. There was a blood-soaked bandage on his right thigh.

"Shot four days ago," the woman replied. She was just a girl actually. Maybe seventeen or eighteen. If she was maybe five feet tall, it wasn't by much. Probably didn't weigh 100 pounds soaking wet with rocks in her pockets. How she'd supported Julie's six foot, two-hundred-pound frame must have been through sheer determination. "Can you help him?" she asked hopefully. "He saved my life."

"I'll do everything I can," Jack promised her. "Dave, help me get him on the Honda. Miss..."

"I'm Nikki," she replied.

"Nikki, you ride with Dave," he instructed her. "Let's get him up. I'll have to hold him and drive. Ready? One, two...three."

Anna and Rebecca were waiting at the door of the shed when the two ATVs arrived.

"He's lost a lot of blood," Jack shouted, as he shut down the engines. "Let's get him inside."

Jack took Julie's arms and Anna took his legs. It was a chore getting him down the stairs, but they managed. Julie moaned once but didn't wake. As soon as they were down the stairs and through the entrance, Dave and Rebecca joined to help, Nikki following close behind. They took him to the common area table where Rebecca had already laid out a sheet from one of the beds.

"Ready, one, two, lift..."

Rebecca immediately began to cut away the bandage and his pants leg with a pair of surgical scissors. "Doesn't look infected. Thank God. I'll give him a shot of penicillin, just in case. When's the last time you started an IV, Jack?"

"Six months? Nothing to it," he replied. Part of the medical supplies included in the Sanctuary's stock was a generous amount of saline solution IV bags. They were outdated of course, but Jack had inspected them thoroughly and discarded less than half that looked suspect.

"I've been trying to keep it clean it," Nikki informed them. "Used up the last of our water this morning."

"You did an awesome job, sweetie," Rebecca replied, continuing to work. "We're going to have to dig the bullet out if we can. I'll give him a local. I'm not a doctor. I don't know how much of a general to give him. Too much with a pulse like his would kill him."

"When's the last time you did anything like this?" Anna asked anxiously.

"Almost thirty years," Becca replied gravely. "He lived." She said, glancing briefly at David.

"Got it," Rebecca said, relief flooding her voice. ".38 maybe?" she said, examining the slug before she dropped it on the table. "Flush out the wound Jack, and I'll close it up. No arteries were damaged. He'd be dead already, otherwise."

"Is he going to be okay?" Nikki asked, her concern evident for all to hear.

"I don't know, honey," Rebecca replied softly. "I've done everything I can. We'll just have to wait and pray."

As soon as they moved Julie to one of the beds, Jack lead the group in prayer, all of them laying hands on Julian Hesterman, Nikki standing at their backs, crying softly.

"Lord Jesus," Jack began, "You are the healing physician. You raised the dead, healed lepers with a touch, and healed others with just a word. We ask you now to heal this good man, my friend Julian..."

Chapter Eleven

Julie and Nikki

"And there went out another horse, which was red; And power was given to him to that sat on the horse to take peace from the earth."

Revelation 6:4

"Hey, he's back," Jack smiled. "How are you feeling?" Jack opened the bottle of water at his bedside which had been waiting for just for this occasion. Someone had been sitting by Julie's side keeping watch since they'd brought him down two days ago. Jack had been on shift only twenty minutes.

"Thanks..." Julie nodded. "Mac is gone," he said softly. "I tried to save him."

"I know," Jack nodded, unable to stop the tears forming in his eyes. "Nikki told us."

Nikki had in fact, told them a lot of things over the last two days while Julie slept. Her name was Nichole Valentine, she was nineteen years old, and she was from Lewisburg. She had been home on Spring break when the Event happened. It was her sophomore year at the University of Alabama at Huntsville. Nikki wanted to be a veterinarian. Julie and Mac had come across her four days ago, right after her family had encounter a group of marauders (*she didn't call them that, but that's what they were*) moving up from Birmingham after the food riots. They had run into her family on Highway 106 as they were headed south to her grandparent's farm in Fayetteville. They were planning to ride out the Event at the farm until food supplies began flowing again. It was just bad luck they ran into the marauders as they were heading north.

They forced her family pickup off the road, shot her father and younger brother on the spot, and would have raped and likely killed her, if not worse. While she was scratching and clawing for her life and virtue, screaming at the top of her lungs however, shots started ringing from out of the woodline. A firefight ensured, killing most of the men who had murdered her family. One of the marauders had taken refuge under their truck. When Julie and Mac had appeared out of the wood line, he opened fire on them. Julie had taken one in the leg and Mac had been gut shot before they managed to take him down.

Julie had let her grieve for as long as he could, and then asked if she knew any place nearby where they could take Mac and try to patch him up. With her dad and little brother dead, and both Julie and Mac wounded, she wiped her eyes, covered her family with blankets from their pickup, and volunteered to drive them back to the nearest town in the Marauder's SUV. Although Julie did his very best, Sergeant First Class Terrance "Mad Mac" McDonald died from his wound two days later in the Bethlehem Baptist Church off Hwy 106. The good folks there buried him in the church cemetery. The church wanted Julie to stay until he had healed himself, but he was adamant about moving on.

With the choice to get to her grandparent's farm, or help Julie because he and Mac had saved her life, she'd promised Julie she'd help him get to Franklin and make her way south afterwards. She owed him. The SUV they'd liberated from her attackers broke down about fifteen miles south of Franklin. They'd walked cross country the rest of the way. The last five miles she'd practically carried the wounded Special Forces Operator.

"We had to try and help," Julie sighed. "Couldn't just slink away while they, well...you know. She's a strong kid. If she's shed a tear since that first day, I haven't seen it."

"You did a good thing, Julie," Jack replied, laying a comforting hand on his friend's shoulder.

"Four tours in Afghanistan without a scratch and Mac gets taken out in Tennessee by a punk on the side of road," Julie said bitterly.

"Hungry?" asked Jack. Julie nodded his head. "We'll bring you something to eat."

"He's awake," Jack announced to the group. They were eating lunch at the common room table. Nikki sprang from her seat and rushed to see him. Jack sat down beside Anna and took one of the chicken fingers off her plate. She lay her head on his shoulder and intertwined her arm in his. Mac's death had hit him hard.

"Someone write this down," David said, wiping his mouth as he finished his lunch. "That girl isn't going anywhere, anytime soon without Julian Hesterman."

"His wound is doing very well," Rebecca observed, casually. "Remarkably well, as a matter of fact. Yesterday, I would have sworn I'd botched it and he'd have trouble ever walking again unassisted. This morning when I checked it, well, I'd say he'll be on his feet again in no time."

"*The fervent prayer of a righteous man availeth much*," Anna replied, patting Jack's leg.

Jack kissed the top of his wife's head. "What do you say we clean up these dishes and go do some studying? I'm thinking the Hook in Magog's jaw will be happening next. God must destroy them soon if Israel is going to burn their weapons for seven years."

"I wouldn't believe it if hadn't seen it with my own eyes," Julie said coming into the common area the next morning during their Bible study. "I'm still not sure I'm seeing this."

Jack smiled as Julie entered, supported by Nikki. He was hardly limping at all. Jack had a feeling she was supporting him now simply out of habit, or just to be close to him. "Have a seat, it's just getting interesting."

"What's going on, Jack?" he said, allowing Nikki to help him take a seat.

Jack was fully convinced his friend could have done it himself. Maybe he was in some sort of subconscious denial. He *shouldn't* be walking so well so soon. "Doing a little intelligence gathering on the coming attack on Israel," he replied.

"Ummm, Jack, even on the run I know the EU and that alien dude signed a treaty with Israel," Julian said. "After what they just pulled off and with the Anunnaki assuring their security, no one is going to attack them for years to come."

"Maybe, maybe not," Jack shrugged. "You poll this room; the maybes will probably win out. Everyone, this is Julian Hesterman, my brother from another mother. Julie, this is David and Rebecca Hitchcock. Dave is former 3rd Group and Becca was IDF, and though she'll never actually admit it to you, probably former Mossad as well. This stunning woman is Anna," Jack said, laying his arm lovingly across her shoulders, "...my wife."

The look on Julie's face was comical. That Jack was married was obviously a bigger shock to him than finding him sitting around in a group reading the Bible. Anna got up from her seat at the table, went over and gave Julie a big hug. A look of jealously quickly flittered across Nikki's face, but it vanished almost instantly. Anna had been nothing but kind, sweet, and generous to her since the moment she'd appeared. It was also obvious to anyone with half a brain, she was totally devoted to Jack Braedan.

"We're so glad you're here, Julie," Anna said, giving him a final squeeze. "And that you're feeling better."

"Ummm, thanks, Mrs. Braedan," Julie said hesitantly.

"Anna," she insisted, retaking her seat by Jack.

"Or Annie Oakley," David grinned. "She's already a better shot than me."

"So...you're gathering intel? In the ummm...Bible?" Julie asked incredulously.

"More accurate than an NSA spy satellite," Jack smiled. "Which are probably looking for people like us as much as they are pointed at the Middle-East right now."

"People like who?" Julie asked, still trying to process it all.

"Christians," Jack and Anna almost answered as one.

"The *Army of God*," David said.

"The *Sword of David*," Rebecca nodded.

"Who...what is the Sword of David?" Julie said, becoming a little overwhelmed.

"Why, you're looking at them," Jack grinned.

Bible study was suspended while Jack filled his friend in on everything that had happened to him over the month since the Event. The rest of the group added things to flesh out the story where they had participated. By the time they reached this moment, sitting around this table, Julian was speechless.

"So, you're a Bible thumper now?" he asked, finally finding words.

"Julie, that's not nice," Nikki admonished him.

"Sorry," he said, "a believer then. In Jesus and all...this?" he asked, picking up a bible.

"In Jesus and all this," Jack nodded. "Although, I don't really know enough to be thumping anyone just yet," he grinned.

"I need a drink," Julie sighed.

"How about some coffee?" Anna asked. "It's a little early in the morning for shots. Even in this crowd."

"Coffee would be great Mrs....umm. Anna," Julie hastily corrected.

"I'll get it, Mrs....umm Anna," Jack smiled. "Go back to that list of countries, Sweetie. I'm still not totally convinced Turkey will be in the mix. They signed the treaty after all."

Their Bible study lasted all the way until lunch on that day.

"So, what you're saying," Julie asked, getting up to get himself a refill of coffee (with no help from Nikki and not even a trace of a limp), "is that Iran, probably Turkey, Libya and the Sudan are going to retaliate against Israel soon? You think Iran is somehow going to talk Russia into joining them? Even with the Anunnaki craft in the capitals of the 10 Zones, and them dealing out space tech and cures for every known disease like Halloween candy?"

"That's what we're saying," Jack nodded. "And some supernatural force is going to totally annihilate them as soon as they cross into Israel."

"Almost totally," Dave added. "Well above 80% though depending on your figures. And not a single bomb will drop on Israel. The destruction will be so great it will take seven months to bury the bodies and the Israelis will burn their weapons and equipment for fuel for seven years."

"And you're also telling me that David and Rebecca here predicted the EU peace treaty and the World Zone Council, before it happened?" Julie asked. "That Azalil is a demon, not some spaceman and Apollos Cassini is going to turn into some sort of dictator?"

"Not some sort, but the worst the world has ever witnessed," David explained. "Worse than Nero, Genghis Khan, Hitler, Stalin, Mao, and the rest combined."

"I've known you for over four years, Jack," Julie said slowly. "I fought beside you, watched you plan, rethink, and plan again. I've never *once* known you to be anything other than a deliberate, thoughtful, leader. You've saved my life more times than I care to count, and I owe it to you to listen to what you have to say at the very least."

"That's all I ask, Julie," Jack smiled. "You're a smart man, smarter than most. You'll see what I've seen, I promise you."

"Nikki," Anna said, joining the discussion. "I know you're worried about your grandparents, it's only natural. We'll keep trying to reach them by cell, but I'm sure they'd want you to be safe. This place is as safe as just about anywhere until things settle down. Safer than most, I'm guessing. You and Julie are welcome to stay here with us if you like. All we ask is that you keep an open mind. Pitch in where you can, just like everyone does. In a couple of days, if you want to leave and go to Fayetteville to be with your grandparents, we won't stop you. We'll even take you there, won't we? Jack?"

"I guess we will," Jack smiled. "Julie, I know you were headed to Mac's place...before. You're welcome to stay here, if you want. I'd say stay at least until you're feeling better, but you're well enough to travel again already, unless I'm mistaken."

"You in the miracle business now, as well, Jack?" Julie asked, rubbing his thigh. There was hardly any pain at all, just a little stiffness.

"I don't do miracles," Jack chuckled.

"Some people in this room would probably disagree with you," David said softly.

***

"Holy.... Jack! Everyone! Get in here!" Julie shouted.

Jack lifted Anna's arm off his chest and rolled over to check his watch on the floor beside the bed. It was a little after 4AM. Julie was always the first one up on the Team. In the week since he'd been here, Jack knew he couldn't have gotten more than five hours of sleep a night. The man was still up reading the Bible when Anna dragged Jack to bed after 11. "Come on, hon," he said, kissing her neck. "Let's go see what has Julie so excited. But put something on first," he grinned, slapping her bare bottom.

"Owww," Anna cried. "Can I at least shower first, Jack Braedan? I probably smell like, well, I probably smell."

"And whose fault is that?" Jack said, pulling on a tee shirt, then standing to put on his jeans. "All I wanted to do last night was go to sleep."

"You sure didn't *act* like you wanted to just sleep," she smiled, rolling over and pulling back the covers. "Are you sure you don't want to stay just a bit longer?"

"Lord, get dressed woman," Jack shuddered, looking at his beautiful wife. "Or we'll both be late, and Julie will burst in here and see something he shouldn't."

"JACK!"

"Moving, Sergeant!" Jack called back. "Get dressed, woman," he said, turning to wink at his wife.

"Moving, Sergeant," she sighed.

"What is it, Julie?" he asked, arriving in the media room. David was already there, Nikki was walking in, rubbing sleep from her eyes.

"Look!" he demanded, point at the television, and turned up the sound.

GNN was in the process of break news.

"....am I hearing you correctly, Elam?" the GNN anchored asked.

"Indeed, you are," the GNN field reporter replied. The bottom of the screen said the man was Elam Levinthal, reporting from Jerusalem. "In what can only be described as a shocking, truly shocking event, an over-night surprise attack on the nation of Israel has apparently been thwarted by...well, a storm of meteors. From the north, south and west, squadrons of bombers and attack fighters were knocked from the sky, as they were only seconds away from initiating an aerial assault on the nation of Israel.

The first hint of this attack occurred at roughly 10PM local time, when Israeli air defense radar suddenly went dark. Sources from inside the IDF are reporting that Russian satellites are suspected of beaming a massive jamming signal that blanketed the entire nation. The Israeli air force scrambled to launch interceptors at the unknown attackers. But before they could become airborne, they were ordered to be grounded, as balls of fire began streaking across the heavens from the east. I witnessed these...meteors firsthand when I ran outside in response to the air raid sirens. I...I believe we have a video coming up right now. It was taken by a quick thinking GNN cameraman."

The screen cut to video. Air raid sirens could be heard wailing in the distance. A shaking camera was pointed at the clear night sky, filming the countless trails of fire in what was probably the most massive meteor shower in recorded history, but they weren't falling to earth. They seemingly appeared out of nowhere in the skies above Israel and began streaking outward. The camera zoomed out to its farthest setting and off toward the horizon the meteors seemed to be exploding in mid-air. Where they struck, flaming debris spiraled down to the ground and detonated further. Caught up in the moment, the cameraman let out a string of shocked curses before someone at GNN thought to cut the sound.

"We are also getting reports from outlying districts," Levinthal continued, "that massive convoys which were thought to be relief efforts headed to the areas most devastated by the Israeli assaults of the preceding weeks were actually, huge military convoys of troops, artillery and even armored vehicles. They had deployed under the cover of darkness and were also massing to attack. But...but this same meteor shower appears to have had a significant effect on them, as well. It is quite frankly, and I hesitate to say the word, a miracle. My sources report to me that with the IDF forces spread so thin in Lebanon, Syria and Egypt, this surprise attack would have likely overwhelmed them in hours. If their aerial assault had managed to succeed, the attackers would have pounded the Israelis to rubble as their military readiness has been significantly reduced since the signing of the EU-Anunnaki peace treaty."

"Thank you, Elam," the GNN anchor replied. "We are cutting live now to Rome where we are informed, World Zone Council Chairman General Cassini is about to issue a statement. Rome, are you there?"

"This is Hans Van der Berg reporting live from Rome," announced Mr. Van der Berg. "Chairman Cassini is indeed preparing to make a statement."

"We're going to the WZC temporary headquarters now, Hans," the GNN anchor announced.

The scene switched to a conference room where Chairman Cassini was at this moment stepping to the podium. "I'll make this brief," Cassini announced gravely. "Events are unfolding now even as I speak. Around 2200 hours in Jerusalem, Israel came under intense satellite jamming in preparation for a surprise attack. If not for a natural phenomenon that WZC scientists have confirmed to me was a likely "aftershock" of solar flares that this world suffered only a few short weeks ago as it passed through the asteroid belt between Mars and Jupiter, the attack would have succeeded. EU defense experts, even our friends the Anunnaki were completely caught off guard. It will not happen again."

"Azalil probably isn't going to be pleased he admitted that" David grinned.

"In response to this violation of the nation of Israel, and in honoring Israeli treaty, forces from Zone 7 and several other districts are launching a retaliatory strike on the offending nations. Zone 7 armor columns are even now advancing from Germany toward Russia. Our planes have struck in targets Iran, Turkey, and Libya. World Zone naval forces are sailing to launch further strikes, as well. Let me assure you, our response will be swift and terrifying. The World Zone Council will no longer tolerate nations who threaten global peace and our fledgling brotherhood of man."

"Let me also assure you observatories around the world, in conjunction with Anunnaki scientists and NASA space telescopes, are diligently seeking for any other events that might threaten the safety of WZC citizens. Further information will be released through WZC news outlets as details become available," Cassini promised. "I will not be taking questions at this time. Thank you. On behalf of The World Zone Council, I wish you peace and safety," he concluded and abruptly left the podium.

"In recap," the GNN anchor said coming back on screen. "The world has again stood witness to the unexpected and devastating forces of nature as a meteor storm…."

David turned off the sound. "Cassini probably soiled his undies after watching the video. It's a terrible thing to fall into the hands of a righteous God. Funny, he didn't mention how this *meteor* storm only struck around the borders of Israel," he remarked.

"I bet it knocked that smug look off Azalil's face as well," Rebecca added.

"Anything else in that book about what's coming?" Julien asked quietly, pale and shaken.

"Lots," Jack nodded gravely. "But I'm afraid nothing good in the immediate future. Let's get the coffee started. Looks like Bible study is starting early this morning."

"How about we pray first?" David suggested. "Father in heaven…."

***

"It's a lot to take in, Jack," Julie sighed. They were outside the Sanctuary, letting Julie stretch his legs a bit under the stars. He had been here almost three weeks now. Even though the night was relatively cool for mid-May, it wasn't the temperature that made Julian Hesterman abruptly shudder. "When this first went down, I thought it was a freak solar storm, overreaching governments grabbing more power and control, and aliens finally making themselves known. Now you're telling me it's all some cosmic battle between good and evil."

"It's not just a cosmic battle," Jack informed him. "It won't be long, biblically speaking, before Michael kicks Lucifer and his angels out of heaven, but there is a struggle going on here on earth as well. Despite what the world believes, the Anunnaki aren't extraterrestrials. They are demons inhabiting manufactured flesh. This is just the beginning. It'll get continually worse until the point where if Jesus doesn't intervene, all life on this planet will perish."

"We used to make fun of this stuff, sitting in the Team room on Sunday mornings," Julie pointed out.

"Hard to make light of these events now that we're living in them," Jack replied.

"So.... according to your Bible," Julie said, thoughtfully, "world war, famine, and plagues are coming next?"

"Cassini's "retaliation" for the attack on Israel will probably get out of hand," Jack nodded. "Maybe there will even be some limited nuclear exchanges. It'll cause oil disruption. Which will further tax the world's power supply, after those solar flares knocked out a lot of electric grids. Which will worsen the food shortages. Which will cause more riots. Which will bring death. A LOT of death. Before the year is up, maybe a quarter of the world's population will be gone."

"That's...that's..."

"Nearly two billion people," Jack nodded.

"Jesus," Julie whispered. "And God's doing this, why? To punish us?"

"He's allowing it," Jack explained. "There's a difference."

"Not to the dead," Julie muttered.

"No, I suppose not," Jack admitted. "Look Julie, since the beginning of history, God has allowed man free will. The freedom to choose his fate. He laid out the straight path and told us there would be consequences if we didn't follow it. Not His consequences, but the consequences we'd suffer because of our own mistakes. He told Adam and Eve in the Garden of Eden, they only have one rule...one...don't eat from the Tree of the Knowledge of Good and Evil. We couldn't even do that right. Lucifer tricked Eve into eating the fruit, and she shared it with Adam. Since that moment, man has been making excuses. Adam blamed Eve and Eve blamed the serpent. Lucifer blamed God for not giving him more power over His creation.

"You know the state of the world, Julie. We've been pushing and pushing against the old, outdated, "religious" morals of the past. All you had to do over the last few decades is read a newspaper or log on to the internet to see some nut job suing or protesting for this or that "right" from deciding to wear a dress, to call yourself a woman and pee in the lady's room, to all kinds of depravities that people wouldn't have tolerated even thirty years ago. In Paul's letter to the Romans, he said that since we are determined to worship created things instead of the Creator, God would give us over to our *reprobate* minds and let the chips fall where they may. The chips are falling now, my friend."

"So, what do we do, Jack?" Julie asked.

"Get right with our Creator," Jack replied. "Pray, learn, and warn people. Survive as best we can. Help where we can. If our study is correct, and you've already seen that it is, things will get bad during the next year. But Cassini will step in with the help of the Anunnaki and take more and more control. Things will eventually settle down, for a time anyway. He'll get the credit and people will *love* him for it, not even realizing he's taken control of what they can eat, where they can work, even how they can think and who they should pray to. By the time the world realizes it, it'll be too late. That's when the world will *really* start to suffer the consequences of our mistakes."

"You've gone all in on this stuff, haven't you?" Julie said, turning to look at his comrade, his leader, his brother.

"What other choice do I have?" Jack shrugged. "After learning what I've learned, it's either resist or join Cassini's World Zone army, by goose stepping through towns locking up Christians. I can't turn a blind eye to what's really going on for a paycheck, a hot meal, and a comfortable bunk to sleep in, can I? You took the first step when you and Mac bugged out rather than swear the new oath. Now that the President is dead, I imagine another oath will be coming soon. This one sworn to Cassini and the World Zone Council. Now, it's time for you to take another look and open your eyes, and your heart."

"I've got a lot to think about, Jack," Julie admitted.

"That's all I'm asking you to do," Jack said, laying an arm across his friend's shoulder. "Now, what do you say we smoke these cigars," he asked, fishing two Cubans out of his shirt pocket, "then go do some more Intel work? If I'm not mistaken, I saw Anna and Nikki in the kitchen working on a blueberry pie when we left."

Chapter Twelve

Jackson

"Hey everyone, drop what you're doing!" David commanded, "We just got an email from the *Army of God."*

"Really?" Jack said, walking into the common room, sipping on his first cup of coffee of the day. "What's it say?"

"Don't know. Haven't opened it yet. From the Arkansas branch," David replied. "Should we wait for the others?"

It was the middle of September. The group had settled into a quiet routine over the summer. The garden they'd planted not long after the arrival of Julie and Nikki, had been a huge success. They'd spent the last week canning green beans, yellow squash, okra, sweet corn, and tomatoes. The potatoes, both sweet and russet, hadn't faired nearly as well. But it was a bumper crop, all things considered. They had managed to replace a sizeable portion of the canned goods they'd consumed from the Sanctuary's pantry, even though they hadn't skimped on the fresh vegetables added to their diet over the last few weeks. Just the right amount of rain, a household full of willing work hands, and the grace of God, had proven to be a potent combination.

"Open it up, Dave," Jack said, sitting down beside him. "Sleepy heads will just have to get over it." The first line of the email had Jack up out of his chair and going to roust the remainder of the group out of their beds.

"Okay, what's all the fuss about?" Rebecca asked, rubbing sleep from her eyes and the last to join them. It was only a few minutes past 6AM.

"Jack, you want to read it aloud?" Dave asked.

He took another sip of coffee, hoping it would mask his excitement.

"We need your help, *Sword of David*," the email began.

"Could be a trap," Julie said thoughtfully, breaking the silence. "*Army of God* went dark after that debacle in Texarkana. Probably were compromised. It's probably the WZC following up on Intel they forced out of them."

At the end of June, *Army of God* had attempted to ambush a World Zone convoy of supplies headed to the Camp Robinson, Arkansas military post. It had been too good to pass up. It had also been a ruse to draw them out. Instead of tractor trailers full of food, the trucks had been packed with WZC army troops. The ensuing gun battle had left 11 dead and a dozen more wounded and captured. Their trial had lasted only a week. The execution of the five members who survived interrogation had been shown on live TV by GNN. The first execution by guillotine in the United States of America.

After the failed ambush, WZC had really cracked down on the "*Regressives.*" That's what GNN called the remaining openly Christian population. Which in truth was quickly becoming a rapidly shrinking congregation after Prince Azalil had revealed in early May the Anunnaki were the progenitors of humanity millennia earlier. The Panspermia Revelation was just another of Satan's lies of course, along with the Big Bang and a host of others. But many of the churches in America, and indeed worldwide, were converting to a new age-Anunnaki hybrid religion after that, and the Pope was their new leader. *Eternal Peace Temples*, they were starting to call them now. It was hard to deny their claim after their scientists had shared DNA manipulation technology with the geneticists of the world. Every week seemed to bring some startling new announcement from the World Zone Health Organization, on the progress of their Human Enhancement Project. There were awed whispers that immortality, or something very akin to it, might be possible in the next three to five years. The Dawn of the New Man it was called by the WZC. Lucifer had made the same promise to Adam and Eve. He was a liar from the beginning!

"Could be," Jack admitted. "But why send it to us? *Sword of David* is a flea on the back of the WZC elephant in the grand scheme of things. We've become farmers, not freedom fighters."

"Don't sell yourself or us short, Jack," Anna admonished him. "You know what we did for the detainees in Franklin spread like wildfire. *Sword of David's* exploits traveled across the South. Hardly a day went by that Jeremiah didn't text us he'd heard from someone who'd heard from someone, who had heard what we did." The mention of Jeremiah cast a somber pale over the group. Jeremiah Graham had fallen off the face of the earth three weeks ago. The young man's fire for the Lord had finally attracted the wrong person's attention after the *Army of God's* failed ambush.

"Sorry," Anna said quietly, realizing the specter she had raised, "but you know it's true."

"All the more reason it could be a trap," Julie nodded, apparently vindicated. "Look at it. Out in the open, lightly guarded, sounds like an easy target. Sounds too good to be true is what it sounds like. Look at that attachment. Overhead drone photos. Guard strength and shift rotation schedules. That's either someone on the inside, some really awesome Intel, or..."

"Or a trap," Jack finished for him. "Look, I *know* all the reasons not to believe this email is authentic. I know all the risks we'll be taking, but a FEMA camp of over one hundred Christians in Jackson," he argued. "You know they are bound for the guillotine eventually if someone doesn't help them. Don't get me wrong, growing food and protecting our own is important, but it's been weighing on me, more and more. We should..."

"I say we help," Nikki announced. Every head turned to her. The meek young girl who had appeared in Franklin dragging a wounded, bleeding Julie in the spring, had blossomed over the summer into a confident, vibrant young woman. In fact, Nikki Valentine had worked as hard as any of them tending the garden, and trained harder than anyone had expected, with weapons and unarmed. She had put on 10 pounds of muscle and 100 pounds of confidence. She was also no longer afraid to speak her mind to a group with much more worldly experience. "You people are the most resourceful, competent men and women I have ever met. We are only six, but we are the *Sword of David*. And yes, Julie Hesterman, I said we! I don't think it was a coincidence you chose the name of a giant slaying king. Those with the ability to help, also have the responsibility. You taught me that, Julie," she concluded with a resolute glare.

"Well, that settles it for me," Rebecca nodded. "I'm in."

"I go where Becca goes," David replied.

"Crops are in," Anna added. "What else have we got to do?"

"Well...." Jack started to reply.

"Besides that," she smiled, patting his cheek.

'If the ladies are all in, how can I say no?" Julie sighed. "What the heck. All this farming has made me fat and lazy. What's your plan, boss?"

"People in our line of work never expect to live forever, Julie," Jack pointed out. "I wager our chances haven't improved under the WZC, but I have already a couple ideas I'd like to run by everyone. It's not going to be as simple as our raid in Franklin, but..."

***

"Looks clear," Julie said, handing Jack the binos.

They were in the wood line, overlooking a large, white board farmhouse in rural Madison County, about a mile South of Highway 198 and just north of the South Forked Deer River. They had been on the road for four days. In the world before the Event and the Anunnaki, Jack and the group would have piled into the Escalade, hit Interstate 840 West to 40 West, and driven the 125 miles to Jackson in a little under two hours. Without special permits however, traveling outside your own county limits had become a challenge under the World Zone Council. It would have been impossible given the fact that the Escalade was not only loaded with 6 people, (four of them wanted by the WZC Security forces) but also enough weapons, ammo, and food to carry out a revolution in Central America in the 80s. Their path had taken them South from Franklin to Spring Hill, then West to Centerville, Linden, Decaturville, and Scotts Hill. It was all travelled on back roads and driven after 11PM with head lights off, using night vision goggles. They hid in whatever cover they could find, sleeping during the day.

The farmhouse was out in the middle a field in Nowhere USA. Perfect spot for Christian freedom fighters to meet and plan the raid on a FEMA detention camp. Perfect spot for an ambush as well, if they weren't on their guard.

"Pretty good spot," Jack said, voicing his appreciation. "They'll see anyone coming from any direction for 500 yards."

"They'll see us coming, all right," Julie remarked. "We're a day later than we expected. Think they waited?"

"They knew it might take longer than anticipated," Jack shrugged.

"So, what do you think, boss?" Julie asked. They had been laying in the wood line watching the house for the last six hours, while the rest of the group hid 200 yards away in a thick copse of trees along the river. They'd seen no signs of movement other than one lone female who'd gone out to a nearby shed and stayed only a few minutes.

"Stick to the plan," Jack said. "We wait until dark and give our signal, (*three flashes from a white lens*) and see if they answer correctly. (*Four return flashes from a red lensed flashlight*) You go meet them, *(that had been a very heated debate among the group*) signal back the "all clear", and we go see what's what."

That was a slight deviation from what they'd discussed with the *Army of God* by email. After their four-flash reply, they were supposed to drive on up to the farmhouse. Jack would have none of that, however. Perfect way to get the *Sword of David* all in one nice little swoop, if it was indeed a trap. When Julie was satisfied that they were on the up and up, he'd signal back (*two flashes followed by a fifteen second pause, then two more*) Anything other than that reply and they would break contact, fade into the night, and hit the farmhouse from the north side just before daybreak to free him, or avenge him. That had stirred another heated debate. Julie had been for the group just disappearing into oblivion and letting him figure a way out. Nikki would have *none* of that. Neither would Jack or the rest of the group. "I will leave no fallen comrade behind" were not just words from a *Hooah* Soldiers Creed poster. Not to "Blackjack" Braedan, and not to the *Sword of David* either.

"That's four," Julie nodded, as his signal was returned almost immediately from an upstairs window of the farmhouse. "Wish me luck, boss."

"I'll pray, instead," Jack replied, laying a hand on his shoulder. "I'll be watching with the .308 until you reach the porch. You have 30 minutes Julie, then we are coming in hard and fast at daybreak no matter what, so make it quick."

"I got this," Julie smiled. "Hey, umm Jack, if this goes south..."

"It won't."

"If it does," Julie said quietly, "Tell Nikki..."

"You love her, I know," Jack grinned. "Everyone knows. You two might as well admit it and get it over with."

"That obvious, huh?" Julie sighed sheepishly.

"Get moving, Staff Sergeant," Jack said. "You can tell her yourself in half an hour."

"I'm Ruth," the woman said, extending her hand to Jack. She was in her mid-to-late thirties, about five-foot-six, short cropped brown hair, with unassuming features except for her winning smile. "Not my real name, of course. Security. Those two gentlemen are Jacob and Seth," she said pointing to the only other people in the house from *Army of God*. "Also, code names."

Julie had reported all clear within ten minutes of entering the farmhouse. Jack had signaled the Escalade and they went forward to the rendezvous, hopeful but still on guard.

The two men inclined their head in acknowledgement, no handshakes. The one on the right was just under six feet, lean build, thick beard streaked with gray, and a buzzed haircut. He was dressed in jeans, heavy boots, and an OD green military shirt. He carried an M4 carbine and had a huge .357 Colt Python on his belt. Jack's experienced eye could tell he had been military, with at least a couple tours overseas. It was in the way he held himself, relaxed, but alert. The other man was probably not older than eighteen or twenty, with sandy hair and features that were once soft, but had been hardened by the last few months after the Event. He carried a lever action Marlin 30-30. He was a bundle of nerves, caressing the Marlin's stock, his eyes shifting back and forth now that his group was outnumbered and outgunned.

"Pleased to meet you, *Ruth*," Jack replied, taking her hand. Firm grip. She had a military look about her as well. "I'm..."

"That's *Adam*," Julie replied for him with a grin. "The red-head is *Eve*. The old guy is *Moses,* of course. That's *Leah*," he said, meaning Becca, "and the pixie is *Mary*."

"And you are...?" Moses/David asked curiously.

"*Luke,* of course," grinned the ex-Delta Force medic.

David wanted to be upset, slightly, but he was more please that Julie could remember so many Biblical names off the top of his head, and he didn't mind Moses so much on second thought. The old part...well, he'd let it pass...for now.

"Sorry for the deviation in plans, *Ruth*," Adam/Jack apologized. "We didn't really know what we would be walking into."

"No big deal," she shrugged. "I'm glad you took precautions. Makes me feel a little better about this entire plan."

"You weren't in favor of us coming, were you," Eve/Anna said. It was not a question.

"Oh, I'm glad for the help," Ruth nodded, "We aren't as strong as the Texas bunch, even after Texarkana, but reaching out to anyone is a gamble nowadays. Welcome to Jackson. There's supper in the kitchen. We were expecting you yesterday. *Luke* told me why you took so long. Made me feel even better about you guys, if it matters. You can stack your long guns against the wall. Keep your side arms. I won't be offended. After you've eaten, we'll get down to business."

Even warmed up, the venison steaks and fried potatoes hit the spot after four days on the road eating MREs. "So, where's the rest of your group?" asked Jack as he finished, wiping his mouth, and taking another sip of warm coffee.

"Right to it, I like that," Ruth nodded. "Got antsy when you didn't show yesterday and went to another safe house. Eggs in one basket and all that. Rest of the group will be in here in the morning. I'll send *Jacob* to let them know you've arrived. We'll go over the plan in the morning, hash out details, then head to the FEMA camp after dark and see what's what. We can make small talk for a bit, but the less we know about each other the safer it will be for all of us. For obvious reasons. I would like to know however, in as nonspecific a way as you can manage, what experience you have at this sort of thing. Other than Franklin, I mean."

"And I'd kinda' like to know what the Arkansas *Army of God* is doing in Jackson," asked Jack curiously. "Email didn't really get into that."

"Hopefully rescuing my husband," Ruth said, with the pain in her voice clear. "Otherwise, we'd have stayed west of the Mississippi."

"Well then, me and *Luke*, I'd say we have about twenty tours between us," Jack assured her. "Not our first dance. *Moses* and *Leah* were both gunfighters in their day. Still have what it takes. I've seen it firsthand. *Eve* and *Mary* are new to this sort of stuff, but we've trained them well so...if your bunch can bring half that to the table, and your Intel is good, I'm actually feeling a little better about this."

"Two tours myself," Ruth replied. "*Jacob* was a door kicker in the Marines. *Seth* is my.... *Seth's* only experience is hunting but he's a good shot. The rest that will be joining us don't have as grand a resume as you guys, but...they are all still alive and uncaught by the WZC. Can't say that about a lot of folks."

"If we are finished with the "get to know you," Ruth said, "It's gonna be a long day tomorrow. Help me clear these dishes? There's a big room upstairs. Hope you brought bed rolls. *Seth* and I will take first watch. We'll wake two of you later. Who wants next?"

"Are you asleep, babe?" Anna whispered, her head resting on his shoulder.

"Praying," Jack replied, stroking her hair.

Julie and Nikki had just started their watch. It had to be close to midnight. Dave and Becca would be next. He and Anna had last shift. They'd wake Ruth just before sunrise, so she'd be awake to observe her group coming and look for anything *"out of the way,"* she called it.

"I just wanted to tell you I love you, Jack Braedan," she said, raising up on an elbow. All he could make out of his wife in the dim light was a tangle of long braids and unruly waves of hair. She'd wanted to cut it all off for this mission, but he'd convinced her that if she went all Celtic Warrior Queen, it'd be much more intimidating. Maybe even paint half her face blue, weave in some bones, and bits of jewelry. She'd almost cried with relief, but he had been serious. She really was his warrior queen. "And I'm proud of you. There hasn't been a single moment since you returned to Franklin that I haven't thanked God that you came back into my life."

"I love you too, Anna," Jack replied, reaching up to caress her cheek.

"Jack," she said, leaning down to whisper in his ear "Do you...do think you can be quiet?"

Dave and Rebecca were across the room. Dave was snoring softly.

"If I need to be," he replied.

"You do," his Warrior Queen whispered, leaning over to kiss him.

"Here they come," Ruth announced. She was looking out the front window through Jack's binos. Two vehicles were approaching, one a late model Land Rover with brush guards, lights, and big mudding tires and the other, was a newer Nissan Tundra four-door. As they pulled up to the house, a dozen men piled out, armed to the teeth, and dressed like some nightmarish caricature of a redneck militia group... If they were WZC, this day wasn't going to start well. Not well at all.

"We're good," Ruth nodded.

Jack clicked the .308 back on safe.

It got crowded quickly in the small main room of the farmhouse, even though half the newly arrived group stayed outside and spread themselves out in a defensive perimeter. The only two that were offered introductions by Ruth, was the leader, made obvious by the deference shown him by Ruth and the rest of the *Army of God*. She introduced him as *Judah*.

"Robert Sawyer," he said, taking Jack's hand. "My friends call me Bobby. Glad to meet you."

Jack raised an eyebrow at the breach of security they'd established.

"WZC knows who I am," Bobby shrugged. "They been looking for me before there was a World Zone, and I figured it might put you at ease a little bit. We really are glad to meet you boys and girls," he added with a grin.

The only other *Army of God* Ruth introduced was *Samson*. He was six and a half feet of muscle, dark skinned, with eyes full of thunder and a grip of iron. Until he smiled and said, "Pleased to meet you," and warmth folded around you like a blanket on a cold winter night.

"Might as well just wear your jersey," Jack grinned. "We met once when you came to Afghanistan with the USO in '15. You flew in our chopper to Jalalabad."

"Hey, I think I remember you," he laughed, inspecting Jack's face closely. "Quick draw with the paper bag when I tossed up my lunch?"

"Happens to most everyone," Jack grinned. "You also made me a cool two hundred with your four sacks against Jacksonville last January. Sorry it didn't work out the next week."

"Seems like another life, brother," *Samson* shrugged. "Hope you tithed out of that?"

"That was the old Jack," Braedan smiled. "In present company, we won't discuss what I did with it. What Old Jack, did."

Julie chucked at the memory. When both Nikki and Anna gave them a disapproving glare, Julie's chuckle quickly turned it into a cough, and he found something on his boot that needed attention.

"*Samson* is kinda hard to miss," Sawyer nodded. "That's why he stays out of sight mostly. We only bring him out with the blitz package.

"Rest of the time, I run the preschool," *Samson* laughed. His laugh was infectious. The kids probably adored him.

"What say we make some coffee and get down to business," Sawyer suggested. "Even with the Lord's help, this day will be full of peril. *Samson,* you want to open with a prayer before we get started?"

"Abba Father," the huge man began, bowing his head. The room followed suit.

The FEMA camp was the city of Jackson's former YMCA sports complex. The detainees were held on the softball field in a dozen, tightly packed Air Force frame and canvas tents. Four guard towers had been constructed around the makeshift camp. Two in the outfield and one each adjacent to the 1st and 3rd baseline dugouts. *Army of God's* Intel said the concessions stand behind home plate was the kitchen, with the announcer's box as the Sergeant of the Guard's headquarters. The fence around the field had been reenforced with three strands of concertina wire. Intel also said that there was a nine-man relief in a nearby gymnasium.

The nearest WZC police station was six miles to the east, with a reaction time of maybe 15 minutes under normal conditions. Those "normal" conditions would be delayed tonight when a detachment of the *Army of God* attacked the Jackson Power and Electric relay station on the north side of town, and made a lot of noise doing it, just five minutes before H-Hour. After tonight, World Zone Council security forces would be swarming West Tennessee. Whether their mission succeeded or not, this was going to be a one-shot deal.

It was almost two hours after midnight, the waning hours of the current shift. Twelve hours on, twelve off, was a taxing duty over an extended period. This was the last day out of seven for this crew. Three hours before their relief began to stir, before their entire crew was rotated out at 6AM, and *The Army of God* and *Sword of David* were counting on it being the low point of this shift's watchfulness before they were relieved.

The soft "*hoot*" of a Tennessee barn owl sounded to the west. To the guards on duty, it would now be a familiar call. An *Army of God* sympathizer had been out for a few hours each night for the last three nights, providing the sounds of the nocturnal hunter. To the assault force, it meant the snipers were in position. When it sounded again, it would be one minute until the "distraction" at the relay station. When it sounded the third and final time, it would signal police were responding and it was time to begin the assault.

The snipers would initiate the attack, picking off the watch tower guards with fabricated suppressors. David and Rebecca were one of those teams, Seth and his spotter were another. The other two teams were nameless *Army of God* members. Jack and Robert Sawyer were the leaders of the eight-person assault force, which would breach the compound with a small C4 and detcord charge, blowing a six-foot hole in the center field fence. Their signal would be when another charge blew the power panel for the field's lights. Ruth and Jacob were a part of the assault, as well as Anna and three other *Army of God* members. Julie and Nikki, along with another young man, *Michael*, would storm the stairs leading up to the announcer's booth and secure it. *Samson* and his four-man team would hit the gym, eliminating any reaction force.

Twenty-three people in all, had spent the last two hours getting quietly into position after their six-vehicle convoy had traveled into Jackson, using three separate routes. They easily avoided all checkpoints and WZC patrol vehicles in route to the FEMA camp. The *Army of God* obviously had a sympathizer or even a member in Jackson WZC security. There were still good people in the world, even after all that had happened in the last six months. As they waited, Jack silently prayed that brave soul would be shielded by the angels after tonight.

A second *"hoot."* Jack's trained hearing detected a muffled rumble to the north sixty seconds later and then the very faint crack of gunfire. No one else seemed to notice. They were probably distracted by the blood pounding in their ears in anticipation of what was to come. Through the trees, he could see one of the guards in the tower along first base line stand up. The guard lit a cigarette and leaned against the half wall of his tower, blowing out a cloud of smoke.

A third *"hoot."* A quiet *"snap."* The guard twisted and tumbled over the wall. Several *"snaps"* quickly followed, as *Ruth* and *Jacob* sprinted from cover and emplaced their charge on the centerfield fence. They rushed back to the relative safety of the tree line just as the charge on the field's light panel plunged everything into darkness. Then, their breeching charge split the night with light and a thunderous boom, and silence was no longer necessary.

It had begun.

The assault team rushed through the breech and into the compound. Sawyer and his wingman ran towards the gate next to the third base dugout below the west tower to cut the lock. It would be to this exit they would herd the detainees. The other members of the assault team, Jack and Anna included, began rushing into the tents, rousting the surprised and frightened prisoners, urging them to run as fast as their feet would carry them to the east. Three blocks away on Sycamore Avenue, two stolen school buses would be pulling into the vacant lot beside the old First Presbyterian Church. It was now one of Jackson's many *Eternal Peace Temples*. They would remain there for exactly 20 minutes. After that, the escaped Christians would have to trust in the Lord to guide them to safety.

Of the entire plan, this part required the most faith, especially for the bus drivers and their armed escort. Yellow Bluebird buses would make an awkward, suspicious target at 2AM, but the First Presbyterian had been chosen carefully. Sycamore Avenue was not any logical route to the YMCA from either the power relay station or the WZC security barracks. With any luck, and the grace of God, the buses would be well out of the city before 3AM and in route to *Army of God* safe houses.

All seemed to be going well, surprisingly well, until a guard in the 3rd base watchtower popped up and sprayed Sawyer and his wingman with a SAW light machine gun. They both went down under the hail of bullets. He turned and began firing long bursts indiscriminately into the tents located below, and the scene descended into bedlam as everyone exposed scattered or went down under the withering fire. Jack dropped to one knee and emptied an entire thirty round magazine from his H&K at the guard. The man disappeared out of sight. Jack reloaded and emptied another magazine into tower, his howl of rage drowned by steady three-round bursts of 5.56-millimeter bullets.

When he didn't reappear, he ejected the empty magazine and slapped in another. Their rescue had descended into nightmare. There were multiple casualties laying on the blood-soaked grass of the softball field. He could hear moans of pain mixed with cries of terror coming from some of the tents. There was a muffled sound of a firefight coming from the nearby gym. A flash-bang went off in the announcer's booth above, blowing out the windows in a shower of Plexiglas. "Anna!" he cried, frantically searching for his wife in the chaos.

"Over here!" she replied, emerging from cover. She was supporting a wounded *Army of God* fighter. He was bleeding from several wounds; one pantleg was drenched black with blood from crotch to boot. He collapsed as Jack ran toward them. Unable to hold the man up any longer, Anna fell to her knees beside him. Jack dropped to her side and checked the man's pulse.

Nothing.

"He pushed me down when the firing started," Anna cried, tears streaming down her cheeks.

"He's gone, Anna," Jack said gently closing the man's eyes, then helped his shaken wife to her feet. "Get them moving. Make it quick. I'm going to check on Sawyer."

She nodded and wiped her eyes, once again his Warrior Queen. "I'm good."

He kissed her quickly and ran.

The gate was open. Thank God. Sawyer was leaning against the fence, still alive but just barely. He coughed blood as Jack dropped to his side. He'd taken at least three rounds to the chest. His wingman was dead, half his face blown away. Sawyer coughed more blood. "*Adam*."

"It's Jack," Braedan said, putting pressure on the worst of his wounds. Blood seeped through his fingers. "Jack Braedan."

"Get them out of here, Jack," Robert Sawyer replied, closing his eyes. "I'm...just gonna rest..." He trailed off. Jack checked his pulse. The leader of the Arkansas *Army of God* had fought the good fight and finished his race.

Jack lowered him gently to the ground. Maybe ten minutes had passed since the raid started. It seemed like hours. Frightened detainees began streaming by, herded by Anna, *Ruth,* and *Jacob*. *Jacob* urged them to follow him as *Ruth* knelt beside Sawyer. She smoothed his hair, sobbing quietly, then took his weapon and handed it to the man standing behind her. He pulled back the charging handle, making sure there was a round chambered, then helped her back to her feet.

"I'm *Boaz,*" he said quietly, offering his hand to Jack. *Ruth's* husband, of course. Jack wiped his hand on his pant leg. *Boaz* took it, unmindful of the blood, and helped him to his feet.

"*Adam,*" Jack replied, just as things went from bad to worse. Sirens in the distance. Too soon. Much too soon.

"Jack! Little help here!" Julie shouted. He and Nikki were supporting *Michael* in a two-person seat carry. His right foot dangled horribly, twisted inward at an angle it had no business being in. He was pale from shock. "Misstep on the stairs," Julie explained. The young man screamed in pain and passed out, as he and Nikki lowered him to the ground. "We need something to make a splint, maybe some internal damage. Won't know until I get his boot off," he finished pulling a knife.

"We don't have time," *Boaz* said. The sirens are much closer now. "Help me get him up."

"I'll carry *Michael,*" announced *Samson*, arriving on the scene, and quickly taking it in. He had a bandage wrapped around one massive thigh, seeping blood. There was only one other man with him. Jack raised a questioning eyebrow and *Samson* shook his head sadly.

"We can't move him until its set!" Julie argued. "A bone splinter could pierce the anterior tibia artery and he'd bleed out before we get to the trucks."

Boaz flipped the selector on his carbine to fire. "Then, step back," he said sadly.

"No!" Nikki shouted. "We don't leave anyone behind, and we don't shoot our wounded!"

"They'll make him talk, *Mary,*" *Ruth* said softly, new tears coming. The aftermath of the Texarkana disaster still weighed heavily on the *Army of God*. "Better this than torture and the guillotine."

Tension mounted as the group argued back and forth, and the sirens slowly got louder. But a calmness had settled over Jack. Couldn't move the young man, couldn't shoot him. There was no earthly option remaining. He suddenly knew in his heart what needed to be done.

"Quiet!" he shouted, as he knelt beside the unconscious *Michael.* He placed his hands gently on the young man's horribly injured leg and began to pray.

"Abba Father," he said, lifting his face to the heavens, "You are the great physician. Through your power, Yeshua Hamashiach healed lepers with His touch."

Samson laid a massive hand on Jack's shoulder, "Through your power, He raised Lazarus from the dead."

"We are unworthy," Jack added. "But your servant, what is his name, *Ruth*?"

"Ethan," she replied quietly, moving to place a hand on Jack's other shoulder. "His name is Ethan."

"Your servant, Ethan," Jack continued, "still has great works to do in your name. We are stained with blood, the blood of Jesus, the blood of your only son and our Redeemer Yeshua HaMashiah, who has washed us clean. We ask you, Abba, in His name, to heal your servant, Ethan." At the mention of his name, Ethan's eyes flew open. He looked up at Jack in surprise.

"Get up, Ethan, we need to be going," Jack said softly, standing up and offering him his hand, he pulled Ethan to his feet.

Boaz and *Ruth* hugged each other. Nikki laughed. Anna was crying. Julie just stared in wonder as Ethan stood there looking confused over what all the fuss was about.

"Well, let's go then," Ethan shrugged, and headed off at a trot.

Samson turned to Jack and placed both hands on his shoulder, his eyes filled with wonder, then pulled him into a crushing bear hug. "Brother," he laughed, setting him back on his feet, "I don't think Ethan is the only one with great works left to do. Praise God! Wait until the kids hear about this!"

"We have to get back to them first," Ruth said. "Shall we?" she asked and trotted out the gate.

The others followed.

Chapter Thirteen

New Family

"Cassini just nuked Riyadh," Dave informed them from the media room. "Counting the suitcase bomb that went off in LA, that's four in the last month."

"Mumbai?" Rebecca asked.

"Five," Dave corrected, turning off the television and joining them in the kitchen. "Smells good. What are we having tonight?"

"Chicken casserole," Rebecca replied.

"Again?" David sighed, though everyone knew it was his favorite.

It was the middle of October, six months since fate had brought them together. The group hadn't been outside the immediate area of the Sanctuary in two weeks, since they'd returned from assisting the *Army of God* Arkansas unit on the FEMA camp raid. It had taken them almost a week to make the one-hundred-and-fifty-mile journey back to Franklin. Between dodging the swarms of World Council Zone army patrols their raid had produced, bypassing roadblocks, and avoiding wandering bands of *Reavers,* (that's what GNN had dubbed the armed bands of scavengers roaming the south and Midwest), it had been a long, arduous journey. They'd helped release over fifty Christian prisoners, but the cost had been high. Half a dozen of the Robert Sawyer's Arkansas followers had lost their lives freeing *Boaz* and the rest.

"It's getting cold out," Julie announced, coming in from the Sanctuary foyer. He and Jack had been *'Up Top'* checking the western perimeter of the Braedan property, since Camera #12 was on the fritz. "It'll likely snow in a couple days." He leaned down and kissed Nikki's cheek, as she sat at the table patching the knee on a pair of jeans. "Glad I decided to get baptized last week before all the ash and dust started clogging up the skies and dropping temperatures."

"I'm glad you quit fighting it altogether, Julie Hesterman," Nikki smiled, not looking up from the jeans.

"And what was I supposed to do?" Julie asked, sitting down beside her, giving her another quick kiss. "After watching Jack pray over *Michael* and heal his broken leg?"

"Ah, twisted his ankle is all," Jack said, coming into the kitchen after hanging up his H & K and removing his boots.

"For the last time, Jack Braedan," Anna scolded from the kitchen. "Stop selling the Holy Spirit short. We all saw, Nikki, Julie, and me. You trying to downplay your part won't change what happened."

"Kid was unconscious," Julie nodded. "Probably never going to walk again *if* he had even survived."

"Just get used to it, Jack," Anna said, bringing in plates and setting them on them table. "You are strong in the Spirit and the Power of His might. Whew," she said, wrinkling her nose after kissing him on the cheek. "Strong is right. Go take a shower before supper. You have time. And no, we don't have *that* much time," she finished, before he could even suggest she join him. "And do me a favor. Trim your beard," she ordered. "You're not a prophet."

"I'm still praying on that," Jack grinned, heading toward their room.

After Jack returned from his shower, the group said blessings and they all sat down to eat. "Has there been any more news on the internet about the Two Witnesses in Jerusalem?" Julie asked no one in particular.

True to the Word of God, only a few days after the thwarted attack on Israel, two men had suddenly appeared before the Wailing Wall, preaching for Israel to come to repentance. It hadn't even made the news for several weeks. This was all due to the astounding story of the sudden destruction of the combined armies and air forces of Russia, Iran, and all the allies they'd managed to con into attacking. Combined with the massive cleanup effort required to find and bury all the dead bodies, the two lone street preachers hardly registered on the GNN radar. That is until the crowds they started attracting began to hinder construction of the new Temple.

When Israeli and WZC police attempted to remove them, fire came down from the sky and literally burned the police officers to ash. For two days the video went viral on the internet and news, as well as a dozen other videos of people filming the duo as they preached and prophesied. Most amazing was that each cell phone captured the pair in the language of its owner. GNN finally forced both stories from the airway with an explanation of incendiary grenades that went off accidentally during their attempted arrest and clever dubbing of the soundtracks by a subversive Christian group. Why no second attempt at arrest was ever made or how the group managed to dub audio on a dozen different cell phones...well...GNN was ignoring the story, so it just fell from public view. It hadn't rained a single drop in Israel since their appearance and any attempt to touch them resulted in the untimely death of police officers.

Cassini and Prince Azalil were strangely silent on the matter. In fact, there had been no Anunnaki presence in Jerusalem since their appearance. Anunnaki craft had left many of the World Zones capitals. Returned to their own world it was reported, to bring back more scientists and doctors to help with the continued effort to heal the planet. Prince Azalil remained however, along with his two hundred most trusted Captains and a few of the pyramid-shaped ships.

"Not since the *Army of God* posted that cell phone video link on their web site three days ago," David shrugged. Some WZC official finally got the bright idea to just take them out with sniper fire from a safe distance. He also thought it would be a good idea to film it all. The police sniper fired at least a ten-round magazine at the pair, each round somehow missing its mark to strike the wall behind them. Until one of the men turned toward the sniper's nest and the camera, pointing his finger. The last few seconds of video feed were of the sniper, spotter, and several others in the room, screaming in pain as they were consumed by flames. How *Army of God* managed to get the video was nothing short of a miracle itself. "Why?"

"Just something I was reading this morning," Julie replied. "Cassini is going to have them killed eventually."

"Not for a while yet," Rebecca replied. "Three more years, in fact."

"How are they going to stand there right where they are building the Temple for three more years?" Julie asked.

"By the Power of the Most High," David shrugged. "Jack isn't the only one who has it," he teased.

Jack let the remark pass. The chicken pot pie was delicious!

"Look, everyone," Nikki interrupted softly, before he could dig deeper into the subject of the Two Witnesses, "I've been meaning to bring this up since last week."

"We have," Julie added, taking her hand.

"Well," Nikki said hesitantly. "It's nothing really..."

"Go on, dear," Anna encouraged her. Nikki had been pensive for the last few days.

"It's just that, well, Julie asked me to marry him and...."

"Praise the Lord!" Jack laughed, getting up from his seat to shake Julie's hand and give Nikki a quick hug. "It's about time."

After the congratulations had died down and everyone had toasted the couple with tea or water, Nikki continued. "But I want my grandparents to be there," she said quietly.

That dampened the mood a little.

"It's a long way to Fayetteville," Jack replied. "Under the circumstances, that is."

"Well, I've been giving it some thought," Julie replied. "I could drive down ..."

"Not by yourself," Jack and David said together.

"Or...or" Julie continued, "We could *all* make the trip. The caddy would fit us easily. It is really getting cold out after dark. You know as well as I do, Jack, untrained *Reavers* and trained soldiers as well will huddle up at night and stay out of the weather. We could leave around 2AM, be there before sunrise, get married, wait until dark, and then make the drive back. No problem."

"Who's going to marry you?" Jack inquired. "Assuming we can do that."

"We were thinking of asking you, Jack," Nikki smiled.

Jack almost spit out his tea. "Me? You can't be serious?"

"You do everything else," Julie grinned. "Break prisoners free, heal busted legs, and convert heathens... Saying a few words should be a piece of cake. What do you say?"

"I did it for you, Jack," David reminded him. "Just repeat after me, 'We are gathered here today in the presence of God and these witnesses...'"

"Oh, why not?" Jack smiled. "I think this calls for a toast, a real toast. I'll get the bourbon. I know you're only nineteen, Nikki, but my bunker, my rules."

"I'll be twenty in a month," Nikki smiled.

"I'll get the glasses," Dave nodded.

"Just five, David," Anna said quietly. "I won't be drinking."

"You okay, hon?" Jack said, looking at his wife curiously.

"Feeling a little queasy. That's all," Anna replied. "Pot Pie not sitting well. Oh, go get the Jim Beam and quit worrying over me. I'll have a watered-down shot, but that's all. And everyone else, no celebrating too vigorously. Looks like we need to convert one of those bunk beds rooms to a double tomorrow, before we leave for Franklin."

"Looks quiet," Jack said, observing the Valentine farm through NVGs. "Lights on in the back of the house."

It was 0630. Still about twenty minutes or so until sunrise. They had left Franklin in the Cadillac just after 2AM. The back of the caddy was loaded down with foodstuffs just in case the Valentines were running low on supplies. They had assured her that they were doing fine, but Nikki hadn't talked to them since before Jackson. Like everyone else, she hadn't used her cell since the raid, afraid of the WZC techs tracking them.

The ride down had been uneventful. They'd taken their time, slow and cautious, moving along back roads as much as they could and avoiding the main highway. They'd passed only a few abandoned cars and seen no sign of *Reavers* or WZC patrols. Julien had been correct when he'd said they'd probably be huddled up or inside to avoid the cold. It was hovering right around freezing. The night was thick with clouds, otherwise there would have been a heavy frost on the ground. Julie would get his snow soon. You could almost smell it coming.

"What do you think?" asked Jack. "Wait until sun rise or move on in?"

"Grandpa has probably been up an hour already," Nikki replied. "Nana will be soon if she isn't up already. Drive up lights on. He'll likely be on the front porch with his double barrel before we get halfway down the drive. It'll be okay once he sees me."

"You're the boss," Jack shrugged. "I just hope he doesn't fire off a blast before he sees it's you."

"He's not excitable," Nikki replied. "Drive in slow. It'll be fine."

They loaded back up in the Caddy and drove the final one hundred yards with headlights on. As she'd predicted he would be, Nikki's grandfather was on the porch before they pulled to a stop, shotgun pointed at the windshield.

"Ain't nothing here worth your life," he shouted, as Jack turned off the engine. "Just turn on around and there won't be any trouble."

"Papa, it's me?" Nikki said, opening the rear passenger door and stepping out so he could see her. "It's okay."

"Nichole?" he asked, lowering the shotgun, but keeping it on a low ready.

"It's me, Papa," she nodded, her voice catching at the end. She ran to him, and he almost dropped the shotgun as she flung herself into his arms. She hadn't seen him since a week before her father, Henry's only son, and her family had been murdered on Highway 106. Their reunion was an emotional one. The rest of the group waited patiently while they cried and hugged it out. When Nikki's grief had run its course, she waved to them motioning them forward. "It's okay, Papa, these are my friends."

"Well, come on in," he said warily. "Get out of the cold."

"Let's go meet the Valentines," Jack said. "Just remember, emotions are likely to run a little...well... high when they find out why we're here. Be on your best behavior, Julie."

"It'll be fine, Julie," Anna assured him, patting him on the shoulder from the back seat. "You're a good man. Just don't mention that you two have been sharing a room. Even if you were sleeping on the top bunk. You have been, haven't you?"

"Yes, ma'am," he nodded.

"You keep those ma'am's and sirs flowing. It'll help," Dave nodded.

The group exited the caddy and made doubly sure Mr. Valentine could see they were slinging their weapons, as they walked up to the front porch where Nikki and her grandfather waited. The men had trimmed up their beards, nice and neat, and Rebecca had given all of them a good haircut. Another of her seemingly endless talents.

"Papa, these are my friends," Nikki said as they approached. "That's Jack and Anna. That's David and Rebecca. And that's Julian, the man I told you about."

"Let's take this inside," her grandfather replied, still eyeing them warily. Especially Julie. "Your Nana will want to meet them too. Come on, folks. Coffee is on. I'll have to make another pot though. Been out of sugar for a month. Black will have to do."

"I think we can help with that," Jack informed him.

"I'm on it," Julie replied.

"I'll get it, Julie," Jack insisted, "you go on in and meet Nana."

When Jack came into the house a few minutes later, everyone was gathered in the living room. He leaned his H & K against the wall where everyone else had placed their weapons and waited. "I've got sugar and powdered milk. There are a lot of other supplies in the SUV."

"Lord bless you," an older woman said. Nana, obviously. She and Nikki were on the couch, still hugging, though the tears seemed to have subsided. Dressed only in a robe and slippers, she hadn't been up long. Nikki's grandmother was possibly in her late fifties, brown hair streaked with gray, and petite like her granddaughter. Southerners would say, "She has aged well." Jack could see Nikki in another thirty years. If they survived this Tribulation, Julie was going to be a lucky man. "Henry likes his coffee black, but I've missed a little sugar in mine horribly."

"Where can I put this, Mrs. Valentine?" asked Jack.

"I'll take it, honey," she replied, accepting the box he was holding. "You have a seat and take a load off. And it's Helen."

Anna patted the cushion beside her. She was in a love seat in the corner. Rebecca sat in a chair with David behind her. Henry Valentine was leaning up against the door jamb leading into the kitchen, eyeing the group. At least, Jack assumed it was the kitchen since that's where Helen disappeared with the sugar and milk. Nikki remained on the couch and Julie was standing at parade rest as far from her as the room allowed.

"You folks all from Franklin?" he asked.

"I am, sir," Jack replied, taking his seat beside Anna. "Anna is too, and the Hitchcock's. Julie is from New Jersey originally."

"Yankee, huh?" Henry snorted.

"Papa, be nice." Nikki said.

"I'm just asking, Nichole," Henry said.

"Yes sir, New Jersey, sir," Julian replied. "Hackensack. But I've been stationed at Fort Bragg for the last four years."

"Nikki said you were a solider," Henry nodded.

"We both were, sir," Jack added. "Until the *Event*."

"So, you boys are deserters?" he asked.

"I swore my oath to the constitution," Jack replied. "When Julie told me what was...."

"No need to explain yourself," Henry interrupted, somberly. "Can't say I much blame you. Things turning out the way they have, you were lucky for the warning. Julian, is it? Relax boy. I got out as a corporal in '91. I was a DAT. Dumb Ass Tanker. Did four years at Ft. Stewart with the 24th. Saw some action in Desert Storm, but I guess Nikki has already told you that."

"She did, sir." Jack nodded. "The 24th was a fine outfit."

"It's Henry, not sir," he replied. "Tank gunners aren't sir, even in today's army. Can I get you a chair Julian? Any farther away from me and you'll be out on the porch?"

"I'm fine, sir...Henry," Julian replied.

"Suit yourself," Henry shrugged. "I said relax. I'm not going to shoot you. Not before breakfast anyway," he muttered.

Julian went pale.

"Papa be nice," Nikki insisted again, walking over to go take Julie's hand. "He saved my life."

"Kept you away from us for six months, as well," Henry replied.

"Papa, I stayed with them because, well...," Nikki tried to explain, "Because well...."

"I have a pretty good idea why you stayed." Henry replied. "Can't really blame you, but it hurt your Nana something fierce."

"Sir..." Julie began.

"We want to get married," Nikki interrupted.

"Do you now?" her grandfather asked, his eyes stabbing Julie like twin daggers.

"Sir," Julian said, finding his voice, "I love Nikki. We've come for your blessing if you'll give it. We're getting married, regardless."

"So, he does have a spine after all," Henry said grudgingly.

"Coffee is ready," Helen called from the kitchen. "I can't carry eight mugs. I'm afraid it's instant," Helen apologized as she poured each cup. "That's all they've had at the Food Mart for the last few months. Lord knows we're glad for even that."

"Thank you, Mrs. Valentine," Jack smiled. "There are two big containers of Maxwell House in the Caddy. We brought some other stuff as well. We aren't planning on heading back to Franklin until after dark if it's okay. We sure wouldn't want to impose on you for chow, as well. We brought plenty. There'll be leftovers."

"Bless you," Helen insisted again. "Sugar, coffee, *and* your own food? Nikki must have let on like we were paupers."

"If I may ask...Helen," David inquired, "what exactly *does* the Food Mart have? We haven't been into Franklin in quite some time."

"Don't want to be picked up in a WZC sweep, huh?" Henry surmised.

"Picked up again is more like it," David replied. "Jack... ummm... liberated us on the day after the *Event*."

"Did he now?" Henry asked. For just an instant, he seemed impressed.

"We rescued more from the FEMA camp in Jackson last month," Nikki said proudly.

"Don't tell me you were part of that madness, Nikki," Henry grumbled. "What are you folks, some sort of vigilantes?"

"We prefer to think of ourselves more like Soldiers of the Cross, Mr. Valentine," Julie corrected.

"A world of sheep and wolves needs sheepdogs, Papa," Nikki said defiantly.

Jack almost laughed. She'd definitely been hanging around Julie too much.

"Never took you for a sheepdog, Nichole," her grandfather replied. There was a note of pride in his voice however, and for the first time he almost smiled.

"This world has changed, Papa," she nodded. "I've changed with it."

"I can see that" Henry said. "So...are you folk's part of the *Army of God* then or that other bunch the *Sword of David*?"

"Well, actually, Henry," Jack said hesitantly, "We, all six of us, *are* the *Sword of David*."

"Outlaws according to the WZC," Henry sighed. "No wonder you haven't been into Franklin in a while. So, tell me how do outlaws come to my home bearing gifts?"

"I was blessed with a father who had some foresight," Jack replied. "We're pretty stocked up. Even for a long haul. Henry, we've already discussed this amongst the group. We've plenty of room at our place. You're welcome to come with us when we head back. And if I may ask, how have you avoided being picked up by World Zone sweeps? You're Christians. Real ones according to Nikki. Why aren't you rounded up already and in a camp?"

"We're small potatoes down here in Fayetteville, son." Henry shrugged. "Even Cassini and his Anunnaki aren't worried about folks like us. Yet. Not when the sheriff is a believer. And while I appreciate the offer," he continued, "I've lived in this house since I was born. It'll take more than a little thing like the Tribulation to run me off. If I understand my Bible son, which I do, one place is likely to be as the safe as the next. We're off the beaten path. For those that wander too close, I've got the double barrel. We've got a well for water, chickens for eggs, a few head of beef cattle. Come Spring, we will have a garden again. We'll do okay."

"Did you say you have eggs?" David grinned.

"That's one thing we have in abundance," Helen smiled, happy for the turn in conversation. "I'll start breakfast. Why don't you go back into the living room for a spell and leave me to it?"

"Do you mind if I help, Helen?" Anna asked. "We were cooped up in the SUV for hours."

"I'll help, as well," Rebecca. "If you don't mind."

"I don't mind a bit," Helen replied. "Nikki, show them where all the things are, while I go out to the chicken coop."

Nikki was about to protest when Henry chimed in, "Excellent idea. Julian can tell me why he thinks I should let him marry my little Nichole, without you around all moon eyed. You boys come as well. You can explain to me why you thought it was a good idea dragging my granddaughter around fighting the WZC."

"All right son let's hear it," Henry said, when the men had moved back to the living room with their coffee.

"I love her, Mr. Valentine," Julie began.

"Love?" Henry snorted. "More like hormones. You've known her for what, five months? Rescued her from *Reavers?* Innocent young woman saved from a fate worse than death, of course she's going to fall for you. Tell me why *you* think *you* love her. Other than her big blue eyes and pretty face."

"She saved my life, as well, sir," Julie replied. "Practically carried me to Jack's place while I was all shot up. She's smart, and funny, and strong. She helped me find the Lord. I guess that's the most important thing. Sir, I don't know what I can say to convince you. I just know I want her by my side for whatever time I have left on this earth."

"If I may, Henry?" Jack asked.

"Speak your piece," Henry nodded. "You are obviously the leader of this bunch."

"I've known Julie for over four years, sir." Jack began. "Fought beside him. Slept beside him in some of the crappiest places on God's earth. With the way the world has turned, you couldn't ask for a braver, more determined man to look after Nikki. Look, sir, I know it may have started out like you said. Nikki took to him because he saved her. He was wounded and she had something to take her mind off her family while she helped him heal. He helped her through a bad, bad time. We all did." Jack waved his hand to include David and Julie, "We've seen the worst of humanity and survived. David lost his legs in Desert Storm but found Rebecca. I buried my parents and found Anna in the same day. I think God planned those things, so we would find the helpmate He had in store for us. I have no doubt Julie was on Highway 106 at the exact moment when Nikki needed him, for the same reason. We all know how short life is. That it can be taken in an instant. We all know there's very little chance that we will live beyond the next few years. I think...I believe, God placed these women in our lives to give us the strength to endure, to remind us that there are still good things in this life. A reason to get up in the morning and keep going. To face what's coming with love in our hearts and not fear."

"You feel the same way, Julian, or is he putting words in your mouth?" Henry asked.

"I couldn't have said what is in my heart any better, sir," Julie replied quietly.

"And this business of dragging her off, attacking FEMA camps," Henry said. "This *Sword of David* nonsense."

"Sir, this world..." Jack began, but Henry cut him off.

"I want to hear it from him."

"Sir, all I can promise you is that I'll give my life protecting her," Julie replied hesitantly. "I believe... we all believe, Nikki included, that if you have the means and the ability to help someone, you also have the responsibility. I know this a dangerous world. Now more than ever. There is darkness all around us. Your Nikki is a light in that darkness. I was on the road to destruction until I found her. I know God brought her into my life, and I thank Him every day for her. If I have just one day left on this earth, I know I want to spend it as her husband. Loving her, as Christ loves the Church. I love her, sir. I don't know what else I can say."

Henry stared into his coffee, weighing his words. After a long moment of silence, he finally spoke. "I suppose there's nothing I can do to stop this, short of tying her up and running you folks off at gunpoint," he sighed. "I'll be frank with you. It hurts, bringing her back to us and knowing you're just going to take her away again, but I'm honest enough to admit she'll be safer with you than here. Ah well, for what it's worth, I'll give my blessing. You taught her how to shoot one of those things yet?" he asked, nodding at all the weapons lined up against his living room wall.

"She's a natural," Julie smiled.

"Nikki takes to anything she puts her mind to," Henry nodded. "If she's set on having you as her husband, there wouldn't be a thing I could do to stop her anyway. Welcome to the family," he said, walking over to take Julian's hand. "But we aren't finished talking yet, son." He promised. "When is this wedding gonna be?"

"Today, sir," Julie replied. "She wants to get married here."

"And the preacher?" he asked. "Not too many real ones left around these parts. Unless you want one of those *Eternal Peace Temple* blasphemers to officiate?"

"I'm not a preacher, sir," Jack replied. "But they've asked me to say the words."

"You're pretty good at talking," Henry nodded. "I'll give you that. I guess you'll do. Helen!" he called into the kitchen, "better make breakfast a quick one. Looks like you have a wedding to plan today."

Nikki came running from the kitchen and rushed into her grandfather's arms. "Thank you, Papa!" she cried. After a quick, fierce hug, she ran to Julie and literally leapt into his embrace.

***

Julian Hesterman and Nichole Valentine were married in the living room of her grandparents' home just after 10AM, on October the 15th, the 196 day after the *Event*. Both bride and groom wore blue jeans and flannel shirts. They exchanged wedding rings donated by Henry and Helen who had been happily wed for 35 years and no longer needed the simple gold bands to show their commitment to each other. Anna and Rebecca were maids of honor, and David stood in as Julie's best man. Jack Braedan, former Delta Force Master Sergeant, leader of the Christian warriors known as the *Sword of David,* officiated. He read from the New Testament, Book of Ephesians, Chapter 5.

"But as the church is subject to Christ, so also the wives ought to be to their husbands in everything. Husbands, love your wives, just as Christ also loved the church and gave Himself up for her, so that He might sanctify her, having cleansed her by the washing of water with the word, that He might present to Himself the church in all her glory, having no spot or wrinkle or any such thing; but that she would be holy and blameless. So, husbands ought also to love their own wives as their own bodies. He who loves his own wife loves himself; for no one ever hated his own flesh, but nourishes and cherishes it, just as Christ also does the church, because we are members of His body. For this reason, a man shall leave his mother and father and shall be joined to his wife and the two shall become one flesh."

"The world claims these words put a woman in bondage to her husband," Jack said, closing Henry's Bible. "But how can a woman be in bondage to someone who is the same flesh? No more than a man can subjugate his own body to himself. From this moment on, you are no longer Julian Hesterman and Nichole Valentine, you are Julie and Nikki. Let no man separate what the Lord, God, *Yahweh* has joined together."

"Julie?" he asked. "Before God and these witnesses, do you take Nikki to be your wife? To love, to cherish, and protect her as Yeshua loves, cherishes, and protects the church? To cling to her in sickness and health, to love her and no other, so as long as you both shall live?"

It was a simple ceremony, but one full of love and respect. It was witnessed by family and friends. And sanctified by the love Julie and Nikki held for each other, and their mutual love for their Creator and Savior. When Julie and Nikki kissed, there wasn't a dry eye in the house, including Henry's.

"I guess that does it," Jack smiled, when they'd finished their kiss.

"Son," Henry smiled, his first real smile of the day. "If you aren't a preacher, you missed you're calling."

"Thank you, Henry," Jack replied. "My mom would have loved to hear you say that."

"Julian," Henry Valentine said, "give Nikki another kiss, then come with me. We need to talk."

"Yes, sir," Julian said, kissing his wife on the cheek. "Coming, sir."

"What do you think they are talking about?" Jack asked.

He and David were drinking coffee, looking out the kitchen window at Julie splitting firewood out back with an axe while Henry watched, smoking a pipe. They'd been out there for an hour now. Julie had split at least a rick of wood. Didn't seem like Mr. Valentine was getting the least bit winded. Julie on the other hand, was working up quite a sweat.

"Same thing Anna's dad would have said to you I suppose," David replied. "If he'd been around on your wedding day. Husbandly duties and responsibilities?"

"I doubt if Julie needs any talk about the birds and the bees. You think he and Helen will be okay here?" Jack wondered.

"Who can say," David shrugged. "He may be right. One place may be as good as another in this world. We've got a bunker, but the Valentines are blessed with an out of the way farm. And the Lord's protection? We are all destined for martyrdom most likely. I'm betting Henry and Helen are prepared for either possibility."

"Still wish they'd come with us," Jack sighed.

"You can't protect the entire world, Jack Braedan," David said, laying a brotherly hand on his shoulder. "God will watch over Henry and Helen, or He will call them home, as he wills."

As they watched, Henry placed his arm around Julie and they both began to pray.

Chapter Fourteen

I'll meet you there

"Babe, are you okay?" asked Jack, knocking softly on the Valentine's bathroom door.

Anna had been in there almost twenty minutes.

He heard the toilet flush, and Anna opened the door. "Just an upset stomach," she said quietly.

"You sure?" he asked with concern in his voice. None of the group had had so much as a sniffle during the *Event*. Not even the usual summer allergy problems that Tennessee was famous for.

"I'm fine, dear," she said, patting his cheek.

"Are you okay, sweetie?" Helen asked as they rejoined the group in the living room. Mrs. Valentine was an observant woman.

"Could I trouble you for some tea maybe?" Anna asked.

"It's no trouble at all," Helen said. "Julian, go on with your story. It's...fascinating. Come along," she said, taking Anna's arm and escorting her into the kitchen.

"You're not putting me on, are you, son?" Henry asked, resuming the conversation.

"I saw it myself, Papa," Nikki assured him. She and Julie were sitting in the love seat, holding hands.

"Saw what?" asked Jack.

"Saw you pray over a boy and heal his busted leg, apparently," Henry replied. "Did you really do that, son?"

Even without Anna in the room to admonish him, Jack didn't try to evade the truth this time. "Jesus healed him." He replied, taking an empty seat. "I just asked him to."

"Kind of like our own spiritual JTAC," Julie grinned.

"JTAC?" Nikki asked.

"It's the soldier on the radio who calls in air support when there's trouble," Rebecca explained. "I like that, Julie."

"I've asked the Lord for a lot of things in my life," Henry said quietly. "Sometimes he answers me, sometime not. But I've never heard the likes of this before. The Lord works in mysterious ways."

"Amen to that, Henry," Jack sighed. "Amen to that."

The conversation lulled then, until David decided to lighten the mood. "Henry, would you like to hear about how our boy Julie tried to catch the raccoons that were getting into our strawberries this summer?"

"Not *that*!" Julian groaned. "I thought that was our secret, Dave?"

"There should be no secrets between husband and wife," Nikki laughed. "Tell us, David."

"Picture if you can then, Julie from Jersey," David grinned, "pitted against one of God's most mischievous creatures..."

"Henry, I need you to take me to town." Helen announced, coming into the room as the laughter died down at the conclusion of David's tale.

"Whatever for, my dear?" He asked wiping a tear from his eye. He hadn't laughed so hard since before the *Event*. "It'll be dark in less than an hour."

"I need to pick up a few things for our new family before they head back to Franklin," she replied.

"What sort of things?" He asked, curious now.

"*Things,*" she insisted. "We will be back before dark. Won't take long."

"Get used to that tone, Julian," Henry sighed, rising from his chair. "Valentine women uses that tone, just do what they want. Or you end up sleeping by yourself on the couch. Would you gentlemen mind taking that wood that Julie split and putting it on the back porch while we are gone? It would be a big help."

"No problem," Julie nodded.

"Rebecca, would you like to ride with us?" Helen asked. "Anna is going too."

"Well, sure. I guess." Rebecca said surprised at the offer.

"Do you think it's safe?" David asked, taken off guard.

"I'll be safe enough with *Sword of David* women, I warrant," Henry shrugged. "But thanks for your concern. Like I said, Fayetteville is small time to the WZC. And the sheriff is a believer. They can take their sidearms. No one will bat an eye."

Jack was looking at Anna with concern. She had been crying unless he was mistaken, but she gave him a reassuring smile. He still raised a questioning eyebrow.

"I'll be fine," she nodded.

"Can I go, Papa?" Nikki asked, a little hurt she hadn't been invited.

"You help your man," her grandmother replied, in the same tone she'd used on Henry. "We'll be back soon. When you're done, go to the cellar and get a couple pints of those blueberries I canned last month. I'll make you a cobbler for the road."

"Everything okay, babe?" asked Jack, as he helped Anna with her jacket.

"It's fine. Really," Anna replied, only worrying him more. "Go help the boys stack that wood, and we'll be back before you know it. I love you, Jack Braedan," she finished, giving him a tender kiss.

"I love you, Anna Braedan," he replied, opening the door for her. Now beside himself with worry.

That hour was the longest of his life.

***

The Valentines, with Anna and Rebecca, returned just before sunset and Jack almost wept with relief. He finally understood what it meant to pray without ceasing. Jack rushed to help them carrying in bags from the Food Mart, which they let him do willingly, but Rebecca all but pushed him aside when he asked what was in the other plastic bags they had brought in.

"Come on in here, Jack," Henry called from the living room. "Let the women handle that."

"You go on," Anna smiled, kissing his cheek. "We *women* will handle this."

Henry was pouring a shot of Jack Daniels into four tumblers as he entered. "I don't usually partake, but it's been a heck of a day."

"To Julie and Nikki," David said, raising his glass.

The four men touched glasses and drank.

"Lord, that's smooth," Henry said. "With Lynchburg right up the road, a man must have a strong constitution to not be swayed by this vice. Another?"

The four men sat in the living room and discussed life, the universe, and other subjects, while partaking liberally of the Tennessee sipping whiskey. They were only interrupted once as Anna, accompanied by Nikki, made their way towards the bathroom.

"I thought you ladies only did that sort of thing at restaurants?" Julie asked, as they passed by.

"Mind your own business, Raccoon boy," Nikki quipped.

David almost choked on his whiskey, as Jack and Henry roared with laughter. Julie muttered something about, "it seemed like a good idea at the time," and wondered silently what he'd gotten himself into this morning.

When they came back through several minutes later, Anna stopped behind Jack, leaned down, and kissed him on the cheek. "I love you, Jack Braedan," she whispered in his ear. It wasn't the whiskey that made him flush.

"Go wash up, gentlemen," Helen announced about an hour later. "Dinner is almost ready."

"Coming with me, Raccoon..." David started.

"Don't you *even,* old man," Julie growled.

It was crowded around the dinner table, the Valentines not accustomed to so many visitors. Helen had set out the "good china" and they sat down to a meal of fried chicken, homemade biscuits, mashed potatoes, and gravy, with green beans from the cellar. Henry gave the blessing, as they all held hands. It was the most enjoyable meal that any of them could remember having in a long, long time. Dinner was just about concluded when Anna excused herself, having only made one polite attempt at her plate.

Jack made to follow her, but Nikki reached over and grabbed his arm. "Sit, Jack," she ordered. "She'll be back in a minute."

He sat. Apparently, the Valentine women's tone worked on just about everyone.

Anna returned as promised a few minutes later, as everyone was clearing off their dishes and helping Helen wash, dry and put away the china. She rushed into Jack's arms, making him drop the glass he was drying, and she burst into tears.

"Honey?" he asked, holding her tightly. "What's wrong?"

She lifted her head, reached up to caress his check, and then turned to look at Nikki. "I'm so sorry, Nikki, I know this was supposed to be your special day."

"Babe, tell me what's wrong!" Irrational fears flooded through Jack's mind. Cancer? Some new virus?

"Plus, again?" Nikki asked. She was smiling, eyes brimming with tears.

Anna nodded.

"Would someone please tell me what is going on!" Jack demanded. He seemed to be the only person in the room who hadn't figured it out yet.

"I'm pregnant, Jack," Anna said softly.

The words swirled in his head. Pregnant? How? Well, he knew how but...now? Heaven's mercy, now? Darkness threatened to take him. How could he... how could they... raise a child in the Tribulation?

"Jack, say something." She said anxiously when he didn't reply.

"I don't know what to say," he replied hesitantly, honestly. "I love you more than life. I want to shout for joy, and I want to weep at the same time. What are we going to do, babe?"

"We are going to pray," Henry announced, taking charge. He walked over to them and placed a hand on each of their shoulders, and unbidden they knelt before him right there on the dining room floor. "Everyone, come here," Henry directed. The group circled around Jack and Anna, each laying a hand on the pair.

"Heavenly Father," Henry began, "You are our rock and our protector..."

When he was finished, Jack and Anna held each other and cried softly, not from worry but from the joy of having such a loving family to support them as they faced an uncertain future. "You two go into the living room and take a moment," Henry said, "Helen, I'll put on the coffee. It's time for that blueberry cobbler that you and Nikki made."

Anna took Jack by the hand and led him the love seat where she crawled on his lap, resting her head on his shoulder. They sat there for a long while, just taking comfort in each other's embrace.

"You're pregnant," Jack said, finally breaking the silence. He placed a hand on her still flat stomach, unconsciously seeking to shield the new life growing inside her.

"I know," Anna said softly into his shoulder.

Moving his hand to lift her chin, he looked into the emerald eyes that had captured him that first moment at *Guns USA.* "This isn't going to be easy," he said.

"I know," Anna kissed him tenderly, then lowered her head to his shoulder once again.

"Our *Sword of David* days are over," Jack informed her. "The world will just have to take care of itself."

"Jack..."

"The world will have to take care of itself," he repeated firmly. "God may have been able to give His Son for this fallen world, but I won't risk our child for it. I'm not as strong as our Father. If we must stay in the Sanctuary until Jesus comes back, and I mean literally, that's what we'll do. We'll do whatever it takes to make this work, to protect our child. Short of renouncing Jesus, of course."

"Of course," Anna agreed, snuggling even closer. From the instant that blue plus sign had appeared on the pregnancy test, she'd worried how he would react when she told him. She didn't know if he'd be angry, filled with fear, naïve, foolish, or full of joy. But once again, she gave thanks to God for bringing them together, for giving her the perfect man to protect her and their child in this dangerous world.

"I wonder if Helen has any pickles in her cellar?" he asked, kissing the top of her head. "Helen! Do you have any pickles in your cellar?"

"I most certainly do," she laughed from the kitchen. "You two about done in there? We're cutting up the blueberry cobbler."

"What do you say, mommy?" Jack grinned, kissing her hair. "Want some pickles and cobbler?"

"Why don't we just start with some cobbler for now," Anna smiled.

"Deal," Jack said, helping her to her feet. "Hey, everyone! We're gonna have a baby!"

"I for one, am surprised it took so long," David called out playfully. "Ow! Well, you know how they...ow!"

"Let's get in there before Becca really hurts him," Anna sighed, taking his hand.

It was the best blueberry cobbler that either of them could ever remember eating.

"So..." Jack said slowly, problems and complications and horrible scenarios running through his head, "what are we going to do for you know... baby stuff?"

"Sufficient unto the day," Henry replied. "You can't worry about the future, Jack. I'll be blunt, if I may?"

"By all means, Henry." Jack nodded.

"It's going to be difficult enough staying alive for nine months to see this child born," Henry replied. "Before the *Event*, this would be one of the most joyous days this house has ever seen, but we are living in uncertain times. We've prayed over you and Anna," Henry continued, "and prayer is a powerful thing. But this group knows what's ahead. The Time of Jacob's Trouble has barely begun."

"That's true enough, Papa," Helen replied. "Doesn't hurt to plan ahead though. Big K has a well-stocked baby section. At least, it did a month ago when we went to get that new pressure cooker when ours went on the fritz. Why don't y'all stay the night? We've plenty of room, and tomorrow we take another trip into town and buy what we can find. It'll at least be a start."

"Well, Helen and I would enjoy the company," Henry nodded, "Look, I didn't mean to cast a shadow over you."

"It's fine, Henry," Jack assured him. "We're fine," he said, taking Anna's hand and kissing it. "If you hadn't prayed over us and we weren't surrounded by...well, our family, I'd be on the floor shaking with dread."

"It's settled then," Helen announced. "You'll stay another night. Let's get everyone settled, shall we? We've got three rooms, not counting mine and Henry's, but the sofa pulls out."

"That'll be us, David," Becca volunteered. "Let the newlyweds and new parents fight over the beds. We'll get Henry to take us back to town tomorrow and see what we can find at the Big K, and then we'll see what the next day brings."

What the next day brought was something no one had seen coming. Snow. Henry was up first, and as he went into the kitchen to make coffee, he saw that the world had gone white. Big, fat snowflakes were falling. An inch or two covered the ground already. "Good thing we put that wood on the back porch." He muttered. "Everyone get cracking!" He called out loudly. "If you want to go to town today, we better leave quickly."

Jack assisted Henry putting snow chains on his Buick. The man was ready for anything, it seemed. He offered to let them take the Escalade, but Henry would have nothing of it. "Buick will be fine." He insisted. "Besides, that monster will attract attention, even in this weather."

After pooling all the cash that the group had on them, which totaled almost three hundred dollars, Henry, Helen, Anna, and Rebecca left at about seven. Meanwhile, everyone else busied themselves making breakfast under Nikki's direction. By the time they returned, it was almost nine and there was at least four inches of snow on the ground.

"Won't be anyone going back to Franklin, today," Henry announced, kicking snow from his boots. "Roads are a mess. Looks like you're stuck here until this clears."

Eight inches fell before the snow finally stopped around noon. But *"stuck here"* was a harsh term for three of the most enjoyable days they'd spent in a long while. They ignored the world beyond the farm, and simply focused on spending time with the Valentines and melding them into their family. No country Bed and Breakfast could have compared to Henry and Helen's hospitality. If only the farm had been better stocked, it would have been a decent place to spend the Tribulation.

If only.

On the morning of the fourth day, the sun poked through the clouds. By 9AM, the temperature had reached almost forty degrees. Jack decided it was time to leave.

Henry protested. Helen cried.

"If we don't leave, we'll eat you out of house and home," Jack argued. They had gone through all the supplies they'd brought with them from Franklin, and no small amount from the Valentine's cellar. "You know it's true, Henry. Six more mouths to feed will burn through your stores in a month."

It was the hard truth.

They invited the Valentines once again to accompany them to the Sanctuary, but Henry stood firm. Anna made Jack promise they'd make a return trip to Fayetteville soon, condition's permitting, with more supplies. Jack made Henry commit to memory the directions on how to get to his bunker if "*things turned*."

Dinner that evening was a solemn affair, and when they departed not long after midnight, there wasn't a dry eye among them. Henry hugged Julian Hesterman, the Yankee from Jersey, so hard you could almost hear ribs crack. "You take care of our Nikki," Henry said softly, tears on his weathered cheeks.

"I will, Henry," he promised, his own eyes wet with tears. "Bye, Nana," he said, hugging Helen. She wept unashamedly.

"You take care of Anna," Helen said, hugging Jack when it was his turn. "The Devil himself won't keep us away when it's time to deliver your child."

"I'll keep them safe, ma'am." Jack promised.

The long, slow ride back to Franklin was quiet. Rebecca drove with David up front. Julie and Nikki rode in the back seat, Julie comforting his sobbing new wife, until she finally fell asleep in his arms. Jack and Anna rode "shotgun" in the middle bench seat, Jack with his H&K locked and loaded, Anna doing the same with her AR.

The roads were ice hardened, but the heavy Cadillac handled them well, creeping along most of the way hardly topping 25 or 30 mph. Its tires were practically new and its super-charged 6.2-liter V-8 engine was a beast. They met only two other vehicles on the entire return trip, on what business they could only speculate, but both passed by without incident. The fact that Jack stuck the barrel of his H&K out the window, plainly visible, probably didn't hurt. Their only other company on the journey was the cold, snow-covered landscape, and dark night.

"Tire tracks in the driveway," Rebecca hissed, as they made their way through the front gate. It was 7AM. There was only a faint glow of orange in the east.

"How many? What kind?" Jack demanded, as he pulled back the charging handle, making sure the H&K was loaded.

"Can't tell," David replied, doing the same for his AR.

"Nice and slow, Becca," Jack cautioned. No one had been on their property since they'd returned from Jackson, although someone had squatted in the house for a few days while they had been away.

Lights off, they crept forward. As soon as the Caddy came around the corner of the house, blue lights split the darkness. Four patrol cars. WZC or local, Jack couldn't tell. But it meant the same thing. Trouble. A spotlight from two different vehicles bathed the Escalade in piercing white light.

"Turn off your engine and step out slowly," commanded a voice over one of the patrol cars loudspeakers.

Jack made his decision instantly. The safety of his wife and unborn child was all that mattered. "Becca, roll down the window and hold out your hands so they can see them. As soon as I jump out, you floor it in reverse and don't stop for anything. You know where the creek meets the road?"

"I do," she nodded. "What are you planning, Jack?"

"Drive it off the road there, cover your tracks as best you can," he continued, "she might make it up the creek, but I doubt it. Ditch her if you must and beat feet to the Sanctuary. I'll meet you there."

"Jack, what do you think you're doing?" Anna demanded.

"Making sure no one follows," he replied. "Keeping our child safe."

"Jack, NO!" she cried.

"Turn off your engine and step out slowly," commanded a voice again, more forceful this time. "You have 30 seconds before we open fire."

"Listen to me!" Jack said, "It's the only way! I'll cover you while you get to the road. I'll hit the woods. They'll never catch me." He had thirty rounds in the H&K and two spare magazines in his cargo pockets. It would have to be enough.

"Coming too, boss," Julie said.

"No!" Jack barked. "Keep 'em safe, Julie. David, you smoke anything that gets by me, but you get them out of here!"

"Will do, Coastie," David nodded grimly.

"I love you," Jack said, pulling Anna to him and kissing her fiercely. Before she could stop him, he opened the passenger door. "Now, Becca!"

Jack was firing as soon as his feet hit the snow, spraying 5.56 mm as he ran. Becca floored the accelerator as return fire shattered the front windshield. Jack dropped to one knee and emptied his magazine. A spotlight went dark as Becca whipped the Cadillac in a 180 degree spin. The powerful engine threw up a blizzard of snow as it sped fishtailing for the gate. Jack quickly reloaded and fired as he ran, rounds stitching the snow behind him.

One of the patrol cars roared in pursuit of the Caddy. Jack hit the snow and rolled, firing from the prone, he put a dozen rounds in the driver's side window. It rolled to a stop, horn sounding as the driver slumped forward. He spared a quick glance down the drive. The Escalade slid and hit the brick pillar on the right as it exited the gate, then it roared off to the east. Jack leapt to his feet, emptying the rest of the magazine at a second vehicle as he ran. The windshield shattered. He ejected the magazine and reloaded in one smooth motion. Firing from the hip in the direction of the other two vehicles, he sprinted for the wood line.

Two strides from the wood line, something smacked him hard in the back of his head and high on his left shoulder. He flew forward, careening off a tree and into the snow. He tried to lift himself up, but his left arm was useless. Blood splattered the snow where he'd fallen. Jack forced himself to his knees, using the butt of his H&K for support. Bullets snapped into the trees around him, whizzing by his head. He made it to his feet and managed two steps before he was hit again, his right thigh blossoming with fire.

He fired a quick burst from his back, rolled painfully, and struggled to his feet once more. He made it to the next tree and fired a three-round burst. Next tree for cover, another three-round burst. Always farther into the woods. Always west, away from Anna and his unborn child. He did this until the bolt locked to the rear and the H&K was empty.

Jack ejected the last magazine. The barrel was too hot to touch. No longer useful for support, he let it drop to the ground, hissing in the cold snow. He struggled to his feet, using a tree to steady himself, then turned and limped painfully deeper into to the woods. He went always west, though leaving a trail of blood behind him that a child could follow.

He made it perhaps another hundred yards and his vision swirled. He dropped to his knees, catching himself with his good right arm, then fell on his back in the snow. Sunlight was streaming through the branches now, glorious beams of light that fell like spears of white fire to the snow. It was so beautiful. He closed his eyes knowing it was likely the last thing he would see on this earth. "I'm sorry, Anna," he whispered.

Jack began to pray, as darkness overtook him. A blinding pain in his shoulder, brought him back. His eyes fluttered open. A booted foot ground into his shoulder and he screamed in pain.

It stopped.

"Ah, still alive? Good," a voice above him said casually.

Jack managed to focus through the pain. His vision cleared. Above him stood an Anunnaki, white haired, eyes as black as the pit. "I should just let you bleed out," the Nephilim continued, "But..." Crouching down beside him, it probed the wound in his shoulder with a slender finger then raised its hand and touched his blood to its tongue. The Anunnaki spit in disgust. "But I have a few questions for you, Nazarene. Be a good soldier and hold on until the ambulance arrives. Can you do that for me, *Sword of David*?"

Jack closed his eyes, and the world went dark.

The last sound he heard was the Nephilim laughing.

The Time of Jacob's Trouble will continue in Nephilim Rising.

Acknowledgements to my biggest fan, James Davis (JD) Webb. Stepsons are a blessing from God and JD is the best.

Special thanks to a very special reader who volunteered her editing services, Laurel Taylor. Also, to the digital artwork on the cover by Pierre-Alain Durand of 3mmi. Check out his artwork on Artstation.com and other sites. I picked an already completed work and Pierre transformed it into a something that captured the essence of the Sword of David perfectly.

Most of all, thanks to YHWH, God of Creation, for sending his son, Yeshua, to redeem us from our sins.

Printed in the USA
CPSIA information can be obtained
at www.ICGtesting.com
LVHW090339080424
776714LV00007B/353

9 781095 986127